Praise for
Shadows on the Sand

"Gayle Roper's mysteries get deeper and develop more tangled threads with each book. The characters and setting are so real I wanted to run out and help them. Happily ever after was in serious doubt. Very well done."

> —LAURAINE SNELLING, author of the Daughters of Blessing
> Series and the Red River of the North Series

"There's nothing quite like a long-awaited vacation, especially when it's served up with a Gayle Roper novel. *Shadows on the Sand,* a tale of faith, forgiveness, and fresh starts all wrapped in a captivating mystery, was just what I needed to return to the real world refreshed and inspired."

> —TAMARA LEIGH, author of *Nowhere, Carolina* and
> *Restless in Carolina*

"With vivid, realistic characters and a tightly woven plot, *Shadows on the Sand* is a novel I couldn't put down. The emotional ride stayed with me long after the last page. Highly recommend!"

> —ROBIN CAROLL, author of *In the Shadow of Evil*

"*Shadows on the Sand* is a rare mix of love story, spiritual warfare, and crime drama all rolled into one fabulous tale. Gayle Roper has once again created fascinating characters and a rich story that kept me up well into the night."

> —MARK MYNHEIR, homicide detective and
> author of *The Corruptible*

GAYLE ROPER

Shadows
on the
Sand

A Seaside Mystery

MULTNOMAH
BOOKS

SHADOWS ON THE SAND
PUBLISHED BY MULTNOMAH BOOKS
12265 Oracle Boulevard, Suite 200
Colorado Springs, Colorado 80921

Scripture quotations or paraphrases are taken from the following versions: The Holy Bible, New International Version®. NIV®. Copyright © 1973, 1978, 1984 by Biblica Inc. ™ Used by permission of Zondervan. All rights reserved worldwide. www.zondervan.com. The Holy Bible, English Standard Version. Copyright © 1991, 1992, 1995 by American Bible Society. Used by permission. The King James Version.

The characters and events in this book are fictional, and any resemblance to actual persons or events is coincidental.

ISBN 978-1-60142-084-8
ISBN 978-1-60142-306-1 (electronic)

Cover design: Kelly L. Howard
Cover photography: Pam Ullman/Getty

Published in the United States by WaterBrook Multnomah, an imprint of the Crown Publishing Group, a division of Random House Inc., New York.

MULTNOMAH and its mountain colophon are registered trademarks of Random House Inc.

Library of Congress Cataloging-in-Publication Data
Roper, Gayle G.
    Shadows on the sand : a seaside mystery / Gayle Roper. — 1st ed.
        p. cm.
    ISBN 978-1-60142-084-8 — ISBN 978-1-60142-306-1 (ebk.) 1. City and town
life—New Jersey—Fiction. 2. Missing persons—Investigation—Fiction. I. Title.
    PS3568.O68S53 2011
    813'.54—dc22
                                                    2011003832

Printed in the United States of America
2011

10 9 8 7 6 5 4 3 2

In memory of Chuck.
They don't come any better.

S o Bill punched him in the nose, Carrie!" Andi Mueller swung an arm to demonstrate and nearly clipped me. "He was wonderful!"

I leaned back and held up a hand for protection. "Easy, kiddo." I smiled at the girl and her enthusiasm.

Andi giggled like the smitten sixteen-year-old she was. "Sorry."

"Mmm." I rested my elbows on the pink marble counter that ran along one wall of Carrie's Café, located two blocks from the boardwalk in the center of Seaside, New Jersey. I was the Carrie of the café's name, and Andi was one of my servers, in fact, my only server at the moment. She'd been with me almost two months now, taking up the slack when the summer kids left to go back to college or on to real jobs.

"Let me get this straight," I said. "On Saturday night Bill, who is your true soul mate, punched Jase, our Jase, for paying too much attention to you at a party." I didn't think my voice was too wry, but soul mates at sixteen made me both cynical and scared, teen hormones being what they were.

Andi just grinned with delight of the even-mentioning-his-name-gives-me-the-vapors kind and nodded as she sat on a stool at the counter. "Isn't it romantic?"

I was hearing this tale today, Monday, because now that the season was over, Carrie's was closed on Sundays. My staff and I had earned our day of rest over a very busy and marginally profitable summer. We might be able to stay open for another year if nothing awful happened, like the roof leaking or the dishwasher breaking.

Listening to Andi made me feel ancient. I was only thirty-three, but had I ever been as young as she? Given the trauma of my growing-up years, I probably hadn't. I was glad that whatever her history, and there was a history, she could giggle.

"How do you expect to continue working with Jase after this encounter?" I was very interested in her answer. Jase was one of three part-time dishwashers at the café. All three were students at the local community college and set their schedules around classes. Jase worked Tuesdays and Saturdays from six in the morning until three, and the last thing I wanted was contention in the kitchen between Andi and him.

Andi looked confused. "Why should I have trouble with Jase? I didn't punch him. Besides he's an old—" She cut herself off.

I wanted to pursue her half-thought, but the door of the café opened, and Greg Barnes walked in, all scruffy good looks and shadowed eyes. His black hair was mussed as if he hadn't combed it, and he had a two-day stubble. He should have looked grubby, but somehow he didn't. He looked wonderful.

All thoughts of Bill and Jase fled as my heart did the little stuttery Snoopy dance it always did at the sight of Greg. Before he could read anything in my face, assuming he noticed me as someone other than the person who fed him, I looked down at the basket of fresh-from-the-oven cinnamon-swirl muffins I was arranging.

Andi glanced from me to him and, much too quick and clever, smiled with a knowing look. I held my breath. She wasn't long on tact, and the last thing I wanted was for her to make some leading remark. I felt I could breathe again when all she did was wink at me. Safe for the moment, at least.

Greg came to the counter and slid onto his favorite stool, empty now that the receding flood of summer tourists left it high and dry this third week in October, a vinyl-covered Ararat postdeluge.

"The usual?" I asked, my voice oh-so-casual.

He gave a nod, barely glancing my way, and opened his copy of *The Philadelphia Inquirer*. *The Press of Atlantic City* waited.

I turned to place his order, but there was no need. Lindsay, my sister, partner, and the café's baker, had been listening to Andi's story through the serving window. She waved her acknowledgment before I said a word. She passed the order to Ricky, our short-order cook, who had stayed with us longer than I expected, long enough that he had become almost as much of an asset to Carrie's as Lindsay was.

My sister gave me a sly smile, then called, "Hi, Greg."

He looked up from his paper and gave Lindsay a very nice smile, far nicer than he ever gave me.

"The sticky buns are all gone," he said in mild accusation, nodding toward the glass case where we kept Lindsay's masterpieces.

She grinned. "Sorry. You've got to get here earlier."

He raised an eyebrow. "Or you could make more."

"I'll take the suggestion under advisement," she said agreeably.

"Haven't you heard the adage about making your customers happy?"

"Yeah. So?"

He laughed and turned a page in the paper. I brought him a glass of OJ and a cup of my special blend.

"How're you doing?" I asked, just as I did every morning.

He gave me a vague smile. "Fine." Just as he said every morning.

But he wasn't. Oh, he was better than, say, a year ago, definitely better than two years ago, but he wasn't well. Even three years after the tragedy that had altered his life, he was far from his self-proclaimed fine. If you looked closely—as I did—you could see the strain never completely left his eyes, and the purple stains under them were too deep and dark, a sure sign that a good night's sleep was still little more than a vague memory for him.

But he was sober. More than two years and counting.

"Keep talking, Andi," Lindsay said as Ricky beat Greg's eggs and inserted his wheat bread in the toaster. "This is better than reality TV. It's really real." She walked out of the kitchen into the café proper. "Bill bopped Jase," she prompted.

"Our Jase," I clarified.

Greg looked up. "Your dishwasher?"

I nodded.

"Hmm." And he went back to his paper.

"And Jase went down for the count." Andi's chest swelled with pride at her beloved's prowess.

I flinched. "Don't you think knocking a guy out for talking to you is a bit much?"

Andi thought for almost half a second, then shook her head. "It wasn't for just Saturday. He knows Jase and I work together, and he was staking his claim."

I'd seen Jase and Andi talking in the kitchen, but there never seemed to be any romantic overtones. "Jase is a nice guy and a good worker. I don't want to lose him because of your boyfriend."

"He is, and I don't want him to go either," Andi agreed. "I like talking to him."

"Me too." Lindsay rested an elbow on the counter and propped her chin in her palm. "I think he's sad."

"What do you mean, sad?" But I'd sensed he was weighed down with something too.

"He's funny and open most of the time," Lindsay said, "but sometimes when no one's talking to him, I see this look of sorrow on his face."

I nodded. "All the more reason to hate that he got punched."

"Yeah." Lindsay got a dreamy look in her dark brown eyes. "But there's something about a guy defending you, even if what he's defending you from isn't really a threat." She sighed.

"Lindsay!" I was appalled. "Get a grip." Though if Greg ever wanted to defend me, I was pretty sure I wouldn't mind. Of course, that presupposed he'd notice I was in trouble. I glanced at him bent over his paper. Not likely to happen. I bit back a sigh.

"Tell me, Andi. Does Bill plan to punch out any male who talks to you?"

"Come on, Carrie," Andi said. "Don't be mad at Bill. You know how guys can be when they've had a few beers."

I did know how guys could be, beers or no beers. "What were you doing at a party where there was drinking?"

She became all prim and prissy. "I did not drink."

"I should hope not, but you shouldn't have been there." Good grief. I was sounding more and more like her mother—or how her mother would have sounded if she weren't missing in action somewhere. Part of that history I didn't know.

"Order up," Ricky announced as he walked to the pass-through. "The food is never better than when I plate it."

You'd have thought he was Emeril or Wolfgang Puck or one of Paula Deen's sons, not a stopgap cook who couldn't find any other job after graduating from college with a psychology degree and who stayed around because he had a crush on the baker.

I grabbed Greg's scrambled eggs and wheat toast and served them. He accepted them with a nod and a grunt.

"So what happened to Jase?" I asked Andi. I found myself hoping Bill had bruised a knuckle or two in his violence, though I was pretty sure it meant I was a terrible person too. I didn't wish for a broken hand or anything that extreme, just something to remind him that punching wasn't the way to handle a perceived rival.

Andi waved her hand vaguely. "Bill and a buddy carried Jase to his car. They only dropped him once."

I imagined the *thunk* of poor Jase's head hitting the ground and flinched in sympathy. No such thought bothered Andi. She was too busy being thrilled by Bill, who rode in like her shining knight, laying waste to the enemy with knuckles instead of the more traditional lance.

"How much older than you is Bill?" Lindsay asked.

Good question, Linds.

Andi studied the cuticle of her index finger. "He's nineteen."

Lindsay and I exchanged a glance. Those three years from sixteen to nineteen were huge.

I couldn't keep quiet. "So he shouldn't have been drinking at this party either."

Andi slid off her stool. If looks killed, Lindsay'd be sprinkling my ashes in the ocean tomorrow morning.

"What does Clooney think of you and Bill?" Lindsay asked. Clooney was Andi's great-uncle, and she lived with him.

Andi cleared her throat. "We don't talk about Bill."

"Does he know about Bill?" Lindsay's concern was obvious.

Andi stared through long bangs that hung over her hazel eyes. The silky hair sometimes caught in her lashes in a way that made me blink but didn't seem to bother her. "Of course Clooney knows. Do you think I'd keep a secret from him?"

"I didn't think you would." Lindsay smiled. "I'm glad to know I was right."

So was I. Sixteen could go in so many different directions, and I'd hate for this pixie to make wrong choices—or more wrong choices.

"Is he going to college?" I asked. "Bill?"

"He was, but not now." Her fingernail became even more absorbing. "He dropped out of Rutgers at the end of his freshman year."

Uh-oh. Dropped out or failed out? "Does he plan to go back? Try again?"

She shrugged. "He doesn't know. Right now he's happy just being. And going to parties. And taking me." By the time she was finished, she was bouncing at the excitement of it all, her strawberry blond ponytail leaping about her shoulders.

Greg looked up from his newspaper. "So this guy took you, a very underage girl, to a party where there was lots of drinking?"

Andi looked at him, eyes wide, acting as if he'd missed the whole point of her story. "Don't worry about me, Mr. Barnes. Or any of you." She included Lindsay and me with a nod of her head. "I can handle any problems that might develop at a party. Believe me, I've dealt with far worse."

I was intrigued. I'd stared down plenty of problems in my time too, and I wondered how her stare downs compared to mine.

She grinned and waved a hand as if she were wiping away her momentary seriousness. "But I'd rather talk about how great Bill is."

"So how great is he?" Lindsay asked. "Tell me all." At twenty-seven, she was an incurable romantic. I wasn't sure how this had come to pass, since she had every reason to be as cynical as I, but there you are.

I frowned at her. "Stop encouraging the girl."

Lindsay just grinned.

I looked at Andi's happy face and had to smile too. "So what's this wonderful guy doing if he's not in school?" Besides being and partying.

"Uh, you mean like a job or something?"

"Yeah." Lindsay and I exchanged another glance. Greg looked up again at Andi's reluctant tone.

"Well, he was a lifeguard over the summer. He's got this fabulous tan, and it makes him so handsome."

Soul mate stuff if I ever heard it. I half expected her to swoon like a nineteenth-century Southern belle with her stays laced too tightly. "What about now? Postseason?"

"And he was the quarterback on the high school football team two years ago when they won the state championship."

"Very impressive. What about now?"

"He was named Most Valuable Player."

"Even more impressive. What about now?"

She began making sure the little stacks of sugar and sweetener packets in the holders on the counter were straight. "Right now he's just trying to figure it all out."

Being. Figuring. And punching guys out while he thought. "You mean he's trying to decide what he wants to be when he grows up?"

She glared at me. In her mind he was grown up. She turned her back with a little sniff and went to clean off a dirty table.

Lindsay swallowed a laugh. "Your sarcastic streak is showing, Carrie."

Mr. Perkins, another regular at Carrie's Café and at eighty in better health than the rest of us put together, rapped his cup on the pink marble counter. He'd been sitting for several minutes with his eyes wide behind his glasses as he listened to Andi.

"No daughter of mine that age would ever have gone to a party where there was drinking," he said. "It's just flat out wrong."

Since I agreed, I didn't mention that he was a lifelong bachelor and had no daughters.

He rapped his cup again.

"Refill?" I asked, not because I didn't know the answer but because the old man liked to think he was calling the shots.

He nodded. "Regular too. None of that wimpy decaf. I got to keep my blood flowing, keep it pumping."

I smiled with affection as I topped off his cup. He gave the same line every day. "Mr. Perkins, you have more energy than people half your age."

He pointed his dripping spoon at me. "And don't you forget it."

"Watch it," I said in a mock scold. "You're getting coffee all over my counter."

"And a fine counter it is." He patted the pink-veined marble slab. It was way too classy and way too pricey for a place like the café. "Did I ever tell you that I remember when it was the registration counter at Seaside's Grand Hotel? And let me tell you, it was a grand hotel in every sense of the word. People used to come from as far as Pittsburgh, even the president of U.S. Steel. Too bad it burned down. The hotel, not U.S. Steel."

"Too bad," I agreed. And yes, he'd told us the story many times.

"It was in 1943," he said with a faraway look in his eyes. "I was thirteen." He blinked back to the present. "It was during World War II, you know, and people said it was sabotage. Not that I ever believed that. I mean, why would the Germans burn down a resort hotel? But I'll tell you, my father, who was an air-raid warden, about had a seizure."

"I bet he was convinced that the flames, visible for miles up and down the coast, would bring the German subs patrolling offshore right up on our beaches," Lindsay said with a straight face. "They might have attacked us."

I glared at her as she repeated word for word Mr. Perkins's line from the story. She winked unrepentantly.

Mr. Perkins nodded, delighted she was listening. "People kept their curtains drawn at night, and even the boardwalk was blacked out for the duration, the lights all covered except for the tiniest slit on the land side, so the flames from the fire seemed extra bright. All that wood, you know. *Voom!*" He threw his hands up in the air.

Lindsay and I shook our heads at the imagined devastation, and I thought I saw Greg's lips twitch. He'd heard the story almost as many times as we had.

Mr. Perkins stirred his coffee. "After the war some investor bought the property."

"I bet all that remained of the Grand was the little corner where the pink marble registration counter sat." Lindsay pointed where I leaned. "That counter."

Again she spoke his line with a straight face, and this time Greg definitely bit back a grin.

Mr. Perkins added another pink packet to his coffee. "That's right. The buyer decided to open a restaurant around the counter and build a smaller, more practical hotel on the rest of the property."

Even that hotel was gone now, replaced many years ago by private homes rented each summer to pay the exorbitant taxes on resort property.

I walked to Greg with my coffeepot. "Refill?"

He slid his mug in my direction, eyes never leaving his paper.

Be still my heart.

2

The café door opened again, and Clooney sauntered in. In my opinion Clooney sauntered through life, doing as little as possible and appearing content that way. I, on the other hand, was a bona fide overachiever, always trying to prove myself, though I wasn't sure to whom. If Clooney weren't so charming, I'd have disliked him on principle. As it was, I liked him a lot.

Today he wore a Phillies cap, one celebrating the 2008 World Series victory. His gray ponytail was pulled through the back of the cap and hung to his shoulder blades.

"You work too hard, Carrie," he told me frequently. "You'll give yourself indigestion or reflux or a heart attack or something. You need to take time off."

"If I didn't want to pay the rent or have insurance or eat, I'd do that very thing," I always countered.

"What you need is a rich husband." And he'd grin.

"A solution to which I'm not averse. There just seems to be a shortage of candidates in Seaside."

"Hey, Clooney," Andi called from booth four, where she was clearing. She gave him a little finger wave. Clooney might be her great-uncle, but try as I might, I couldn't get her to call him Uncle Clooney. Just "Clooney" sounded disrespectful to me, but he didn't seem to mind.

"Hey, darlin'." Clooney walked over to Andi and gave her a hug. Then he came to the counter and slid onto the stool next to Greg. He did not take off his cap, something that drove me crazy. I've developed this manners thing, probably because my childhood was so devoid of anything resembling pattern or politeness. I know people thought me prissy and old-fashioned, but I am what I am, a poor man's Miss Manners.

Clooney pointed at a muffin, and I placed one on a dish for him. He broke off a chunk, then glanced back at Andi. "She tell you about that fool Bill?"

I grinned at his disgruntled expression. "She did."

"What is it with girl children?" he demanded. "I swear she's texted the news around the world."

"She thinks it's a compliment—her knight defending her."

Clooney and Greg snorted at the same time.

"Slaying a dragon who's threatening the life of the fair damsel's one thing," Greg said, actually looking at me. "Decking a kid for saying hi to a pretty girl is another."

"Your past life as a cop is showing," I teased.

He shrugged as he turned another page of the paper. "Old habits die hard."

The door opened again, and in strutted the object of our conversation. I knew it had to be him because, aside from the fact that he looked like a very tanned football player, he and Andi gazed at each other with love-struck goofy grins. I thought I heard Lindsay sigh.

Andi hurried toward the kitchen with an armful of dirty dishes from booth four. She squeaked in delight as Bill swatted her on the rump as she passed. Clooney stiffened at this unseemly familiarity with his baby. Mr. Perkins tsk-tsked his disapproval.

"Can I have breakfast now?" Andi asked when she reappeared empty-handed.

The wait staff usually ate around ten thirty at a back booth, and it was ten fifteen. We were in the off-season weekday lull between breakfast and lunch, and the three men on their stools were the only customers present. I nodded.

Bill looked toward the kitchen. He appeared overwhelmed at the prospect of food, unable to make a selection. He draped an arm over Andi's shoulder as he considered the possibilities, and she snuggled against him. Clooney's frown intensified.

Bill was a big guy, and it was clear by the way he carried himself that he still thought of himself as the big man on campus in spite of the fact that he was now campusless and unemployed. As I studied him, I wondered if high school football would end up being the high point of his life. How sad that would be. Clooney drifted through life by choice. I hoped Bill wouldn't drift for lack of a better plan or enough ability to achieve.

Careful, Carrie. I was being hard on this kid. Nineteen and undecided wasn't that unusual. Just because at his age I'd already been on my own for three years, responsible for Lindsay, who was six years my junior…

Bill gave Clooney, who was watching him with a rather sour look, a sharp elbow in the upper arm and asked, one guy to another, "What do you suggest, Clooney? What's really good here?"

Clooney's relaxed slouch disappeared. I saw the long-ago medal-winning soldier of his Vietnam days. "You will call me 'sir' until I give you permission to call me by name. Do you understand, *boy*?"

Bill blinked. So did I. Everyone in Seaside, no matter their age, called him Clooney.

"Stop that, Clooney!" Andi was appalled at her uncle's tone of voice.

"Play nice," I said softly as I realized for the first time that I didn't know whether Clooney was his first name or last. I made a mental note to ask Greg. As a former Seaside cop, he might know.

"R-E-S-P-E-C-T, darlin'." Clooney gave Andi an easy smile. He gave Bill a hard stare. "Right, Bill?"

Bill blinked again. "Y-yes, sir."

Andi took her beloved's hand and dragged him toward the back booth. "Ignore my uncle. He's having a bad day." She glared over her shoulder at Clooney, who grinned back at her.

"She's got spunk, that one," he said with pride.

"How'd she end up living with you?" I'd been longing to ask ever since Clooney showed up with Andi just before Labor Day and asked me to give her a job. I did, and I guess I thought that gave me the right to ask my question.

Clooney disagreed because he said, "I think I'll have one of your amazing Belgian waffles with a side of sausage."

"I'm on it." Lindsay headed back to the kitchen before I said a word. "Got it, Ricky?"

"Got it." Ricky tested the waffle iron with a flick of water. He smiled as the water jumped and evaporated. He was a handsome kid with dark Latino looks of the smoldering kind, a young Antonio Banderas. Unfortunately for him, his smoldering looks appeared to have no effect on Linds.

Another victim of unrequited love.

Andi came to the counter and placed an order for Bill and herself. I blinked. We could have served the whole dining room on less.

Mr. Perkins eyed me. "Are you going to make him pay for all that? You should, you know."

True, but I shook my head. "Job perk. He's cheaper than providing health benefits and not nearly as frustrating."

"So say you." Clooney settled to his waffle and sausage.

I watched the parade of laden plates emerge from the kitchen and make their way to the back booth, making me reconsider the "cheaper" bit. Andi took her seat and stared at Bill as if he could do no wrong in spite of the fact that he leaned on the table like he couldn't support his own weight. Didn't anyone ever tell the kid that his noneating hand was supposed to rest in his lap, not circle his plate as if protecting it from famished marauders or little girls with ponytails?

"Look at him," Clooney said. "He's what? Six-two and over two hundred pounds? Jase Peoples is about five-eight and one-forty if he's wearing everything in his closet."

"Let's forget about Jase, shall we?" Andi's voice was sharp as she came to the counter and reached for more muffins. "The subject is closed."

I grabbed her wrist. "No more muffins. We need them for paying customers. If Bill's still hungry, he can have toast."

"Or he could pay." To Mr. Perkins a good idea was worth repeating.

Andi laughed at the absurdity of such a thought.

Ricky had left his stove and was leaning on the pass-through beside Lindsay. "Four slices coming up for Billingsley."

"Billingsley?" I looked at the big guy as he downed the last of his four-egg ham-and-cheese omelet. With a name like that, it was a good thing he was big enough to protect himself.

"Billingsley Morton Lindemuth III," Ricky said.

"I should never have told you." Andi clearly felt betrayed.

"But you did. And you got to love it." Laughing, Ricky turned to make toast.

"He hates it," Andi said.

I wasn't surprised.

Greg drew in a breath like you do when something terrible happens. We all turned to stare at him.

"What's wrong?" I asked.

He was looking at the front page of *The Press of Atlantic City.* "Jase Peoples."

"What?" I demanded.

Clooney grabbed the paper and followed Greg's pointing finger.

I could see the picture and the headline above it: "Have You Seen This Man?"

3

C looney began to read aloud:

Jason Edward Peoples, 25, of Seaside, NJ, was reported missing
Sunday night by his parents, Joseph and Margaret Peoples.

"He never came home Saturday night," a distraught Joseph
Peoples said. "Or all day Sunday."

Clooney interrupted himself. "I'd think lots of twenty-five-year-old
guys didn't come home to Mom and Pop on Saturday night."

There were general grunts of agreement from Greg and Mr. Perkins.

"But he'd been gone for several years," I said. "I imagine they were
afraid he'd taken off again."

"Keep reading," Lindsay ordered from her listening post.

Peoples was expected at a large family gathering held in his honor
Sunday afternoon, according to police. He never appeared.

"Since the last time he was seen was during a fight at a party
Saturday night, we are investigating," said a police spokesperson.

"We called his cell phone when he didn't come home as
planned," Margaret Peoples said. "We called him all day Sunday.
He never answered. He'd never have missed the party. After all,
it was for him."

Jason Peoples had been out of contact with his family for
several years. He returned to Seaside a month ago.

"No one has seen him since someone picked a fight with him at that party," Joseph Peoples said. "What if he's hurt and needs help? You can understand why we're so worried."

The police are asking anyone with information about Peoples' movements to contact them immediately.

There was a moment of silence. Then we all turned as one and looked at Bill, who had walked to the counter as Clooney read.

He stared back, his face white.

Clooney made a growling noise deep in his throat. "You need to contact the cops, boy."

Bill stood and held his hand up in front of him as if to ward off Clooney's words. "I don't have to do anything. I didn't make him disappear! I'm not going to the police."

Andi flew to his side. "He didn't do anything wrong! I know. I was there."

Greg stood, pinning Bill with his gaze. He might no longer be a cop, but at the moment, that authority sat easily on his shoulders. "Someone will give details of the fight, including your name, Bill, if it hasn't been done already. It'd be good if you went to the police on your own rather than wait for them to come looking for you."

Bill stared back, bristling with attitude. "I gotta go. I got"—he seemed to be searching for a word—"*stuff* to do." He made for the door.

"Bill!" Andi bolted after him.

"Later, cupcake." He pushed the door open, intent on escape.

She followed him outside and grabbed him by the arm. He turned. They stopped in front of the picture window where we could see them. He stared down at her, one unhappy camper.

"What?" I could read his lips with ease.

She spoke to him with urgency, her hands flashing.

His frown deepened, and he said something that displeased her. One hand went to her hip, and she poked him in the chest with the other. I had to admire her chutzpa.

He grabbed her by the wrist, and she flinched. She tried to pull free, but he held on, leaning down and yelling in her face.

Clooney was off his stool faster than a runner off the blocks at the sound of the starter's pistol, Greg right behind him, but Bill was already moving. He pushed Andi away with enough force that she stumbled and almost fell. He strode away without a backward glance.

Clooney shoved the door open, his angry gaze on the retreating Bill. "You ever touch her in anger again, kid, and you'll answer to me!" He reached for Andi. "Are you all right, sweetheart?"

She ducked away and glared at him. "Stay out of it, Clooney."

Her unexpected anger sparked his. "Fat chance of that!"

"I can handle him!" She pushed past her uncle and made her way back inside, rubbing her wrist.

Muttering to himself, Clooney followed and caught her by her apron strings. "Let me see!"

She held out her arm with an impatient sigh. "I'm fine."

He ran his fingers over the bruise already forming. "No, you're not." He grabbed her in a hug. "Stay away from him, honey. He's a bad one."

"He's not," she said, her anger gone, her voice teary. "He's just upset."

"No matter how upset a man is, he never manhandles a woman," Mr. Perkins announced from his stool.

Andi rolled her eyes.

Clooney growled agreement. "If he comes near you again, I'll have to teach him a thing or two."

Andi pulled away and glared at her uncle. "I don't want to hear anyone talking against him." She grabbed his arm. "I mean it, Clooney."

He folded under her angry look. "Yeah, yeah."

She turned to Mr. Perkins. "Got that?"

She stared at him until he said, "Yes, I got it."

She nodded, then ruined her defense by rubbing her wrist as she stalked off to hide in the ladies' room at the back of the dining area.

The café door opened, and a pale couple entered. I walked to them, smiling. "May I help you?"

"We're looking for Carrie Carter."

"That's me." I upped my smile.

The man looked quite ill, his skin gray, his eyes bloodshot and circled with deep violet. He gave a halfhearted smile that faded quickly to sadness. "We're Joe and Margaret Peoples."

Jase's parents! I lost my smile. Had they come to tell us what had happened to Jase? If their expressions were anything to judge by, the news wouldn't be good.

"Please, have a seat." I ushered them to table one, glad the café was almost empty.

"We're sorry to bother you." Mrs. Peoples was pale too but in the way of someone who was troubled, not ill. She folded and unfolded a tissue with nervous fingers. "We just want to ask some questions. If it's okay."

"Of course it's okay"—I slipped into the third chair at the table—"though I don't know how I can help you."

Margaret was lean to the point of gauntness, and I wondered how much of her build was due to worry over Jase when he'd been missing the first time. For a mother, that was more than enough to put you off eating.

But why would anyone run away from nice people who cared for him?

"They're trying to tell us he went back to that cult." Joe's concave chest puffed up, indignant at the thought. "But he didn't. I know he didn't."

Greg slid into the fourth chair at the table. "How do you know that, Mr. Peoples? What makes you so sure?"

"Joe," the older man said. "Call me Joe."

"This is Greg Barnes," I said. "He knows Jase too, and he's concerned about him, as we all are." I decided that mentioning Greg was a former cop might intimidate the retiring couple.

Joe didn't seem to care who Greg was. He just wanted an opportunity to talk about his son. "When he came home, he was disillusioned."

"Not home from the café." Margaret was quick to clarify. "Home from that terrible place. He liked it here."

Joe nodded. "Disenchanted. And very sad. That's how we know he didn't go back."

"More than disillusioned, Joe. He was contemptuous." Margaret's voice took on that contempt. "'I hate The Pathway.' That's what he said. 'Hate.'"

"And he said it more than once," Joe said. "I'd ask him why, if it was so terrible there, did he stay all those years?" He stared at the tabletop as if he were envisioning the conversations.

"'Because I was stupid.' That's what he said." Margaret gave an emphatic nod to underscore the comment.

"But he never told you what made him finally leave?" Greg's voice was gentle.

Joe's shoulders sagged. "Just like he never told us why he left home the first time. Or this time."

"He didn't leave us again, Joe. He didn't." Margaret patted her husband's shaking hand.

"Then where is he?"

Joe looked about to cry. How many nights had they wept together or separately for their missing child? I wanted to wrap my arms around Joe and comfort him, not that he wanted consolation from a stranger. His sorrow was of a depth and breadth beyond my power to help. Only God gave solace on that level.

Margaret cleared her throat and looked at me. "We thought he might have said something here that would give us some clue as to where he went." She glanced at her husband. "I don't think we can survive his disappearing again."

She meant that Joe couldn't survive. His heart had broken once, found joy in their son's return, and if that heart broke again, the blow might well be lethal.

"He didn't say anything to me." I wished I had something of substance to offer. "We talked about schedules and college classes, impersonal things like that. We'd only known each other a short time."

Margaret nodded as if she expected this answer.

"But you should talk to my sister, Lindsay, and our cook. They were in the kitchen with Jase more than I was. And our waitress, Andi. She and Jase talked a lot."

Joe nodded, seeming hopeful again. "I'd like to talk with them. I know it's a long shot, but…" His voice trailed off.

But what else could they do? I looked at Greg and saw the sympathy in his eyes. He knew about losing children. He squared his shoulders, and the sympathetic parent disappeared. In its place was the cop looking for information.

"When Jase left to go out Saturday night, did he tell you where he was going?"

Joe nodded. "He said he was going to that party. 'I hope everyone's not too young,' he said. But a couple of the guys in his classes were ex-military doing college older, like Jason. They were the ones who invited him."

"Did he plan to meet anyone specific that you're aware of?"

"He never mentioned anyone beyond these guys," Joe said.

"And you've talked to them?"

Margaret nodded. "And we gave their names to the police."

"According to the paper, there was a fight," Greg said.

Margaret nodded again. "It's ridiculous. Jason wasn't a fighting kind of guy."

Just the thing a mother might say, but thinking of the slight, pleasant young man, I tended to agree with her. I'd never seen any tendency toward temper, certainly not toward physical confrontation.

"His friends said there was a fight, Marg." Joe sighed. "You have to accept that."

Margaret got a mutinous look, and I thought that even a video of Bill knocking Jase down wouldn't convince her. "One person attacking another isn't a fight."

"That's a very good point, Margaret," Greg said, and she looked at him gratefully.

I pushed back my chair. "Come. Let me take you to the kitchen."

The conversation with Lindsay and Ricky was brief and went as I expected.

"I'm so sorry," Lindsay said. "I wish there was something I could tell you that might help, but all we ever talked about was work or his classes. He was a pretty private person."

Ricky added, "But we liked him. He was a nice guy."

Margaret and Joe both looked pleased at the compliment and more discouraged than ever.

"We knew the chances of learning anything helpful were slim." Margaret took her husband's hand. "But you understand. We had to ask."

"Of course you did." I wanted to cry for them.

"We're all praying for his return." Lindsay had tears in her eyes.

Nodding numbly, Joe and Margaret Peoples left the kitchen. Greg and I trailed behind.

"Andi." I signaled to her as she came out of the ladies' room, and she came hurrying over. I indicated Joe and Margaret. "Jase's parents have come to ask if we know anything that might help them find him."

Her eyes went wide with what looked like panic. Was she afraid of what would happen if they knew she was the one who caused Jase to get attacked? And that the bully who did it had been right here mere minutes ago?

"Uh," she said.

Margaret smiled at her. "If you think of anything, please let us know. We need to find him." She looked at Joe. "We *must* find him."

The front door slid shut behind them after they left, and we were all silent in a combination of fear for Jase and respect for Joe and Margaret. Their pain had been palpable, and it left a bruise in the air.

After a few minutes Ricky cleared his throat. "I hate to bring things back to the mundane, but I got Billingsley's cold toast here." He held it out through the serving window. "If I heat it up, does anyone want it?"

No one seemed interested, so I took it. I sat at the counter and ate it with a cup of coffee, a touch of cream, no sugar. Conversation seemed to have dried up in the aftermath of the Peoples's visit. Lindsay and Ricky became busy in the kitchen, Clooney stared at nothing, and Greg began working the cryptogram on the *Inquirer* funnies page. Mr. Perkins fidgeted, wanting to say more, but since no one would look his way, he was forced to content himself with finishing his coffee.

I opened my Sudoku book to the challenging section and began searching for number sequences as I munched Bill's toast. I'd gotten Andi to try the easy puzzles, and she seemed to like doing them.

"My goal," she said, perky as ever as she appeared beside me, "is to finish a puzzle without looking at the answers in the back of the book." She made believe she hadn't been distressed to see Jase's parents. At least I hoped it was make-believe.

"Sounds good to me." I wondered if she knew more about Jase than she'd said. Was that why the panic? Or was it something altogether different, something I had no idea about? What was her story? Where were her parents? Why was Clooney the one who stood up for her? And why would no one talk about her unusual circumstances?

Andi interrupted my thoughts. "Did you ever use numbers to make a secret code when you were a kid?" She wrote 1ND3 in the margin of my Sudoku page. "You know, 1 equals A. Like that."

I shook my head. Secret codes were too much like fun, something missing from my childhood. "A-N-D-C?"

"What?" She stared at 1ND3 with a frown. "No, not that way. My friends and me used to do it with just the vowels: 2 equals E, 3 equals I. So 1-N-D-3 is A-N-D-I."

"Ah, got it."

"We thought we were so clever. Of course, we were in second grade."

"You were clever. I bet no one ever decoded your notes."

"Not that it mattered," she said. "We never had anything very interesting to write about. I mean, second grade. But when we got older, our codes got more sophisticated. First it was all the letters of the alphabet and their number equivalents, then symbols to represent certain letters, then a mix of numbers and symbols." She grinned. "We could write anything about anyone, and they'd never know. When the teacher confiscated stuff, she couldn't read it either. Neither could Becca."

"Becca?"

Her face darkened. "My goody-goody older sister."

So there was a sister, and one who was resented. It was the first piece of personal information Andi had ever revealed beyond her age and social security number. A million new questions raced through my mind, but before I could ask one, Clooney spoke.

"So solving a Sudoku is like decoding a note?" He was clearly skeptical about any redeeming value in the puzzle.

Andi nodded, then seemed to remember she was miffed at her uncle for not liking Bill. She sniffed. "Only it's more challenging because of the limitations of the form." She spun away to wipe down all the tables.

"'The limitations of the form?'" He stared after her, as if she were as difficult to decipher as the codes written by the Navajo code talkers from World War II. "Where did she ever get that line?"

"Not from me," I assured him.

He watched as I rubbed my eraser over a square to get rid of the three possible numbers and leave the one that was correct—I hoped. "Why do you like those things so much?"

I shrugged. I had no idea. I'd never tried to analyze why.

"Carrie likes unraveling things," Greg said. "Fixing things. Being the one in charge. Proving she's able. She likes to beat the puzzle just like she likes to beat life."

I stared at him, and he looked almost as surprised as I felt. He'd given what I thought was a very accurate read, and it was disconcerting to know he understood me that well. I thought he didn't even see me.

"Huh." Clooney looked from Greg to me and back. "Impressive."

"Very," I agreed.

Greg colored. "You sit on a stool long enough, you notice things."

Clooney gave first Greg, then me his most charming smile, and I braced myself for a con. Clooney that personable meant he wanted something.

"You two are obviously *very* smart."

I shook my head at the blatant flattery, and Greg raised an eyebrow.

"How about I let you two homeschool Andi?" Again the very charming smile. "That should be challenging enough for both of you and have a beneficial purpose." He glanced at my Sudoku book. Unspoken: which the number puzzles clearly hadn't.

"Is she a difficult student?" I asked.

"She's just had things so rough these last few years that she has a hard time with focus." He took his hat off, and for a moment I had hope he'd leave it off. Then he slapped it back in place, pulling his ponytail through the back. "She needs to catch up with her class."

Clooney held out his cup for a refill.

"I bet you're a good teacher." I filled his cup. "A great teacher."

"If you want her to be a beachcomber calculating the value of the things she digs out of the sand." That was how Clooney spent much of his time when he wasn't driving the town's bright red trash truck.

Ricky appeared at the serving window. "My afternoons are free." The café only served breakfast and lunch. "I could tutor her. How much you paying?"

"It's all about helping a needy girl." Clooney made *pro bono* sound a privilege.

"Won't buy groceries or pay the rent."

"You eat here, kid," Clooney said. "You don't need grocery money."

"Rent. I need rent." Ricky started to turn back to the kitchen and lunch prep.

"You good at math, especially algebra and geometry?" Clooney asked.

"Even calculus," Ricky said. "Math minor. I'm sure we can reach a price that's agreeable to us both."

Clooney looked so deflated at the thought of paying, I couldn't help laughing. I patted his hand.

Greg slid off his stool. "Just be glad you've got her to worry about. You're a fortunate man."

There was a short beat during which both Clooney and I were brought up hard against the fact that Greg no longer had his daughter to worry about. Or his son. Or his wife.

I wanted to cry as I saw Greg's shoulders hunch and his jaw clench.

L ife wasn't fair. Or God was out to get him. Either way, he was knee-deep in chicken waste.

You get a little physical with someone and they die on you.

He shuddered with the wave of rage that swept over him. He stared at the ocean. What he needed was a hurricane so he could experience the force and frenzy of the water and wind. Exorcise his personal fury.

He hadn't meant to kill. He hadn't. But the stupid person up and died anyway. What was he supposed to do about it now? Dead was dead.

One thing for sure. They weren't taking him down over it. Okay, maybe they wouldn't say it was murder, it being an accident and all, but manslaughter could take him down too. Hard and fast. And he had no desire to fall.

His jaw hurt. He must be grinding his teeth in his sleep. He opened and shut his mouth, rotated his jaw. If anything, the throbbing increased, and with the pain his rage heated and burned.

He shook with the intensity of his hatred.

Greg felt more than heard the hiccup in the conversation, the "uh-oh, did you hear what he just said?" It happened less often these days than it had even a year ago, but every time it did, the barb of pain struck deep and true. He never knew what to do either, to ease his own ache or to relieve the distress of those who suddenly heard what had been innocently said and had taken on a macabre meaning when they thought of his circumstances.

All he'd meant to do was remind Clooney how lucky he was to have Andi. That was all. Probably. He didn't think he'd even been thinking about Serena or Greggie or Ginny when he spoke, at least not on any conscious level.

Okay, so it bothered him to hear people complain about what he now saw as privilege. Not that Clooney was griping seriously. Still, Andi was here, vibrant and thriving. Pouty, not yet too insightful about character or behavior, especially of the male of the species, but living, breathing. Alive.

Clooney recovered before Carrie. "She'll make me old before my time is what she'll do," he said with an overdone frown.

When Carrie spoke, he'd have thought she missed the awkward moment if it hadn't been for the slight shake in her voice. "If that gray hair of yours is any indication, Clooney," she said, "you're well on your way to ancient without her help."

Clooney laughed too loudly.

Greg stood beside his stool, staring at his empty plate lying on the counter. He'd eaten all his eggs and toast like a good little boy, and he didn't even like eggs, no matter how they were prepared. For some reason they caught in his throat, threatening to make him gag. Yet he ate them day after dismal day.

He just couldn't face a cereal bowl. His had been waiting for him when he'd gone back into the house that terrible day, a soggy, bloated presweetened mess floating on soured milk.

"Dad, you'll rot your teeth!" Greggie and Serena had loved to tease him as only five- and seven-year-olds could. "Just because Grandmom never let you have anything but shredded wheat or bran flakes is no reason to be bad now that you're big."

"It's a good enough reason for me," he'd say as he poured his Lucky Charms or Cap'n Crunch, licking his lips in anticipation of that first sweet burst on his tongue.

"It's okay," Ginny would tell the kids. "He's the one who pays the dental bills." And she'd pour them their Cheerios or Raisin Bran while she smiled at him.

She had the best smile, the kind that dripped with love and warmed your soul. He never could figure how he'd been lucky enough to get her to marry him. And she'd given him Serena, already a beauty with a steel-trap mind, and Greggie, blessed with Ginny's warmth and charm.

On his fifth birthday all Greggie wanted to eat at his party were Count Chocula and chocolate Pop-Tarts.

"Sugar, like Daddy," he said.

The party was a raging success, at least in Greggie's young mind. Ginny had a hard time making the candles stay upright in the Pop-Tarts, but Greggie hadn't cared. He had sugar like Daddy.

As Ginny poured the Count Chocula into the kids' bowls, she'd shrugged. "At least the milk is good for them."

Greg knew that not facing a cereal bowl was ridiculous, as foolish as trying to drink away the pain had been. Still, he came to Carrie's every day and ate eggs.

He stepped away from his stool. "I gotta go. I have to evict a guy named Chaz Rudolph over at the Sand and Sea."

"Sounds like a fun day," Clooney said. "Want help?"

"Yeah." Mr. Perkins sat up as straight as his arthritic back would allow and held out his hand in a gun. "Go ahead, punk. Make my day."

Greg had to laugh, something he still didn't do much. "Listen, Dirty Harry, I appreciate your offer. You too, Clooney, but I think the constable and I can manage on our own."

"I know Chaz Rudolph." Andi leaned on the counter beside Carrie. "I don't like him." She wrinkled her nose.

Greg didn't like him either. "How do you know him?"

Something in his voice must have alerted Clooney, who went as still as a hunting dog on point.

Andi shrugged. "I met him in here."

If Andi met Chaz here, that was okay. No danger. All kinds of people had to eat, even scum like Chaz. As Greg relaxed, so did Clooney. Were all adult males as twitchy about their young female relatives? Would he have been such a guard dog with Serena? With all he'd seen as a cop, probably worse. Oh yeah, much worse.

He walked to the cash register and paid Carrie for his eggs.

She handed him his change, her smile warm and encouraging. "Hope it goes okay. See you tomorrow?"

He nodded, still amazed and appalled at his little dissertation on Carrie's strengths. He hadn't thought he knew her at all except as a pleasant blond woman with pretty blue eyes who ran a nice café. Generic stuff. When had he discerned all those character traits and qualities, and why was he so sure he was right? Not that it mattered, of course.

He exited the café and walked into the sea-scented air. He loved living on a barrier island sandwiched between ocean and bay. The Atlantic always calmed him, always soothed him, even when it raged in a nor'easter or a hurricane, even back on his worst days, when he walked for miles along the tide line regardless of the weather. The sea was consistent, dependable in a world gone mad. The tides ebbed and flowed in an eternal pattern. The waves rose and broke, whether gentle in the summer sun or raging, spume flying, in a storm.

And on the other side of Seaside, the bay spread like a blue magic carpet on which he could float in his old, dinged Starcraft, suspended over a teeming, unseen world. He could lie back on the seats and watch the herons soar gracefully overhead, long spindly legs trailing, or wonder at the patience of the cormorants as they spread their wings to dry, or laugh at the gulls screaming at each other as they fought over a scrap of food.

There was no place he wanted to be except Seaside.

As he drove his pickup the two blocks to the rental units located in the block behind the boardwalk, he sighed at the thought of the cocky, scrawny, nasty kid he hoped had left of his own volition.

He hated evictions.

No, wait. What was he thinking? He hated everything about his property manager's job. It was an honorable job, a worthy job. Many were challenged by it, enjoyed it. It just wasn't for him. But what was?

He'd had his dream job, but his awful circumstances had killed it. He'd known from the first night in his ghost-filled house that he was no longer emotionally stable enough to be a cop.

"God, why?" he'd cried as he stood by Serena's bed with its Pepto-Bismol pink quilt pulled up over lumpy sheets. "She was my little girl, my princess!"

In Greggie's room he stared at the cardboard box full of Legos. He felt his heart catch. "We never built that fort, Greggie. I'm so sorry!"

He wasn't able to go into the master bedroom. It smelled too much of Ginny.

Earlier that evening, when he'd sat slumped on the living room sofa, his father's arm across his shoulders as tears ran down the older man's face, Greg had closed his eyes in pain. And the flames came, crackling, swirling, devouring. He leaped to his feet with a cry and ran outside. He went to the beach for the first of many nights spent walking, walking, his father trailing a few feet behind.

He'd gotten through his family's funerals, though if he heard one more person say how wonderful it was that Ginny, Serena, and Greggie were in heaven, he'd scream. "God, I don't want them in heaven. I want them here!"

He managed to hold on through the big trial at which he testified and put Marco Polo away for many years. Then he turned in his badge. He refused to risk the lives of others because his heart, his very ability to think, to reason, had imploded.

The loneliness and the lack of purpose drove him to drink, literally.

"I used to be a cop, a husband, a father, a Christian," he told his father. "What am I when I've lost all those markers except 'Christian'? And when God lets you lose all that defines you, what does it mean to be a Christian?"

His father didn't give trite answers. "All I can say, Greg, is that when you're at your most alone, you aren't."

Greg had fallen into managing property through a contact at church, and while it wasn't what he'd ever pictured himself doing, at least he was good at it. And it wasn't emotionally demanding—which was a good thing. His emotions had died that long-ago morning.

Most of the time all he had to do to keep his job—and life—simple was make sure everyone's complaints were acknowledged and all the repairs made promptly. Anyone who stayed in one of the apartment or condo complexes he was responsible for soon learned that he took good care of both the renters and the buildings. Doing so meant no confrontations, no messy emotions. Good ol' detached Greg would take care of everything.

"Hey, my faucet's dripping. It drives me nuts."

"Greg, my toilet won't stop running."

"I want to paint my place, Mr. Barnes, and I want you to pay for the paint."

"I can't get the air conditioner to come on." Or the furnace to work or the sink to unclog or...

Most of the complaints were handled with ease. Most of the people were pleasant enough, especially since he never had to see most of them face to face. They worked during the day, and he was in and out of their units without having to talk with them. Just the way he liked it.

Ginny'd die laughing if she could see him these days.

"Greg, it's my turn," she used to butt in when he was going on and on about something. "Take a breath and let me give my opinion."

Now he hardly said anything unless there was no choice. It was like the little black cloud that hovered over him day and night sucked up all his words and transformed them into an invisible dark energy that vibrated about him all the time, buffeting him, draining him.

Except when he went to Carrie's. For some reason, when he walked into that place, the black cloud stayed outside. No dark energy pulsed inside those walls, and he felt comfortable there. Weird. But nice.

He pulled into the parking lot for the Sand and Sea Apartments and parked in a far slot next to the constable's car.

The law required that an officer of the court be the one to enter the unit to see if it had been vacated. The landlord might have to pay to file all the proper papers with the court, might have to wait the appropriate amount of time before eviction occurred, might have to change the locks or pay to have them changed, and might have to store at his own expense any furniture left behind pending a sheriff's sale, but in this instance Greg couldn't enter the unit on his own.

He stared at the eight-unit building, unwilling to get out of the car and see if Chaz Rudolph was still in residence. There were four units on each of the two floors, and Chaz's unit was the one on the first floor to the left of the back entrance.

"You can't make me leave!" he'd railed just two days ago in a nearly incoherent, highly profane phone message about persecution and unfair treatment. "I lost my job!"

No surprise. With the summer kids gone, his drug business had dried up. So sad. In the old days, Greg would have taken great pleasure in busting him. But the guy was crafty and clever. Sly. He always managed to deal without being caught. Of course, it was just a matter of time before he became overconfident and careless. With guys like Chaz, it always happened sooner or later.

But it hadn't happened yet, and today Greg had to evict him. Then Chaz would leave Seaside and set up shop somewhere else, polluting another town with his presence and his drugs until another landlord evicted him for nonpayment if the cops didn't get him first.

Greg slid from his truck and walked to the back entrance of the complex, where Constable Blake Winters waited. Blake was a retired cop, a large man who had eaten more than his share of doughnuts and pasta through the years. He wore a badge on the pocket of his plaid shirt, but he wasn't armed. Of course, he could have been carrying concealed.

Greg and Blake entered the building, turned down the hall, and knocked on Chaz's door.

No answer. Relief washed over Greg. Maybe this wouldn't be so bad after all. Maybe Chaz had gotten smart and left all on his own. Greg pulled out his master key and handed it to Blake, who opened the door.

Both men froze.

Chaz stood in the middle of the living room, in his hands an upraised wooden chair like the ones Greg's parents used to have in their dining room. He was a skinny kid of about twenty who was using too much of his own product. It showed in his pasty complexion and twitchy body. His dirty dark hair fell over his glazed eyes.

Greg sighed as he eyed the chair. He should have known. At least it wasn't a handgun of some kind, a very good thing since he didn't wear his Kevlar these days.

Blake took a step into the room, looking authoritative even without a uniform. "Put it down, Rudolph. You know you can't go around bashing people."

Chaz glared, unimpressed. "I'm not leaving here. You can't make me."

"Yes, I can. You know I can."

"Not without a fight." Chaz licked his lips.

In anticipation or fear? Greg hoped fear. Hopped-up eagerness for a fight was the last thing he wanted to deal with. He stood in the doorway, ready to come to Blake's aid if necessary.

In the years he'd been a property manager, Greg learned that people responded to an eviction notice in one of two ways. They nodded, heads bowed, knowing they hadn't paid their rent, couldn't pay their rent, deserved to be cast out for not keeping their part of the bargain set forth in the lease. These people left with slumped shoulders and fear in their eyes. Greg always felt like the lowest of heels with them, like it was somehow his fault they couldn't pay. He worried about where they would go, how they would live.

Then there were the others. They were confrontational, belligerent. They felt they were being treated unfairly and made things as difficult as they could. Some chose to be destructive in their misguided effort to pay you back for getting upset that they hadn't paid their rent for the past three or four or six months.

Chaz obviously embraced the latter school of thought, and the poor apartment had taken the brunt of his rage. Greg saw holes in the wallboard, and he noted the baseball bat lying on the floor under one. There were dark spots ground into the beige rug, and he was willing to bet they were body waste. Through the opening to the kitchen, he could see the hot-water faucet wrenched from its moorings and the resulting fountain, most of which seemed to be falling into the sink. Still an impressive amount of water rolled across the counter and spilled down the front of the cabinets in a miniature Niagara. The oven door hung drunkenly, one side ripped free.

"Did you clog the toilet too, Chaz?" Greg asked. "Socks? Washcloths? Pampers?"

Chaz glared, chair still raised. "Where'd I get Pampers?"

Not a denial. Greg sighed, thankful he had a reliable plumber on speed dial.

Blake pulled out his cell and hit 911. "We need help with an eviction, and we want to press charges against one Chaz Rudolph, present address Sand and Sea, apartment A, Seaside, for willful destruction of private property and making threats of bodily harm against an officer of the court."

Blake listened a minute, then hung up. "You've got less than five minutes before the police get here." He stood back from the door. "Out."

Chaz looked shocked. "You can't have me arrested! I didn't do nothing!"

Greg looked from one blatant act of destruction to another. "Four minutes."

Chaz lowered the chair, then raised it again. He brought it down with a great crash against the coffee table. A chair leg splintered. The coffee table collapsed. Chaz, triumphant, looked at Greg and Blake.

"Three minutes," Blake said.

"And that isn't my furniture," Greg said. "You rented it."

With a snarl fit for a threatened tiger, Chaz lunged for the door and lurched down the hall. "I'll get you for this!"

"Yeah, yeah." Greg followed to be certain the idiot drove off the lot, Blake right behind him. "Call me to set a date to clean the place out, Rudolph."

Chaz climbed into a bright yellow Hummer without responding.

Greg shook his head. The summer must have been quite profitable. Too bad Chaz wasn't smart enough to turn in the Hummer and get a Kia. Then he might be able to pay his rent.

Chaz hit the gas, and the Hummer roared backward. Blake nodded with satisfaction and turned back to the building. "Time to change the locks."

Greg checked his watch, thankful there was no car in the slots behind Chaz. "Locksmith's due any minute. I'll turn off the water and call the plumber as soon as Rudolph's gone."

He watched as Chaz paused to shift gears. The Hummer leaped forward, but it didn't turn to drive from the lot.

It drove straight at Greg.

6

I leaned on the counter at the cash register after Clooney and Mr. Perkins left. The café hadn't been totally empty since midspring, and the quiet was nice—provided it didn't presage a bad fall and winter. There was a fine line between a more relaxed pace and a dismal pace.

"Hey, Carrie," Lindsay called. "I'm taking ten to run up to the apartment. Everything's good to go for lunch. Ricky's got the tomato basil and the vegetable beef soups simmering. The quiche is ready for the oven and will go in as soon as the black forest cake and apple caramel pies are done."

I glanced at the glass case where a fresh fruit flan was already on display, its circles of strawberries, blueberries, kiwis, and bananas shining under their clear glaze.

"Chicken salad's ready to go, and the pork barbecue is simmering." She pulled her apron off and laid it on the counter. "I'll be back before you even know I'm gone."

I glanced at the clock. Not quite eleven. All of a sudden taking ten sounded wonderful. Only I wanted thirty. I wanted to walk to the boardwalk, sit on a bench, and let the ocean purl and purr while I threw my head back and listened to its murmur. I should be cleaning the bathroom at the back of the café, but the mess there wasn't going anywhere. The tangy scent of salt water won over the acrid odor of bleach hands-down.

"Go on up, Linds. Only take thirty."

"Really?"

"Yep. I'm putting the 'Back at 11:30' sign on the door."

"Yes!"

Her feet pounded up the steps to our apartment. She'd collapse on the sofa with our Maine coon cat, Oreo, lying on her like a great black hairy afghan. Lindsay would murmur how wonderful Oreo was, and she'd purr, her golden eyes closing in delight, her white ruff and whiskers the sole breaks in her midnight pelt.

"Why'd she go up there?" Ricky looked at me with sad eyes. "We could have talked, her and me."

I couldn't very well tell him that she needed a break from his adoring gaze, and the one place she knew he wouldn't try to follow was the apartment. He was allergic to cats.

"Andi, feel free to put your feet up or go for a walk," I said. "Whatever. Just be back by eleven thirty, okay?"

"I'm going to sit down and do a Sudoku." She grabbed her book and walked to a back booth. She turned to me just before sliding into her seat. "He didn't do anything wrong."

Bill. "Then everything will be fine." I sure hoped that was so, but the bruise coloring her wrist gave me pause.

"Yeah, everything will be fine." She sounded as if she was trying to convince herself.

I walked to her and wrapped my arms around her in a gentle hug. She didn't hug me back, but I didn't let it bother me. I remembered the long-ago days when I was just Andi's age and the former owner of Carrie's had hugged me. I hadn't responded either—I hadn't known how—but I'd loved those hugs.

If I could be there for Andi as Mary Prudence had been there for me, even if just a little, I'd feel I was doing something to give back all that had been given to me.

"Carrie likes unraveling things. Fixing things. Being the one in charge. Proving she's able."

Greg was right. I was the one who always took charge, but then someone had to seize control of the runaway train that had been my early life. I just hoped there was a bit more to me than being a control freak. Like love. Or humor.

I hung the eleven-thirty sign on the door and started for the boardwalk two blocks away. I paused at the first cross street and looked back over my shoulder. Carrie's Café. The sign had a Caribbean blue background with navy letters outlined in sea green.

Oh, Lord, I still can't believe it!

I thought of that long-ago morning when we ran away, Lindsay and I. Mom had swayed in the doorway of the bedroom we girls shared. Sunlight shone through the old sheet I'd tacked to our window for a curtain, making her skin look pastier than usual. Her hair was wild, her eyes bleary. She looked ready to collapse. If the alcohol didn't get her, malnutrition would.

"Carrie!" She tried to look angry, but her facial muscles weren't cooperating. "Bobby says you came after him with a knife!"

Bobby, Mom's latest, leaned on the jamb of Mom's room, fat belly hanging over his boxers, a nasty smile on his fat face. Well, he had to explain the cut on his arm somehow, and he wasn't about to say he'd asked for it.

I felt then ten-year-old Lindsay slide under the covers until she was invisible. She was shaking, and I hated Bobby for making her afraid.

"He came into our room last night," I said.

Mom shrugged. "So? He just wanted to say good night."

I stared at her. "Mom, that's not what he wanted!"

She laughed. "Don't be stupid, Carrie. What could he want with you or your sister? He has me."

I might not be beautiful and Lindsay might be scrawny, but we looked alive, which was more than I could say for her. The dead street lady I'd seen last winter on my way to school looked better than she did. She'd had me when she was my age and was now thirty-two, but she looked at least fifty. Old. Old, old, old.

"I want you to give me your knife." She held out her hand, and it trembled. She needed a drink already, and it was—I checked my alarm clock that I'd stolen from the mom-and-pop store down the street—7:10 a.m.

I shook my head. "Just tell Bobby to stay out of our room, and there won't be any trouble."

"This is Bobby's house too," she said, "and he can go anywhere he wants. Maybe next time he'll turn the knife on you."

Bobby stared at me, his porky eyes hungry, his intent clear.

"Just let him try."

In a huff she spun to leave. The quick movement made her dizzy and she grabbed for the wall to steady herself. Now that she faced him, Bobby turned injured victim, clutching his bandaged arm, his face a study in pain.

"Come on, my beauty." He held out his good arm. "I've got just what you need."

Disgusted with both of them, I flopped back on my pillow. Lindsay squeaked as I squished her.

I moved aside. "Come on up for air, Linds. We've got to talk. It's time."

I had watched enough TV to know what happened to girls who ran away to the big city, so we ran away to Seaside. We'd heard stories about the place all our lives. When Mom got soggy drunk and no man was around to occupy her, she'd get melancholy, remembering all the halcyon summer days before her father took off and her mother jumped in front of a bus.

"Back when my daddy was working, before we moved to Atlanta, we lived in Camden, New Jersey, and we'd go to Seaside for two weeks every summer." She'd smile and look pretty for a moment. "We'd stay at the Brookburn, this boardinghouse that had one-room apartments with little refrigerators and two-burner stoves, and I had a cot tucked in a corner. We'd sit on towels on the beach and go in the ocean, which was green, not blue like you see in pictures. Daddy would hold my hands, and I'd jump the waves. At night we'd go on the boardwalk and I'd ride the merry-go-round. Once Daddy took me on the Ferris wheel, and you could see out over the ocean all the way to Europe. At least that's what he told me."

Then she'd start to cry and drink until she passed out.

Her stories made me want to live in Seaside, and Lindsay shared that dream.

"Someday, Linds," I'd tell her as we sat in the library, using the free computer and staring at the sites on the Web full of pictures of pretty beaches and glorious sunsets. Whether we looked at the brilliant transparent blue of the Caribbean or the hypothermic opaque green of the North Atlantic, the sea tugged at us like the cycles of the moon pulled at it.

"Someday," she'd whisper back, her chair pulled close to mine.

Thanks to Bobby, the day came. It was late spring, a good time to run away.

"I'll get a job easy," I told Lindsay as we stuffed what few things we had in our backpacks. "It's a resort. Resorts need summer help. I can be a waitress or a chambermaid or a cashier. It doesn't matter."

"But you're only sixteen," Lindsay said, scared.

"I'll say I'm eighteen and just graduated from high school. I'll say our mom is in the Army on an overseas tour and our dad's dead."

Lindsay looked impressed with the lie. "But where will we sleep?"

"We'll get a room." I tried to sound confident. I'd already decided we would sleep under the boardwalk if we had to. Anything was better than here with Bobby or the men who would come after him.

I packed my knife with care, wrapping it in my other pair of jeans. The thought of meeting dangerous men eager to prey on naive girls didn't frighten me. I'd been keeping my mother's various "friends" at arm's length for years, sometimes with words or tears, more often with my large kitchen knife with which I slept. During the day I hid it under a floorboard so no one could steal it from me. I kept Lindsay close every night too, putting her between me and the wall so no letch could get to her except through me and my knife.

Usually waving my weapon around and threatening to cut off parts of a man's anatomy were enough. Bobby was the first one I ever had to cut, and I'd only succeeded in driving him off because of surprise. When he came back, and I knew he would, he'd be prepared.

I would not give him that chance.

It took us two days to get to Seaside by bus, tickets paid for with money I filched from Bobby's wallet, which he'd conveniently left on the kitchen table when he went to the hospital to get his arm stitched up. No wallet, no money, boom! You pick your hospital right and you get a free ride.

The first thing we did when we hit Seaside was go to the beach.

"The ocean!" Lindsay cried and ran to the water. We couldn't stop laughing as we took off our shoes, rolled up our jeans, and went wading. The water was so cold our ankles hurt, but we didn't care. We hooted and splashed and chased each other like a pair of little kids. Then we collapsed happily in the sand to catch our breaths.

Later that day when we decided to explore Seaside, we walked past a little restaurant called the Surfside, where I spotted a Help Wanted sign in the window.

Heart pounding because, certainly, it couldn't be this easy, I ducked around the side of the building and pulled a clean T-shirt from my backpack. It was Barbie pink with a purple flower on its front, and it read Seaside in shimmery purple letters under the flower. I'd snitched it from one of the few open stores on the boardwalk, and I thought it was one of the prettiest things I'd ever owned.

I pulled out my brush and dragged it through my hair. I was a natural blonde in a world that wondered if blondes had more fun. I could have an-swered that question if anyone had bothered to ask me. No. No way. Not by any stretch of the imagination.

"Do I look okay?" I asked Lindsay. My nerves were jumping so badly it was a wonder I could stand still.

She nodded. "You look beautiful."

I snorted at that overstatement. "You have to wait here for me."

She looked at me with large, teary brown eyes.

I gave her a quick hug. "Don't worry, Linds. I'm not going to pick up a guy or go to the bar." That's what our mother did when she put on a clean shirt—if she had one—and brushed her hair. "I'm going to answer that Help Wanted sign back there."

Lindsay's shoulders relaxed, her trust in me total and weighty. What if I failed her? What if we had to go back home? I stiffened my spine. I couldn't afford to fail.

"What kind of a job do they have?" Lindsay asked.

"I don't know, and I don't care." I swatted at the sand clinging to my jeans. The denim was damp from the knees down, but at least it was no longer dripping. I hoped the person inside that restaurant would think the holes in the knees were the kind you bought, not the kind that came be-cause you didn't have enough money to buy new when the old got raggedy. At least I'd stopped growing about four years ago, and though the jeans were threadbare, they were the right length.

Saying a prayer to a God I wasn't sure existed but I was still careful not to offend because you just never knew, I went inside.

And Mary Prudence Hastings entered our lives.

Smiling at the memories, I crossed the last street before the boardwalk and found myself beside the Sand and Sea. The building was an older one that had gotten a facelift of gray, weathered-looking siding covering its original stuccoed cinder block. All eight units faced the ocean—if you didn't take into account the shops that lined the boardwalk, impeding your view. Still the advertising could legitimately say, "ocean view," a real find if you liked your view to be slices of sea glimpsed between buildings. I could see Greg's pickup in the far corner of the parking area.

As I smiled at the thought of him, the back door of the building slammed open, and an irate Chaz Rudolph stormed out. I recognized him from the café. He was a skinny little guy, and his arms flew as he screamed obscenities. Greg followed him out, all purpose and intense scowl. A man with a badge followed. The constable, no doubt.

Greg stopped on the narrow strip of sandy gravel between the apartment building and the parking lot, arms crossed, legs spread, watching Chaz.

My heart did its usual foolish happy dance, and I sighed. How could I be so idiotic, suffering from a ridiculous case of unrequited love at my age? Such heart palpitations were for sixteen-year-olds like Andi, swooning over unworthy swains like Bill. Or even guys like Ricky, enamored with an older woman like my sister. I was supposed to be mature, to have my act together. All those years of counseling had to be good for something, like discerning the realistic from the unrealistic.

I tore my gaze from Greg and watched Chaz climb into a yellow Hummer. I blinked. Chaz could afford a Hummer, even a used one, but not his rent? His view of reality was more skewed than mine.

Chaz shot Greg a final dirty look, then backed the Hummer out of his slot with a heavy foot and a complete disregard for the neighboring cars, which he sprayed with gravel. The constable went back into the Sand and Sea, but Greg stayed to watch his ex-tenant off the lot. Chaz paused to shift gears, then roared forward.

Right at Greg.

7

I screamed as Greg tried to jump out of the way.

The Hummer bounced over the little concrete barrier that was supposed to keep residents from parking too close to the building and roared
across the narrow strip of dirt edging the parking lot. With a great crashing
noise, it rammed the Sand and Sea, a yellow behemoth bent on destruction.

I stared in shocked disbelief, unable to process what I was seeing. Still,
I managed to scream long and loud. At least I assumed it was me yelling like
a banshee. No one else was around to break the sound barrier.

I lost sight of Greg as he dived for cover. *Oh, Lord! Oh, God! Please don't
let him be hurt!*

The ice paralyzing my limbs melted in the hush following the crash. I
started running. "Greg! Greg!"

Not that there was no noise. I could hear falling building parts, the
rumble of the Hummer's engine, and the slap of my feet, but by contrast to
the fearful roar of the crash it seemed deathly quiet.

As I ran, I could see Chaz in his Hummer, still embedded in the building, pushing the now-deflated air bag out of the way. He looked at what he
had done, looked at the guy with the badge rushing from the building with
a gun in his hand, and threw the Hummer into reverse. At the movement,
his face crumpled as if he were in pain, which he would be after being hit in
the face and chest with the air bag. He stepped on the gas, and with a great
roar the car tore itself loose from the building and flew back across the lot.

"Halt!" the man with the gun yelled as he pointed his weapon.

For the briefest of moments, Chaz and I stared at each other as he fought with the gearshift. I had a vision of him going for me as he had for Greg, eyewitness that I was, but he jerked the wheel and squealed out onto the street, disappearing toward the bridge that would take him off the island.

"Shoot him!" I yelled at the constable as he raced after the Hummer into the street. "Shoot him!" I had never known I could be so bloodthirsty.

"Can't." The constable gave a frustrated snarl. "Too populated." He slipped his gun into his trouser pocket and jogged back to the apartment.

Of course he couldn't. What was wrong with me? I hadn't even noticed the older couple walking down the street or the young mother and her two little children who rounded the corner of the building.

The constable knelt by Greg. "You okay, Barnes?"

Greg didn't respond, just lay there in the strip of dirt by the complex, eyes wide. In pain, in disbelief, or in death? My heart climbed to my throat where it threatened to choke me.

I fell to my knees beside him. "Greg, can you hear me?" *Oh, God, let him be okay!*

I flinched at the bleeding gash on his cheek, and a lump was rising on his forehead. Blood seeped from the many abrasions on his arms and cheek, all angry and painful looking. None appeared to my inexpert eye to be life threatening, but what if the Hummer had hit him? Were there internal injuries I couldn't see? Broken ribs? Pierced lungs? What if there was a life-threatening hematoma forming under that bump on his forehead?

I looked at the constable, who was just standing there, and found him hanging up his cell.

"Nine-one-one," he said. "They'll be here pronto."

Greg frowned. "They were coming for Chaz anyway."

"Yeah," the constable nodded, "but now they'll hurry."

I took a deep calming breath. Greg was conscious. Conscious was good.

And he could talk. Talking was excellent. Slowly my heart returned to my chest and began beating in regular rhythm again.

"Ambulance?" the constable asked.

Greg shook his head and grimaced. "Nah. Just a bump or two. I think I hit one of the parking barriers on my way down." He pushed himself to a sitting position, grabbing his shoulder as he did. He tried to rotate it and made a face.

"A bump or two, my eye. You need to be checked out," I said.

He put out a hand. "No."

I hadn't realized he could be so stubborn.

He stared in disgust at the great hole in the side of the Sand and Sea. Siding, cinder block, insulation, drywall, and glass littered the dirt and bled into the parking lot. "Would you look at that!"

I gave up on him and medical care as a lost cause and looked at the wrecked building. I could see all the way through the apartment to the front window.

"There's broken furniture in the living room." I knew the Hummer hadn't done that.

"Yeah." Greg tried rotating his shoulder again. "Chaz protesting his eviction."

A cop car pulled into the lot, lights flashing but no siren. Officers Maureen Trevelyan and Rog Eastman climbed out.

Rog surveyed the damage and shook his head. "Talk about irate tenants."

"He tried to run Greg over!" My indignation must have been a little over the top because they all looked at me with strange expressions. I dialed back my outrage. "Well, he did. I saw it all."

"But he missed, I see," Maureen said as Greg pulled himself to his feet and leaned against the nearest car. I stood too, my arms spread as if I would catch him if he fell. There was a bruise already forming on his forehead bump, and his cheek was turning purple beneath the bloody cut.

"Was he after you, or were you just in the way when he went for the building?" Maureen asked him.

Greg shrugged and winced at the movement. "Hard to tell."

"Think about it," Maureen said. "You too, Carrie. There's a big diff between attempted homicide and willful destruction of property."

"So what was he driving?" Rog asked.

"A yellow Hummer." Greg, the constable, and I spoke in near unison.

The constable added, "Heading toward the bridge."

"His name's Chaz Rudolph." Greg gave them the license number.

I stared. "You memorized the license number of a car about to run you over?" The man was amazing.

"When it first showed up on the lot, I automatically committed it to memory." He looked at Maureen and gave a half smile. "Old habits."

She nodded.

"Its front end is all messed up," I added.

Rog glanced at the building again and laughed. "I bet." He leaned in the squad car and spoke into his radio, ending with, "Cover the bridge exits."

Greg lurched a bit as he tried to take a step, and I grabbed his arm. "Are you sure you're okay?"

"I'm fine." He forced a smile as he contemplated the building. "What an idiot!"

"I've pulled a couple of people from cars in living rooms when they've lost control or couldn't stop on a slick road," Rog said, "but on purpose is a new one for me. And just when I thought I'd seen it all." He grinned at Maureen. "Days like this, I love my job."

Maureen grinned agreement as three people ran into the lot and joined the young mother and the older couple who'd stuck around to see if there would be any more excitement. Reality TV was never this interesting.

Maureen's smile dimmed as she watched the gawkers. They all had cell phones in hand and were texting madly, even the older couple and the young mom. Her kids were busy scooping cinders and sand into a small mountain.

Maureen gave a frustrated laugh. "They're tweeting and facebooking."

As if to prove her correct, one guy called, "He couldn't get across the Ninth Street Causeway. People blocked it. He turned south on Bay toward the Thirty-Fourth Street Bridge."

Greg snorted. "Amateurs playing at being cops."

"Voyeurs." Rog shook his head. "Someone's going to get hurt one of these days. They may think it's fun and exciting, but the bad guys don't. If one of the gawkers is in the way, look out, baby." Irked though he was, he went to his cruiser and relayed the Thirty-Fourth Street Bridge information to the dispatcher.

"Regular guys blockaded the causeway?" I was stunned. I couldn't imagine putting my car in the path of Chaz and his Hummer. Of course, the tweeters out there hadn't seen what the Hummer had done to the Sand and Sea. Still a Hummer is a Hummer, all big and bad. I was surprised Chaz didn't use it to ram his way past the blockade.

Two cars pulled into the lot, and a twenty-something climbed out of each, one male, one female. They huddled with the other watchers, whispering and pointing when their thumbs weren't dancing on their keypads.

Rog was grinning as he rejoined us. "Dispatch already knew. Several phone calls to 911 from people tracking the Hummer. I bet he's got a line of cars behind him, all tweeters and their friends. He hasn't got a chance."

"Sort of a wedding party motorcade without the crepe-paper streamers," I said. "Or horns. Or bride and groom."

Greg put his hand to his head.

I forgot the tweeters. "Headache?" Dumb question. Why else would he hold his head?

"Oh, yeah. I never should have left the café."

Café! I glanced at my watch. Eleven thirty-five! "I've got to go. It's lunchtime."

"I need to talk to you more," Maureen said.

"Sure, but can you stop at the café? I'm seriously understaffed and need to be there."

She nodded. "I'll drop in after the crime scene techs finish here."

I smiled my thanks and looked at Greg. "You stop in too. Someone's got to clean those scrapes."

He waved his hand like he was erasing the cuts and blood. The heel of his palm was red and weeping.

"You haven't seen yourself, bub. Stop in." I turned away before he could say no. What was it with men? When it wasn't "if you build it, they will come," it was "if you ignore it, it will heal."

As I hurried down the street, several of the texters followed me, joined by a gray-haired lady who zipped right along with the crowd in her motorized scooter. Cilla Merkel, a café regular.

"Did you see it happen?" one tweeter called to me. "I know some lady in a blue top was a witness to that mess. SweetCilla said so. She heard the lady's screams and saw the whole thing go down from her place across the street in that apartment building."

I glanced down. I had on my blue Carrie's Café shirt today. It felt very strange knowing that my screams were responsible for all these people. I glanced at Cilla and gave her a did-you-have-to look. She grinned back.

"Yeah, my Twitter source said blue shirt too," another texter called. "Said her name's Carrie. You Carrie?"

"So what did you see, Carrie?" a third yelled. "Did you scream because he tried to run over you too?"

I began to feel a bit heckled. "Don't you people have jobs?" I asked over my shoulder. "Shouldn't you be at work?"

"Yeah," Number One said. "What's your point?"

There was a rumble of agreement from the rest of the tweeters as we reached the café.

I turned to them. "You're welcome to come in if you want to buy something to eat. If not, stay out here. Okay? Just remember I don't know anything, and nothing's going to happen here except lunch."

"But you haven't told us what you saw."

And I wasn't going to. "That's because I think I should tell the police first."

There was another rumble but not of agreement. They saw me as unreasonable. I studied the motley crew of twenty- and thirty-somethings and Cilla who was old enough to know better, though I supposed she was the only one not cutting work to trail me. The older couple must have been smart enough to continue their walk to the boardwalk. The young mom was here, her two kids hanging from her legs.

"Come on, guys. If you hang outside my door in a big clump, you're going to scare off my customers."

They looked around as if searching for said customers and finding none.

"They'll be here," I said somewhat defensively. "Lindsay's quiche is famous in these parts."

"It's wonderful," Cilla agreed. "My favorite. You got tomato basil soup today? It's Monday."

I gave her a faint smile and addressed the others. "Maybe you could wait across the street by the drugstore." People had to go in to get their medicine regardless of street crowds, right?

"I'll go in and get lunch," Cilla said to the tweeters. "I'll let you know if anything happens. Anything at all." She waved her iPhone.

There was a chorus of "Promise?" and one "You sure you know how to use that?"

Cilla skewered the doubter with a steely look that had him taking a step backward.

"Hey," Number One said. "This is SweetCilla." Like she was royalty.

The doubter looked instantly impressed. "I'm so sorry. No disrespect intended."

Cilla waved a hand, forgiveness granted. Queen Cilla.

As I let the door fall shut behind me, I nearly ran over Lindsay, Ricky, and Andi staring out at our visitors. Linds had her smartphone in her hand, and Ricky was standing too close to her under the guise of reading over her shoulder. His own phone was still in its holder clipped to his belt.

Andi, pink phone in hand, vibrated with excitement. "You saw Chaz try to kill Greg?" Her hazel eyes were wide.

"He was mad about being evicted, and he rammed the building."

"He wasn't after Greg?" Linds held out her phone. "Cilla said it was attempted murder."

"She did, huh?" I replayed the scene in my mind, and I realized I couldn't say whether Chaz wanted to harm Greg or not. He seemed nutty enough to do something that rash, but I didn't *know* that was what he intended. If you're nuts enough to ram a building with your shiny yellow Hummer, you might be crazy enough to go after a person too. But the word was *might*.

"I don't know," I said, and the three looked disappointed.

The door opened, and Cilla drove in. She smiled sweetly. "Don't you worry, Carrie. I won't bother you."

I gave her my hostess smile. "Take any seat you'd like." I waved my hand to show her the possibilities, and there were many since no one in Seaside seemed to be taking an early lunch.

"We follow you on Twitter, Ricky and I," Lindsay told Cilla. "I've learned more about Seaside past and present from you than anyone else."

Cilla nodded, as regal as Elizabeth II, taking the compliment as her due. The only thing missing was the royal wave. "I just sit at my window or on the boardwalk and report what I see."

Even I recognized an understatement.

Cilla rolled up to table two, her eyes sparkling with life and intelligence and her gray hair curled around her very attractive if somewhat wrinkled face. She was a widow, and I wondered why no man had stepped up to take Mr. Merkel's place. Probably no one her age could keep up with her.

"I'll take Lindsay's quiche with fruit on the side and a cup of tomato basil. Oh, and a sweet iced tea, BTW."

BTW? Give me a break!

The door opened, and two of the texters came in.

"You have to order food," I said as I shooed my staff back to work.

"We have to eat lunch sometime," said the taller of the two, "so we decided to eat it here." They slipped into a booth. In another minute all the street group were inside, seated and scanning menus, even the young mom with the two little kids.

As soon as they placed their orders, they began texting, though I couldn't imagine what they were talking about. *I ordered quiche* or *I'm having grilled cheese with ham and tomatoes*? Nothing else newsworthy was happening unless you counted someone dropping a tray of silver in the kitchen with a horrendous crash. Today's dishwasher?

Which reminded me, if Jase wasn't going to be here, I had to do something about tomorrow. And where was he? *Lord, let him be okay, okay?*

Whenever one booth or table emptied, another group of tweeters appeared. Aside from the little bleeps and chimes that denoted new messages, the place was eerily quiet. The upside was that they were too preoccupied to notice the slow service.

"Since he couldn't get over the bridge and out of town, he's speeding south into Avalon on Ocean Drive," one texter announced just in case the others had missed that information.

Ocean Drive was a highway that linked the run of barrier islands that edged South Jersey, protecting the mainland from the ravages of the ocean's temper. I sometimes wondered what would happen to the highway and all the islands if the predictions of global warming came to pass. The highest point in Seaside was less than ten feet above sea level, and it wouldn't take much to devastate the town. In a storm several years ago, the ocean and bay met in Harvey Cedars, an island community several miles north of Seaside. Would such a thing happen permanently up and down the coast someday?

"It's a good thing it's off-season and there aren't many people and cars around," Cilla said when I refilled her sweet iced tea. "I can't imagine the confusion and danger if the place was crawling with summer people."

I had to agree. The thought of that huge vehicle speeding through streets swarming with vacationers was enough to give me the shudders.

The café door opened, and Mary Prudence, Lindsay's and my fairy godmother, walked in, making her way through the three parties waiting for tables.

"What are you doing here?" I asked. "Not that I'm not always glad to see you, but what's up?"

"I read on Twitter that things were slightly nuts here. I thought I'd better come in and help you out."

"You're on Twitter?"

"Sure. Isn't everyone? I follow SweetCilla. She's been reporting everything ever since you screamed."

Uh-huh.

"And I follow Mary P," Cilla said.

"And I follow both," called a slick-looking guy whose suntan was fading toward winter wan.

A flurry of "me too's" and "so do I's" sounded.

I looked at Cilla with her gray hair and Mary P with her carefully tinted hair. How weird that they knew more about technology than I, who was at least thirty years younger than Mary P and closer to forty for Cilla.

"So what can I do to help you out?" Mary P slipped her smartphone into its holder clipped to her belt.

A stray piece of information finally connected. "Carrie's Café is being mentioned on Twitter by name?"

Mary P nodded. "Facebook too. You couldn't pay for publicity like this."

Wow. Maybe there was something to social networking after all.

She wrapped an apron around her ample middle. "You want me to do counter or tables?"

I smiled at her. It was like old times, only then she was the boss and I the employee being told my wait station.

"I'll take the counter and the register," I said. "You and Andi take the tables and booths."

With a nod, Mary P went to talk with Andi about division of labor.

"They got him," Lindsay yelled to the customers.

"Yeah," called a guy with black glasses and a terrible haircut. "The Wildwood PD was waiting for him at the south end of town."

"He smashed up a cop car when he tried to run a barricade," Cilla said. "Marleysghost has pictures on YouTube!"

Everything stopped as everyone, including the cook, the baker, and both my servers went to Marleysghost's YouTube post.

"Ricky," I yelled. "All the cheese in the grilled cheese for booth one is melting out of the sandwich! And smoke's beginning to swirl. Quick or we'll have the smoke alarms blaring!"

Ricky grinned at me and cocked his head toward our customers. "They'll never notice."

How true.

He flipped the sandwich, and it was fine—which I knew. I'd just been trying to keep his mind on his job.

When Maureen and Rog came in around one thirty to hear my version of the incident at the Sand and Sea, I thought my remaining customers would twist their heads off their shoulders as they tried to watch what we were doing and eavesdrop on our conversation. When we went to the back of the café and my office, there was a collective groan.

"Don't worry," Lindsay called to them, waving her smartphone. "I'll keep you updated."

Not if I didn't keep her updated.

I closed the office door behind the three of us, relieved to be free of being reported on. Who knew being a celebrity was so wearing? But if it meant more business…

"I've got a question for you guys," I said. "How come there isn't an army of texters out there looking for Jason Peoples?" I'd been thinking about that for the last hour. "If some idiot ramming a building got everyone so excited, you'd think a missing person would make them froth at the mouth."

"Good question." Rog looked around my cluttered office. "We'll have to get SweetCilla and Mary P on it. Our sources haven't come up with much."

"Tell me you don't follow them on Twitter," I said.

"You'd be surprised what those two ladies have uncovered." Maureen looked around for seats.

I indicated my desk chair. "Yours, Maureen." I pulled a pair of folding chairs from against the wall, offered one to Rog, and took the other.

Maureen sat with caution in the desk chair, well used when I got it. It only wobbled slightly. "As to Jason Peoples, we do know he had a fight with a guy, big and with dark hair, first name Bill. We're looking for that guy as a person of interest, but we don't know much else."

So Bill hadn't followed Greg's advice and gone to the police. I wasn't surprised. My feeling was that Bill would buck authority without a second thought, convinced that he, ruler of his small universe, knew better than they. After all, their only purpose was to interfere with his life.

Maureen appeared frustrated. "No one at the party knew this Bill, or so they say. They're all telling us he crashed the party with some pretty girl with strawberry-blond hair and he got into the fight over her."

I flinched. Andi. "You're looking for Bill Lindemuth."

Maureen looked blank, but Rog, a lifetime resident of Seaside, perked up. "The football hero of a couple of years ago?"

I nodded. "He was in the café this morning for breakfast."

"Yeah? How do you know he's the guy we're looking for?"

I hesitated for a moment, feeling like a traitor but knowing I had to tell them what I knew. Finding Jase was more important than the almost certain possibility of angering Bill or upsetting Andi.

"You need to talk to my server, Andi Mueller. She's a friend of his. In fact she's the girl he was with at the party. But she's only sixteen. Take it easy on her."

8

Greg Barnes stood alone, staring at the damage done to the Sand and Sea. The locksmith had come and gone, but what good was a new lock on the front door when the wall was an open invitation to the crooked and the curious?

He'd called his boss to report what had happened, and with any luck he'd be gone before Josh showed up.

He sighed. Sooner or later he'd have to talk with the man. He just preferred it to be later. After all, it was imperative he go to Home Depot over on the mainland for a couple of sheets of plywood to cover the hole. What if the weather turned? What if night fell and bad guys or nosy kids climbed in? His duty as a property manager demanded he leave ASAP.

As he tried to work up the energy to get in his pickup and drive to the store, a black Cadillac Escalade pulled into the lot. He sighed again as he watched the unfamiliar car park. Another nosy tweeter?

He rubbed his forehead. Much as he hated to admit it, he hurt, but no way would he go to a doctor. Too time consuming. Maybe he should stop and let Carrie tend his wounds. Somehow thinking of her concern for him made him feel a little less achy.

He studied the Escalade. Nice car, *very* nice car. Big. Shiny. New. Much classier than the Hummer that had shouted, *"Notice me, notice me; I'm special and so's my driver."* Of course anyone driving an Escalade wasn't the retiring sort either.

He blinked as Josh Templeton, sleek and buffed, climbed out, sporting new dark glasses and an extra measure of attitude. Huh. Too late to run. And Greg would have to rethink that classier thing.

Josh strode across the lot, his hair moussed to perfection, his trousers sharply creased, the polish on his tasseled loafers getting dusty in the cinders and sand. He stopped beside Greg and studied the hole without a word, though he vibrated with anger. Even his jowls, developing in spite of his attempts to stay young forever, seemed to shimmy with fury.

Greg took a deep breath and waited with patience for the explosion. It was inevitable, and since he was the one standing here, he would be the one getting the blame. The fact that he hadn't been the driver of the car would matter little to Josh.

Well, he could take it. He had no choice if he wanted to keep his job. On the bright side, Josh would be his boss for only two more days.

"What were you thinking, Barnes," Josh snarled, "to let things get this out of hand?"

Greg took a minute until he trusted his voice. "I'm fine, thanks for asking. The blood, abrasions, cuts, and bruises aren't all that major, though I was worried for a minute there when he drove straight at me."

Josh scowled and waved the air as if brushing away a gnat. "Get over yourself. You're fine. You screwed up. You might as well admit it."

Greg sighed. What was the use? It was a good thing Scripture said to *love* one another, not *like* one another. He could behave properly toward Josh in an agape love, polite sort of way—his mother and Ginny had trained him well, as had the instructors at the police academy—but he couldn't bring himself to like the man. At all. Sometimes it felt more like a case of loving your enemy.

"I did not screw up." A bit of self-defense was appropriate. After all, he had Carrie and Blake, to say nothing of the tweeters, as witnesses.

Josh spun to him, mouth open to rebut.

Greg held up a hand. "I will not discuss culpability with you, Josh. I know what I know. I was here. You were not. Blake Winters was here too. Talk to him if you want an unbiased report."

Josh looked around. "Where is he?"

The subtle thread of disbelief about Blake's presence when the incident occurred angered Greg, but he held his temper. It wasn't a war worth fighting. It was just Josh being his usual disagreeable self. "He left after the locksmith changed out the locks."

"Like new locks are going to keep people out." Josh swept his hand toward the hole. "It's a highway through there."

"It won't be after I cover it." Greg was proud of the even tone he managed.

Another car pulled into the lot, and a man Greg had never seen before climbed out, cell phone in hand.

"Wow! That's impressive!" The man studied the hole. "They weren't kidding."

"They weren't," Greg agreed, knowing who "they" were.

"You okay?" the stranger asked, eying Greg's scrapes and bruises.

A total stranger had more courtesy than his boss. How sad was that? "I'm okay."

The man nodded. "Looks painful."

"Who are you?" Josh demanded.

"Mac88. Who are you?"

Josh turned on Greg. "What kind of an idiot name is Mac88?"

Greg mentally rolled his eyes.

"Hey, buddy, watch your mouth." Mac88 scowled at Josh.

"He's a tweeter," Greg explained. "Mac88 is his Twitter name." Did that mean there were eighty-seven other Macs on Twitter or that he was born in 1988? Or on the eighth day of August, the eighth month?

"Facebook too," Mac88 said.

Josh studied the lanky guy with the BlackBerry and sniffed. "I was right. He's a twit." And he turned his back.

Greg bit back a smile at Mac88's outraged expression.

Josh resumed his rant. "You were in charge of this eviction; therefore, this is your fault, Barnes. I expect you to take care of all this mess. Get estimates on repairs, select the cheapest, and get this fixed by tomorrow."

"It may take a bit longer, what with insurance and all." To say nothing of contractors with previous commitments.

"Tomorrow!" Josh puffed out his chest, the very picture of self-importance. "The sale is finalized tomorrow, as you well know." Josh was selling every property he owned, and he'd transferred the responsibility for the negotiations with the representative of a consortium of buyers to Greg. All Josh planned to do was show up tomorrow to sign on the dotted line—or lines, as the case may be—and collect his money.

Which explained the new Escalade. How like Josh, buying the pricey car before he had a check in hand. It seemed he'd never heard the one about "many a slip twixt cup and lip."

"Fred will be in town early tomorrow," Josh said as if he, not Greg, had been the one to work with Fred through the purchase process. "He'll give you a call. Just make sure he shows at one for the meeting with my lawyers. I've got to go."

And he climbed into his Escalade and went.

Greg breathed a sigh as the black car disappeared down the street. Josh always got on his nerves, had from the first time they met.

"He's a real winner." Mac88's voice dripped with dislike. "I'm going to Carrie's Café to see what's happening there."

Greg had never heard a more appealing plan.

9

It was midafternoon, and I was waving a relieved good-bye to the last of the tweeters, ready to flip the lock, when Greg pulled up to the curb. I pushed open the door and waited for him on the sidewalk.

"Hey, look," one of the tweeters exclaimed. "It's the guy the Hummer guy tried to run down."

Greg looked pained as all eyes fixed on him. "How do they know that?" he asked me.

I shrugged. "I'd guess one of the tweeters at the Sand and Sea posted a picture of you."

"He's also the one whose family got blown up," another called. "Check this link."

Greg looked as if he'd been slapped.

"Quick!" I grabbed his arm as their heads bowed and they watched something about the event of three years ago, probably footage on YouTube. I pulled Greg inside and turned the door's lock.

They looked up, eyes bright with curiosity. Intent on coming back in the café and getting up close and personal with the object of their nosiness, they moved as one, like kernels of caramel corn stuck in a clump.

"I'll take another Coke," one called as he pulled on the door, remembering my admonition about having to buy something to be admitted.

"Yeah, me too," several said, expressions becoming those of desperate people dying of dehydration after enduring days under the blazing Saharan sun.

"And I'll tell everyone what a wonderful place this is," another called, holding up his iPad.

"Don't let them in!" Lindsay called from the pass-through. As if I would. "There's nothing left to feed them. They're worse than a horde of locusts!"

"Sorry," I called through the door, giving the tweeters the evil eye. "We close at two and it's now three."

"Not fair," they called, looking crestfallen.

"Come back tomorrow." I waved and turned my back.

Greg studied the swirling mass pacing outside the door, thumbs working their keyboards both real and virtual. He seemed to have regained his balance. "See the tall, lanky one? Mac88. He followed me here."

I nodded. "Feels creepy, doesn't it?"

He reached for his sore shoulder. "Maybe he'll follow me to Home Depot and back, and I can get him to help me nail the plywood over the hole."

"You're too hard on them." Mary Prudence came up beside me. "It's a way of staying connected in an increasingly fragmented society."

I laughed. "Mary P, where did you read that?"

She gave me an impish smile. "Who knows? But it sure sounds good, doesn't it?"

"Without Twitter how would we know the cops got Chaz?" Lindsay called from the kitchen.

"TV? The newspaper?" I offered.

"Yeah, but when? Tonight or tomorrow? Now we don't have to worry about whether he got away or not. Think of the anxiety not suffered."

I rolled my eyes. "I'm sure you would have been just one bundle of nerves."

She grinned. "Sister of mine, you are an anachronism."

"Anachronism. Yowzah, Linds, I'm impressed." I looked at Greg's face in the light streaming in the big front window. "That box of vocabulary flash cards was worth the money after all. And you," I said to Greg. "Upstairs so I can clean those cuts out without a national audience."

Several of the tweeters were watching us, thumbs flying as they did so. One had his cell raised and was snapping pictures. I could just imagine their posts. Grouchy lady. Injured man. What fun they must be having.

"I washed my face." Greg twisted away from my ministrations. He grimaced and grabbed his shoulder.

"Maybe, but you've still got lots of little cinders embedded."

"They'll work their way out. I've got to go get that plywood."

I looked at him in exasperation. "If you don't want to be disinfected, why did you come here?"

He glanced out the window at our voyeurs. "Sanctuary."

I laughed. "Granted."

"Should you be driving?" Mary P peered at him. "You've got a good-sized egg, all black and blue."

His hand went to his forehead. "It's not bad. I'm not concussed."

"So says the man who can't see the injury. Drive him, Carrie," Mary P said. "With that shoulder he's rubbing, he'll need help even if his head's all right."

"I can manage a sheet of plywood fine." He sounded insulted.

Mary P laughed. "I'm not impugning your manhood, you know."

He looked unconvinced.

Drive him. Did I dare? "I have to close out for the day." I indicated the cash register.

"Push-tush," Mary P said. "I can do that with my eyes closed."

She could. She'd done it for years when Carrie's Café was the Surfside. The question was: Could I do it? Could I spend an hour or more alone with Greg and not give myself and my ridiculous infatuation away?

I glanced at him. He looked as balky as a mule on a path he didn't want to traverse. He did not want help. Or was it *my* help he was balking at?

"When you go, Carrie, don't forget fluorescent bulbs," Lindsay called from the kitchen. "The one over my prep table is starting to blink."

I glanced at my sister, who was standing in my line of sight but not Greg's. She was grinning and making "go" signals with all her might. Ricky appeared behind her and made little wiggly movements with his eyebrows that I suspected were supposed to be suggestive but made him look like he had a tic.

One couldn't have a secret around this place. It was mortifying. But the light bulbs were all the excuse I needed.

"It's me or Mac88 and friends." I pointed to the sidewalk and the milling tweeters.

Greg looked ready to protest again, then gave another shrug and another wince. With a rueful smile, he handed me his pickup keys.

I'd never driven such a large vehicle before, and the lanes on the causeway, which always felt narrow because of the age of the bridge, seemed extra snug. I gripped the steering wheel as if holding it tightly would keep us in our lane.

"Relax."

I glanced at him. He was leaning against the headrest, his eyes closed.

"How do you know I'm tense? You're sleeping."

"I'm not sleeping, just resting. And I can feel your tension. The cab is crackling with it."

"Is not."

He snorted at my defensive lie, and a small smile curved his lips though he didn't open his eyes.

"So tell me, Carrie Carter. Where do you come from? I know you're not a Seaside native."

I always hated this question. "I grew up in Atlanta."

His eyes popped open, though he continued to lounge against the headrest. "Really? You don't sound like a Southern belle."

"Atlanta's not the South, despite its geography. People there come from all over."

"And your family came from?"

I had no idea where my father came from, since I had no idea who he was. Though my mother never took us to her home or spoke of family there, at least she gave me a place to name. "My mom's from Camden, New Jersey."

"And you ended up in Seaside because she came here on vacation as a kid? You're keeping the family heritage alive?"

I grabbed at his comment with both hands, a witness happy to be led. "That's true. She talked about Seaside a lot. It made Lindsay and me want to come, so when we decided to move, ta-da, we chose Seaside."

"Just you girls but not your mom?"

The trouble with getting to know people better was that they always asked hard questions. "Not our mom."

"Or dad?"

"Or dad." I'd met Greg's brothers and parents when they came to visit him and hit the café for a meal. How could someone with a wonderful family like his understand mine?

"How long have you been here?"

"It seems like forever," I said evasively.

"How long?" He was watching me, without doubt hearing the reluctance in my voice.

I sighed. I couldn't lie to him. "Seventeen years."

He straightened and stared at me. He'd done the math. "You were a runaway?"

I swallowed. "Why do you say that?"

"You're what? Thirty?" He frowned. "That would make you thirteen?"

"I'm thirty-three. I was sixteen."

"Oh. Big improvement."

I shrugged. What could I say?

"And you brought Lindsay with you?"

I nodded.

"How old was she?"

"Ten."

He stared at me, and I felt my stomach twist. I couldn't imagine what he was thinking. Or maybe I could. Runaways were pathetic druggies. Runaways became child prostitutes. Runaways became thieves. I felt certain he'd met all these sad kids in the course of his career in law enforcement and some with stories more tragic than even I could imagine.

"It must have been bad," he said finally, "if you took your little sister along."

Tears burned my throat at his understanding. "It was," I managed, glad to see Home Depot looming. Enough soul baring for the moment. I was happy to concentrate on the challenge of maneuvering through the parking lot. Fraught with potential calamity as it was, with cars and pickups backing up at me as if I were at a demolition derby, it was much safer than talking about my past.

With great relief I pulled into a parking slot that had empty spaces on both sides. As I eased the keys from the ignition, I breathed a huge sigh. Not one crumpled fender, either Greg's or some stranger's. If I looked at the driving situation in a glass-half-full kind of way, I was already halfway home.

I climbed down from the cab, and we walked toward the store together. Though neither of us said anything, it felt very couple-y to me. Since Lindsay and I had done much of the work in turning the Surfside into Carrie's,

I'd spent a lot of time at Home Depot and Lowe's. I used to watch the shopping couples as they talked, debated, and argued over which items to purchase. Then I'd go off with my sister and buy our supplies.

Today I was shopping with a guy, and it felt good. Not that it was the same as being a real couple. But it was a one-small-step-for-man type of thing, and I was determined to enjoy it.

All right. I was pathetic, but at least I knew it.

Greg stopped just outside the store's door. "I'm sorry you got roped into this."

Did he mean he was sorry he got roped into having me along? "It's okay. I like Home Depot."

He looked at me in surprise. "Are you serious? I thought all women hated it. Ginny did."

"Lindsay doesn't like it much either, but I do."

He still looked skeptical.

We walked into the store and went to the lumber section. Along the way I snagged one of those carts that allowed you to rest sheets of plywood or paneling on their side. I trundled it after Greg, who was now about half an aisle ahead of me. That felt oh so couple-y too. The only other thing more couple-y would be if one of us started looking up and down the aisles for the misplaced other.

"Can I help you, ma'am?" a man in a Home Depot apron asked.

"He'll tell you what we want." I pointed to Greg, who was leaning over the pile of plywood.

As the man went to talk to Greg, I heard what I'd said. "What *we* want." I was thirty-three, and there'd never before been a *we*, at least a male-female *we*, where shopping was concerned. How sad was that? And, frankly, there really wasn't a *we* now.

It wasn't that men had never shown an interest in me. Several had through the years, but it was back when I was still convinced that all men were drunks, reprobates, and lechers.

In time I'd realized that romance, at least for me, was a matter not only of a man who made my heart trip but also of timing and healing. I just hadn't been ready earlier. Too many childhood issues to resolve. I sighed. Now I was finally ready, but the object of my affection wasn't.

Lord, Your Word says our times are in Your hands. Will I ever be in a situation where my timing and a guy's timing—Greg's *timing*—*are in sync?*

When Greg and the Home Depot man started pulling plywood from the pile, I wheeled my cart to them. They slid two sheets on, and I began spinning the cart around so the steering wheels were in the back.

The Home Depot man grinned at Greg. "You've got her trained real good."

I glared at the man though he didn't see. I didn't care how couple-y I ever became, *trained* would never be an operative word. Greg saw my expression, knew how ticked I was, and smiled broadly.

I scowled back for effect. Three cheers for me. I made the man smile for a second time today! A record.

We stopped to pick up the fluorescent bulbs I suspected Lindsay didn't need, and after a small skirmish over who was paying—Greg won—we left the store. With me on one side and Greg on the other, we slid the plywood into the bed of the pickup.

I wasn't as nervous driving back to Seaside, and I almost felt comfortable when I pulled into the Sand and Sea lot. Much of the debris Chaz had caused was already cleaned up, and we dumped the little remaining in the Dumpster at the far side of the lot. We lugged the plywood sheets from the truck to the building, and Greg pounded them into place with masonry nails. With every blow, he winced at the stress on his shoulder. I made believe I didn't notice.

"Can't someone just pry off the boards?" I asked. "To get inside, I mean."

"They could if they were determined to, but why would anyone want to?"

"To get Chaz's stuff?"

He laughed. Laughed! I felt a flicker of pride, like I'd just baked a cake as wonderful as one of Lindsay's. Three times!

"Believe me," Greg said, "no one wants any of his stuff, not even him."

"What happens to it all?"

"I'd bet most of it's rented, but what happens is that I set a date with him to let him in to get his things or for the rental company to come pick up their stuff. If he or they don't come, I put everything in storage until we can arrange a sheriff's sale."

"Well, he won't come. He'll be in jail."

Greg carried his toolbox to the truck, me trailing him. "He'll be out on bail as of tomorrow morning." He sounded resigned. "The only good thing is, he won't be able to leave the area, so some other town will be spared his presence."

"Bail? He tried to kill you!"

"Did he?"

Again that uncertainty. "Weird," I said. "Weird, weird, weird."

"Agreed. Now let's get you home."

We climbed into the cab, this time with him in the driver's seat.

"Pull down the alley," I said as we approached the café. "And don't forget that you're coming up to let me clean out those cuts of yours."

He made a face, but he followed me as I led the way up the stairs to the second-floor apartment Lindsay and I shared.

How couple-y.

They say it's hard to dispose of the dead body of someone you killed. Whether you meant their death or not is irrelevant. Corpses tend to bleed all over you and the surroundings. They're a dead weight, ha, ha. They release strange fluids and gases. And they get stiff as boards, making lugging them a challenge.

And other people are nosy. They spy on you and see you dragging your dead husband or wife to the family car for a trip to the nearest wooded area. Or at a stoplight they notice that your companion never blinks or moves from his propped position in the passenger seat. Or blood drips onto the street from the body stashed in the trunk.

Well, who were "they" to say it's so hard? That's what he wanted to know.

Whoever they were, they hadn't asked him if he agreed. Granted, he didn't have as much practice at disposal as one of those deranged serial killers. Half those guys didn't seem to care about getting rid of their bodies. They left them lying around for anyone to find. It wasn't because hiding the body was hard. Oh no. It was because they were lazy.

He would never be so careless, not about bodies or anything. That was why he was so good at what he did. He thought things through, and he always found a satisfactory way of handling every situation, even the ones where death happened.

So "they" should be talking to him. Maybe he didn't know as much as some, but he had more experience with disposal than the general population.

And he was proud of how successful he was at it.

11

H ave a seat." I indicated a kitchen chair. "I'll get the Bactine and stuff."

Greg looked uncertain as he sat, and I couldn't resist. "You're not afraid of a little Bactine, are you?"

"Of course not." But he didn't sound too convinced.

I glanced over my shoulder at him as I pulled the first-aid supplies from the shelf where we kept them in a large cardboard box with flaps tucked into each other. "You ever had Bactine sprayed on you before?"

"Sure, I've used it."

"On yourself?" I carried the box to the table. "You just tortured your kids with it, right?"

"Well, actually Ginny did all the torturing. It's what moms do."

I had a brief vision of my mother and thought I knew too well about mothers and torture. Ginny did not fit the mold at all.

I flipped open the box with a flourish. With a graceful leap, Oreo jumped up to inspect the contents. We had quite a collection of Band-Aids, ointments, meds, and a large spray bottle of Bactine since it wasn't uncommon to injure ourselves in the line of café duty. I had a giant first-aid kit in the kitchen downstairs too, but this stash was for Linds and me after café hours.

Oreo put out a paw and batted at the antiseptic.

"See?" I said. "Even the cat knows the power of Bactine."

Greg still looked skeptical. "Pretty cat. Does it always sit on the table?"

"She thinks she owns the place and sees no surface as off-limits. She's an indoor cat, so we just ignore her when she jumps on whatever." I thought of Ricky. "You allergic?"

Wouldn't that kill any romance in a hurry? How could I choose between Oreo and some man, even Greg? Oreo had seen Linds and me through years of emotional need and healing. There were times when nothing felt as right as hugging a furry, warm animal.

"Not allergic." Greg reached out and lifted the cat onto his lap. She settled down and began to purr as he stroked her.

You've got to love a man who loves your pet.

Greg sat patiently as I washed the scrapes on his face and arm with a warm, soft, soapy cloth. His eyes closed and seemed to relax. When was the last time someone had taken care of him?

"Don't fall asleep on me."

He gave a slight smile, but he didn't open his eyes. "Not a chance with the dreaded Bactine yet to come."

I swiped an antiseptic wipe over his cheek, and his eyes flew open at the cold. They locked on to mine. They were so dark the irises blended seamlessly with the pupils. Beautiful.

He blinked and looked away, his throat working. Oreo looked up to see why the stroking had stopped.

I took a deep breath and reached for the Polysporin. I put dabs on the scratches covering his cheek. Then I picked up the Bactine.

"Prepare yourself." And I shot it all up and down his scraped arm.

At the first burst, Oreo leaped to the floor, surprised by the *fsst* and afraid of getting wet. Greg's brow puckered, preparing for pain. I guess he thought it would be like alcohol or something, and when all he felt was cold again, he looked at me, uncertain.

"Ginny wasn't a torturer after all." I smiled, then turned to the fridge, pulled out a packet of frozen peas, and wrapped it in a dishtowel. "Here. On your cheek and forehead, though I imagine it's several hours too late to do much good."

As he gingerly pressed the peas to his face, I heard someone coming up the back stairs, and it wasn't Lindsay. Too heavy a step. There was a brief knock, and the back door opened. Mary Prudence walked in.

"Now I remember why I moved to a single-story place." Puffing, she lowered herself into one of the kitchen chairs. "Those steps are killers."

I gave her a hug. "Thanks so much for your help today. I'd have been in real trouble without you." I poured her a glass of iced tea and gave one to Greg too.

Mary P took a long drink. "You need another server. And I'm not applying for the job."

"I know. I've got a Help Wanted sign in the window, but so far no takers."

"Someone will show. Someone always does. All you've got to do is pray them in."

Which was what she'd done with Lindsay and me.

"So how'd the shopping go?" she asked Greg.

"Plywood's nailed in place, thanks to Carrie's help. At least it'll keep the weather out."

"And we got Lindsay her light tubes," I said.

Mary P nodded, her attention on Greg. She leveled her pointer finger at him. "All right, now give. Tell me everything. I read the exaggerated and ridiculous stories posted on Twitter"—she held up her iPhone—"but I want the real scoop. Did some guy in a yellow Hummer ram the Sand and Sea and try to kill you in the bargain? Or did he try to kill you and ram the Sand and Sea when he missed?"

"Good question," Greg said. "The guy is nuts enough for it to have gone either way."

Mary P held out her glass for more tea. "I once met a guy who told me the most cockamamie conspiracy theory I ever heard. When I questioned the logic and logistics of his little hypothesis, he looked me in the eye. 'I read it on the Internet, and you know everything there is the truth.'"

"Ri-i-ight," I said while Greg grinned.

"And they're saying it was attempted murder." Mary P leaned forward. "Was it?"

"Who knows?" Greg launched into the eviction story and Chaz's reaction. Midway through the telling, absorbed in the tale, he lowered his hand and let the peas fall from his face.

"Uh-uh." I lifted his hand with the peas to his forehead again. I held it there perhaps a beat or two longer than necessary for him to get the idea, foolishly thrilled for another legitimate chance to touch him.

He ignored me, but I thought there might be a little hitch in his voice. If there was and I wasn't imagining it, it was without doubt because I was hurting him by pressing on the bruise. Certainly my touch didn't do for him what touching him did for me. Life as I knew it just didn't work that well.

Then I glanced at Mary Prudence and had to apologize to the Lord for that last thought. Life sometimes worked quite well. If ever someone was where I needed her to be when I needed her, it was Mary P, God's gift to us Carter girls. If it weren't for her and her husband, Warren…

"If I get this job," I told Lindsay just before I entered the Surfside, "it means you'll be alone for several hours each day."

"That's okay. Alone here isn't as scary as alone back home."

And wasn't that the truth. "As soon as I get a paycheck and some tips, I'll get us a room. You'll be safe there."

"How long?"

"One week. Two tops."

She straightened her skinny shoulders. "Don't worry about me, Carrie. I'll be fine. We'll be fine."

"I love you, kid." I gave her a fierce hug. I couldn't let her down! *God, if You're there, don't let me let her down.*

I walked into the Surfside and found my savior in Mary Prudence and through her, my Savior.

I told Mary Prudence—or Mrs. Hastings as she was to me then—my made-up story about being eighteen and having a mother in the military. She raised her eyebrows but said nothing. To my great relief she hired me to work breakfasts and dinners with four hours off in the middle of the day. Then she did something that floored me.

"Here's your first week's wages." She handed me a fistful of bills.

I stared at them. Food for Lindsay! A room! *God, maybe You're there after all. Maybe. In case You are, thank You!*

"Now you'd better show up tomorrow." Mary P waved her pointer finger under my nose. "I don't tolerate thieves, and taking that money and not showing would be stealing."

"I'll be here at six thirty tomorrow morning. I promise!"

I rushed to the alley where I'd left Lindsay and showed her the money. She started to cry. I shoved the money in my pocket and hugged her.

"It's going to be okay, Linds. You'll see. It's going to be okay."

"Can we go eat right now?" she asked through her hiccups. "A real meal?"

"We can. And then we'll find us a room. All we need is a bed and a bathroom. That shouldn't cost too much."

"I think you should come back to the Surfside for your meal."

We both jumped and looked to the end of the alley where Mary P stood, feet apart, hands on her hips. She looked like a triangle with legs, backlit as she was.

I had been thinking more McDonald's than the Surfside for our budget's sake. "How much?"

"Meals are free for our staff."

I could eat free? My stomach growled as it had when I was in the restaurant and smelled all the wonderful scents coming from the kitchen. The big box of saltines and the jar of peanut butter I'd cadged from the store back home had lost their appeal a day ago.

But what about Linds? I looked at my sister.

"And their families," Mary P added.

Lindsay grabbed my hand. I fought against tears. I hadn't cried in years, and I wasn't about to start. But kindness was new to me, and I didn't know how to react.

"Come on, both of you," Mary P said. "I'm not certain which one of you looks hungrier." She stalked back to the restaurant.

"Me," Lindsay called with ten-year-old openness as she ran after the woman. I was just embarrassed that our need was so obvious.

Mary P held the door for us. "Pick whatever you want from the menu. Mr. Hastings will make it for you."

My mouth was watering so much I had to keep swallowing.

"Then you can tell me your real story."

My mouth went dry.

I grabbed Lindsay and pulled her to me. "Thanks, but we got to go." I reached in my pocket for the money to give back to her.

"No!" Lindsay looked like a kid who'd had her birthday cake snatched from under her nose—not that she'd ever had one.

Mary P looked at me for a minute and read my panic. "If you want to tell me, that is. You don't have to."

I managed to breathe again.

She fed us well, but I didn't tell her our true story. If I did, I knew children's services would be there for both of us, and who knew what would happen then? Chances were good we'd be separated. People'd be much more willing to take a cute ten-year-old than a sulky sixteen-year-old. No sir, the truth was too risky. The truth stayed locked up inside. I stuck to the military mother until I turned eighteen for real. Mary Prudence merely raised her eyebrows whenever I had cause to mention her, which wasn't often and was only in response to a direct question from someone about my family. Neither she nor Warren commented on the absurdity of a parent deployed for years with no leaves and no attempts to provide income or a home for her daughters.

During that summer, Lindsay and I lived in a single room on the top floor of a boardinghouse that catered to summer lodgers. Most came for a week or two, but we planned to stay until the place closed for the winter.

I found myself another part-time job on the boardwalk, serving lunchtime hot dogs and Cokes to sandy people spending the day at the beach. It meant I didn't have a free moment, but at least Linds and I got lunch every day. I was allowed one hot dog and a drink, and I got very good at slipping Lindsay one of each when the boss wasn't looking. Then the end of summer loomed.

"I have a friend at church who has a little apartment at the top of her house she'd like to rent. She doesn't want to live alone, but she's not looking for a baby-sitter either," Mary P said to me just after Labor Day. "Interested?"

Was I ever! I'd been lying awake at night worrying about where we'd go after the boardinghouse closed in two more weeks.

And so we met Bess Meyerson. "Just like the old-time Miss America," Bess said, but since neither Lindsay nor I had any idea who the old-time Miss America was, we weren't impressed. All we knew was that this Bess Meyerson was not Miss America material. She was older than Mary P, well into her seventies, and as skinny as Mary P was round. Not slim, mind you. Skinny. And wrinkled. I'd seen pictures of Shar-Pei dogs with fewer wrinkles.

But when Bess smiled, she had that same magic as Mary P. Her face lit up, and you couldn't help smiling back.

"It's Jesus," she told me one day when I mentioned her smile. "He gives me joy unspeakable and full of glory."

I blinked but said nothing. How could I respond to such an outrageous statement?

Our new apartment was painted white, all white, and it looked so clean! There was a bedroom and a bath, a tiny living room, and an even tinier kitchen. If you opened the bedroom window, you could hear the ocean a block and a half away, smell its briny scent. And if you climbed out the window, you could sit on the almost flat roof of the second-floor porch.

"We've got a balcony." Lindsay grinned at me. "I'm so happy!"

So was I, though I wasn't effusive about it like my sister. Sometimes I envied her her resilience and ability to forget the ugly things we'd left behind, but most of the time I was too tired to do more than tuck us in.

I continued to work at the Surfside, realizing how fortunate I was to have gotten a job at one of the few restaurants that stayed open the whole year. As in most shore-resort towns, the vast majority of businesses, including eating establishments, were closed by the end of September until the following May or June.

When Lindsay was old enough, she went to work for Mary P and Warren too.

"Mr. H., can I help with dinner prep?" she asked one day, and it soon became obvious that she had a flare for food.

"I love the kitchen," she told me. "And I *love* to bake."

Warren quickly saw her culinary promise, and soon she acted as the

Surfside's equivalent of a sous-chef and baker while I took over more and more of the dining room responsibilities.

Now the restaurant was ours. I reached across the table and patted Mary P's hand. I couldn't imagine where we'd be without her.

She smiled. "What's that for?"

"For being you." *I love you.*

I turned at the sound of Lindsay's footfalls on the stairs, and my eyes caught Greg's. He was studying me with a thoughtful expression.

Thoughtfully was better than absently, wasn't it?

12

Greg kept giving his head mental shakes. Was he really sitting with Carrie Carter in her personal living space, not the café? Sure, Mary P was here and Lindsay was walking in the door, but he was sitting at Carrie's table, drinking Carrie's iced tea, letting Carrie tend his—his what? Wounds sounded too extreme, regardless of what they were saying on Twitter and Facebook. All he had were a few scrapes and bruises. No big deal.

But Carrie had treated them with such care.

And she'd enjoyed Home Depot!

Man, Lord, what am I thinking?

He stood. "Well, I'd, ah, better go."

He was pretty sure that was a flash of disappointment on Carrie's face, though she was quick to hide it. He couldn't decide whether that was good or bad. He held out the now-defrosted packet of peas. Carrie took it and put it back in the freezer.

"You're not allowed to leave." Lindsay pushed him back in his chair. "I haven't had the report straight from the horse's mouth yet." She sat across from him beside Mary P. "Come on, Greg, Carrie. I want to know what really happened."

Greg began telling the story again as Carrie paced, in spite of the empty chair beside him.

"So it wasn't that big a deal," he finished.

"Ha!" Carrie said behind him. "The guy could have killed you! I know. I was there. Only your quickness saved you."

"But he didn't."

"When he drove at you—" She began to pace faster.

"Sit, Carrie," Lindsay ordered. "You're driving me crazy."

So Carrie sat, back straight, eyes fixed on her sister, hands folded on the table like a kid ready to say grace. To him, she seemed on edge, not the usual easygoing Carrie of the café. She'd been tense when they'd gone to Home Depot, but he'd chalked that up to driving the truck. What did she have to be stressed about now? And she seemed determined not to look at him.

What did he expect? He'd kept his distance for all the years he'd been coming to the café. Of course, it wasn't just Carrie he'd kept at arm's length; it was any woman.

It had taken his breath when he discovered that as soon as Ginny was dead, there were women who saw him as available. They didn't seem to understand that loving someone didn't stop just because that person died. Deep and true emotions continued, even seemed to intensify, with the absence of the loved one and the stark realization that she was now gone forever. If anything, the fact that he was grieving seemed to bring out the nesting, mothering instincts in these women. They wanted to take care of him, coddle him, *marry* him.

Ginny and the kids weren't gone a month when he got his first invitation to dinner from a single woman. And they kept coming. After he refused enough of them, word seemed to have gotten around, and he'd been left more or less alone by the women themselves. That's when the dinner invitations from families who just happened to have single or divorced daughters began in earnest. He'd even gotten a couple from families with unhappily married daughters. It was like they expected him to fall in love with one such sad woman and ask her to leave her husband for him, therefore curing all her ills.

Ri-i-ight.

Not that Carrie had ever been one of those women. She'd always been polite and kind, never pushy. Sometimes he wondered if she might have a bit of a crush on him. After all, she tended to blush whenever he spoke to her. Then again she might be allergic to him and the flush was the first step in getting hives or something. Wouldn't that knock his pride down a notch or two?

Because he felt foolish to even think of Carrie and crushes, he had held himself more aloof than usual around her. Until today. He had to admit he'd enjoyed his time shopping with her. He'd enjoyed her attention to his injuries. He'd even enjoyed her distress at Chaz's near miss.

So what did that mean? What did he expect from her now? That she'd get all teary and tell him how glad she was that he'd escaped death because—because what? Life wasn't worth living without him? She'd have died if he had?

No, what he wanted was for her to sit beside him and smile at him. Not just smile like she smiled at Mr. Perkins and everyone else who came into the café, but *smile*. At him. For him.

He swallowed hard as it hit him that he wanted to matter to her differently and more deeply than anyone else, even than her sister or Mary P.

His stomach cramped. That couldn't be right. It couldn't. It would be unfair to Ginny, disloyal, unfaithful.

Which was stupid.

Ginny was dead. Three years dead.

Greg still got the sweats whenever he thought about that day. And he had suspected nothing. He should have. He should have!

"You've got me blocked in," Ginny had said, her voice rushed. "I've got to get the kids to school."

He pulled his keys from his pocket with no shiver of premonition and tossed them to her. She caught them, grinned, and blew him a kiss. As she and the kids went chattering out of the house, he took a bite of his Cap'n Crunch, savoring the taste, when his world exploded in a fireball.

There were no screams, at least not from Ginny and the kids. Just his own anguished cries. Just the shrill shouts of the neighbors and the shriek of the sirens of the first responders. And the mocking whispers of flames writhing and dancing in the bright morning sunshine.

If only he hadn't ignored the threats, hadn't treated them like so much hot air from a buffoon who thought he was John Dillinger. If only he'd realized the depths of brutality and utter lack of morality in the man whose goal in life was to become a crime kingpin. If only he'd realized it didn't take a large following to have men who would seek vengeance on their leader's behalf, men who knew how to make bombs.

If only. If only.

Marco Polo was little more than a street thug, but he'd attracted a band of loyalists who followed his every wish. If his charisma had been coupled with matching intelligence, the man would have become a real-life don to rival the fictional Don Corleone or Tony Soprano.

When Greg first heard of him, he'd joked about the man's name. "His mother must have failed history to name a son Marco when he has the last name Polo."

Well, Marco got the last laugh if you didn't count serving life with no possibility of parole.

So here Greg sat, wanting Carrie to smile at him, all the while overwhelmed with guilt about what he knew was a very normal feeling.

I like her.

Greg couldn't breathe. It was Ginny's voice.

I do.

"Ginny?" But it couldn't be.

Her name as he said it was a mere whisper, little more than a breath, but

Carrie heard it. She turned to him with a shocked, sad expression, not the smile he'd wanted. He tried to smile at her, thinking maybe then she'd smile, but he couldn't. His facial muscles weren't working.

Go for it, Greg. With my blessing. It's time.

It was the bump on the head. It had to be. He felt like Scrooge blaming Marley's ghostly appearance on a bit of potato because Ginny's voice was every bit as impossible as Marley's materialization.

His phone vibrated on his hip. He grabbed at it, grateful for something to break this painful moment.

The caller ID read Fred Durning.

"I need to take this call." He stood. "It's a guy about the closing on the property sales tomorrow."

"Sure." Carrie pointed toward the front of the apartment. "The living room's through there."

He nodded. At least she hadn't sent him out the door. He slid his phone open as he walked into a warm, inviting room. Why it appealed to him he couldn't have said. He just knew the room stilled the chaos swirling inside.

"What can I do for you, Fred?"

"Hey, Greg. Tomorrow's the big day. When and where can we meet?"

Someplace neutral. Someplace friendly. "How about we start with a cup of coffee at Carrie's Café?" He gave the address. "Ten o'clock sound okay?"

Appointment made, Greg slid the phone shut and just stood there. He stared at the rug, a light gray. He had to go back to the kitchen, back to Carrie. He wanted to, but at the same time he didn't. He'd spent three years keeping life as complication free as he could manage. He'd liked it that way, and Carrie was a complication with a capital *C*.

But the voice was right. It was time to move on, to live again. As it said in Ecclesiastes, there was a time to mourn and a time to dance. Had he at last come to the dancing time after the long, black stretch of mourning?

"Everything okay for tomorrow?"

Carrie stood just inside the room, caught in a stray beam of sun, like a carefully staged frame in a film. Her shoulder-length blond hair gleamed and her steady navy blue eyes studied him. She was slim, a little taller than Ginny had been, and at this moment she appeared so female he didn't know how to react. Or rather he did, and that scared him.

"Everything okay?" she asked again.

He blinked and held out his phone. "I'm meeting the guy tomorrow at the café."

She smiled but it didn't reach her eyes. "That's nice."

"Make certain there are a couple of sticky buns for us, okay?"

"Sure. Not a problem."

He had to walk back to the kitchen, but he'd have to pass her in the narrow doorway to do so, feel her body heat, smell her scent. But he couldn't stay flatfooted in her living room, staring at her like some lost Rain Man. "Um, I've got to go. Get back to work."

She nodded, turned, and walked into the kitchen. He followed her, feeling the fool, but at least he didn't have to walk past her.

"See you later, Mary P, Lindsay," he said. They smiled and waved. Carrie held the back door for him, and he had to pass her after all. It was as if she'd burn him if he got too close. Which was ridiculous. She was just Carrie. Sweet Carrie. Lovely Carrie.

He swallowed hard. Had he been so conscious of Ginny when they first dated? He must have been, right? He couldn't remember. All he knew was that Carrie Carter, in one afternoon's time, had struck him a heart blow without even knowing it.

She followed him onto the porch, where she was forced to stand close because of the landing's small size. The air snapped around them.

"Thanks for all your help," he managed. He pointed to his battered face. "And for your peas."

She waved his thanks away. "Always glad to share a vegetable with a friend."

A friend. "Look, Carrie," he began but didn't know how to continue.

Look, Carrie, saying Ginny's name didn't mean anything? Because it did, but not as Carrie clearly thought.

Look, Carrie, I think there might be the very real possibility of something between you and me? And Ginny approves?

"And you know this how?" she'd ask.

"She told me." And wouldn't that sound just fine. Carrie'd be certain he'd suffered a concussion after all. Which he must have.

"It's okay, Greg. It's okay." Again that sad smile.

And Carrie went inside, closing the door softly.

13

After an evening spent staring at the television with no recollection of what he'd seen, Greg took himself off to bed. He read until his eyelids drooped. He read on until he found himself dozing, the book sagging in his hands. Quickly he put out the light and lay down.

As soon as he'd snugged the covers over his shoulders, his eyes flew open. He stared into the darkness with a weary sigh. His mind hadn't gotten the message that he wanted the oblivion of sleep. Instead it played and replayed the day on a full-color loop—the accident, Carrie, Home Depot, Carrie, *Ginny*, Carrie's sad expression—over and over and over.

Trying to break the cycle, he counted backward from a hundred. Not so much as a yawn. He counted forward to a thousand. He prayed for everyone in his family. He sat up and read some more. He thought for a moment around two o'clock that he was drifting off, but the thought seemed to kick-start the loop to double speed, making Carrie race around as if running for her life.

He gave up just before dawn. He untangled his legs from the disheveled bedding and got to his feet. He pulled on an old pair of jeans and a Seaside sweatshirt, and grabbed his fleece pullover and Phillies cap.

Dawn was just lighting the sky when he stepped into his Starcraft. The peace he found on the water was just what he needed to get his mind back in neutral. One night thinking about a woman and he was as jumpy as Oreo when Carrie sprayed the Bactine.

Bad example. Bad! He was here *not* to think about Carrie. He turned his eyes toward the bay, which lay like a smooth sheet of silver in the gray morning mist. He guided his boat from its slip and turned east into the rising sun. A few fishermen and charter fishing boats kept him company as they headed for open water.

When they reached the channel where the bay and the ocean met, he turned back, lining the buoys up for red right returning. He didn't want the excitement of the colliding currents. He wanted tranquility, ease, disconnection.

He still knew peace on the water because Ginny never went fishing. She didn't mind cooking what he caught, but she wasn't interested in the catching. The bay held no memories of her to blindside him, only pleasure and serenity.

After he went under the Ninth Street Causeway and was halfway to the Thirty-Fourth Street Bridge, he killed the engine and pulled out his pole. He dropped his line over the side without anchoring. This early in the day he felt safe letting the boat drift with the tide as it receded. He crossed his ankles on the seat facing him and laid his head back. The gentle movement of the boat was soothing, and he thought he fell asleep for a few moments. After the night he'd had, he wasn't surprised.

But he needed to be alert. All it took was one cowboy in a cigarette boat going full throttle to create catastrophe. He sat up and took a pull on the hot coffee he'd grabbed at the Dunkin' Donuts drive-through. The pair of chocolate iced doughnuts were good, though Lindsay's sticky buns, grilled and spread with butter and reserved for him, would be better.

A gentle breeze ruffled his hair, and he smiled. *In spite of the new complications I haven't sorted out yet, Lord, life's good. Not great exactly, but good.*

And good was a vast improvement from the terrible it used to be. He must not wish for more and disturb this pleasant lassitude. Good was good enough.

He took a deep breath of the tangy air and watched sea gulls wheeling overhead. A blue heron stood immobile in the shallows at the edge of the marshy area to his left, and buffleheads and scaups glided over the wind-ruffled water. A cormorant sat on a piling, black wings spread as he dried them in the sun, now fully risen.

All he needed for perfection was a bite.

The Starcraft's bow nudged up against a small island covered in sea grasses and got stuck in the mud. Greg reeled in his empty line and set his pole aside. He reached into the storage pocket in the boat's side and pulled out a collapsible oar. With a twist he extended it.

He knelt on the seat in the bow and leaned out to push the boat free of the islet.

He almost fell overboard when he saw the hand tangled in the grass, open palm flung skyward. The body to which the hand was attached lay submerged, bumping gently against the mud and grass with the movement of the water.

Greg recognized death but still reached out and felt for a pulse. With sorrow he also recognized the victim in spite of the damage done by the water and the nibbling sea creatures. His memory flashed on Joe and Margaret Peoples, their sorrow-filled faces, and their premonition of disaster. He knew the devastation about to suck hope and happiness from them. The only positive about this scenario was that he wouldn't be required to be the one to inform them of their son's death.

Scratch that. Their son's murder. The coroner would need to make a final determination, but the marks about Jase's neck told their own tale.

But he'd have to tell Carrie and the others at the café. It'd be best coming from him, and it'd save someone on the force from that difficult duty.

Some days life hurt.

He grabbed his phone and called 911.

The SPD Marine Unit arrived first, and Greg moved his boat out of the way as he watched the officers assess the situation. Soon crime scene techs were doing what they could while the Coast Guard, Fish and Game guys, and the SPD talked jurisdiction and the coroner declared Jase dead, not that there was any doubt, but the law had to be satisfied.

Activity swirled around Greg, but he was no more than the one who found the body. Sure, several of the professionals going about their various chores acknowledged him by name, asked how he was. A couple of them even said they missed him. But he was outside the loop, merely the one who reported a tragedy, the one to be questioned about how he made his discovery.

He was amazed at how much the exclusion hurt.

14

Harl Evans grinned as he looked at the bay stretching before him. It was a pretty scene on this warm October Tuesday—tall grasses rising from the islands on which the Ninth Street Causeway rested, the water reflecting the deep blue of the sky. A few motorboats made foamy wakes as they sped past, and a couple of catamarans with colorfully striped sails heeled in the soft breeze. He inhaled the scent of the marshes, a singular smell that was strangely pleasing to a man raised in backwoods Maine. The sun poured down on him, making him feel toasty and warm. He loved warm. It filled him with something approaching happiness. He loved hot even better—which was why he'd ended up in southern Arizona, as far from his home as possible.

Those cold Maine nights when he'd been a kid had been agony.

"Can't we put more wood in the stove, Pop?" he'd asked as a young boy.

"What's your problem?" Pop would retort. "Can't you deal with a little chill? Put on another layer."

Somehow "a little chill" seemed a gross understatement when there was rime forming on the inside of the windows across the room.

"That wood supply's got to last the entire winter, Harl. I ain't cutting any more, not in snow like we got."

"We could buy a couple of cords," he suggested once when he was about seven. He'd heard one of the kids at school talk about buying wood, and he'd been amazed that people did something so sensible.

"We ain't spending what little we got on what's out there for the taking,"

Pop snarled. Trouble was, Pop wasn't taking, so Harl dragged fallen logs home through the thigh-deep snow and did his best to split them.

"Watchin' you with that ax is better'n watching TV," Pop said. "Ain't laughed so hard in years."

Harl bit his tongue to keep from suggesting yet again that Pop apply for a job at the lumbermill in town. Pop's anger and the sharp blows he rained on Harl for what he called disrespect were powerful deterrents. It wasn't until Harl was an adult that he understood that Pop couldn't handle a time clock and a regular job. He just wasn't smart enough, and his heavy drinking didn't help. Doing summer maintenance at the Happy Days Campground was all he could manage, and that was done on his own unpredictable schedule.

Pop kept him home from school when the snow got deep, and Harl didn't even have those few hours of warmth provided by the old hissing and groaning radiators in Moosehead Elementary.

"This room is always so hot," his teacher complained.

Harl smiled and slid his desk closer to the radiator.

"You are a waster of resources, Harl," Pop constantly growled at him when he returned from foraging in the woods with a fresh supply of downed limbs and rotting logs. "You are a weakling, a wimp, and no son of mine. For generations we Evanses have been strong, men of character. What's a little chill to us? You make me ashamed."

Then they were even. Pop's laziness and inability to cope with life shamed Harl.

"I don't want to freeze to death in my own house," Harl said. "Talk about stupid."

"Don't you call me stupid!" Pop's fist came up.

"I'm not! I'm saying freezing is stupid."

"You just don't unnerstand your heritage and the ways we Evanses become men."

For once Pop was right. Harl couldn't equate chilblains with manliness, so he kept chopping wood and building roaring fires.

Early in the winter of his sophomore year, he cut a hole in the upstairs hall and installed a grate to let the heat rise. Pop nearly had a cardiac when he found what Harl had done.

"You put that floor back," he ordered.

Harl had expected this reaction. "Can't. I burned it."

Blind with rage, Pop swung.

The old man had been using the same move for years, and Harl dodged it with ease. He grabbed his father by the shirt front.

"Swing at me again," Harl said in a low, tight voice, "and I'll hit back."

Pop's face turned red and his teeth drew back in a snarl, but he didn't strike out again. Instead he left the house and didn't return that night.

The next day when Harl came home from school, a piece of plywood was nailed over the grate. Since Pop had already left for the taproom, Harl ripped it free, chopped it up, and fed it to the wood stove, stoking the fire hotter and hotter.

Pop came home late and, groggy with drink, had fallen asleep. There would never be a better time.

Harl fed the fire until it was a small inferno. He stepped back, leaving the door of the stove open as someone might if they wanted extra heat, watching, waiting. One coal leaped out, then two, then more and more, all pulsing a fierce red and fiery gold, sizzling, smoldering on the wood floor. When the floor exploded in flames, he smiled. He took his father's bank card and all the money the old man had in his wallet. He then stood in the frigid air and watched the house and Pop go up in the crackling, soaring flames, for once not feeling the bite of the cold due to the warm satisfaction flooding him at the success of his vengeance.

When he was certain nothing would save the old place or the old man, he drove Pop's car to the nearest ATM and took out as much money as possible. He tossed the card in a nearby Dumpster so he wouldn't be tempted to use it again and give the police something to trace. He headed south, toward warmth even in January, and never looked back.

He smiled now as he watched the bay. He liked this little town. It wasn't as warm as southern Arizona, but he did like the wildness of the oceans' waves and the peace of the bay's calm, neither a feature that Arizona could offer.

He looked over his shoulder. Mike was fussing with one of his fishing reels. What was it with the man and fishing? Harl didn't see the attraction. He also didn't understand why a man who liked deep-sea fishing would settle in Arizona.

In the background the television droned on about the discovery of the body of the missing local guy in the bay. Not that such a grizzly find dimmed the scene's beauty in Harl's eyes. Nothing could do that. Nor did the retrieval of the body concern Harl. In fact he felt quite complacent. As far as anyone knew, he was at the compound keeping silence with Mike at the retreat house as they sought God's leading for The Pathway.

Right.

Retreating to pray was Mike's customary cover for his fishing trips. It wouldn't do for his followers who lived in austerity to know of his excursions aboard rented luxury yachts. Oh, they weren't big yachts, just small, well-appointed ones. Mike didn't want to draw unnecessary attention when he anchored in some marina.

Nor would it do for his followers to know what some of their donations were funding—and fishing trips were the least of it. Harl grinned what he liked to think of as his shark's grin.

Was there time to sneak away for a walk on the beach, another feature Arizona lacked? But then Seaside didn't have looming saguaro cacti, arms outstretched, thorns ready to impale you.

He thought for a moment about how different the two locales were, then smiled as he thought of the one feature they shared. Gullible people.

15

As I stumbled down the back steps in the early Tuesday morning light, bleary eyed from tossing and turning all night, I was still wrapped in sadness. In my head that little whisper reverberated louder than a rock band at full throttle.

"Ginny."

Greg had sat at my kitchen table and whispered his dead wife's name. I could stick bamboo shoots under my fingernails and experience less pain, less despair.

Even when Lindsay and I had been faced with living on the street, I'd had hope. We had escaped our own personal hell, were free, on our own, safe. Nothing we'd find in the wide world could compare to the dangers in our home.

We left all that evil for a better life. By God's grace we found it. And I wasn't ungrateful. Truly I wasn't. Still my heart wept as I went in the café's back door, my hopelessness jabbing, stabbing as I swallowed the tears burning in the back of my throat. Blessings in one area of life didn't prevent sorrow in another.

I felt as if I had been robbed of my deepest hope, a foolish hope perhaps, an unrequited dream, but a hope nevertheless. And one word had done it.

"Ginny."

I couldn't imagine being loved like that, three years gone and still my name on someone's lips. *Oh, Lord,* I wailed silently as I poured coffee and served Ricky's food and Lindsay's baked goods. *Why not me?*

I must have sighed because a gnarled hand reached over the pink marble counter and patted mine.

"It'll be okay, Carrie. Whatever it is, it'll get better."

I looked into Mr. Perkins's kind, concerned face and wanted to lay my head on his bony shoulder and weep. "I'm okay." I forced a smile.

He touched under his eye, and I lifted my free hand to my eye.

"Just had a bad night," I said, unhappy that it showed so clearly in the dark circles I'd tried to disguise with eraser stick.

He nodded. "All that excitement yesterday."

"Yesterday was wild." I forced another smile.

The door opened and Greg came in, so handsome in spite of being bruised and scabby. The hematoma from the bump on his forehead had settled into a lovely black eye, which should have made him look disreputable but didn't. My heart did its usual Snoopy dance, apparently unaware of the hopelessness of the situation, something my mind grasped with great sorrow. Clearly I needed better communication between body parts.

Mr. Perkins patted my hand harder. I looked at him with something like panic. He knew?

My face burned. It was a sad day when one's deepest secret was known to all, because if Mr. Perkins figured it out, how many others had also guessed? Ricky? Clooney? I already knew Lindsay, Mary P, and Andi suspected. Could life get any worse?

I pulled free and reached for the decaf coffee before I thought. I almost poured it over Mr. Perkins's hand as he covered his cup protectively.

"Carrie!" He looked at me, appalled. "The real thing!"

I gave him a weak smile. "I'm sorry. I don't know what I was thinking. We've got to keep your blood pumping."

I filled his cup with my special blend, knowing I'd have to say something to Greg and sure that everyone was listening.

"Hi," Greg said with a warm smile. I felt I should look behind me to see who he was smiling at. If he wasn't careful, I'd think he was glad to see me.

"Hi." Courtesy of a brain freeze, I couldn't think of anything else to say. I grabbed an empty cup.

He slid onto his stool, his smile gone as quickly as it had bloomed. He was barely settled before I handed him his coffee. He nodded his thanks.

"The usual?" I managed. Good. Two words. My brain must be thawing.

He nodded again.

"Got it," Lindsay called. "Ricky, the usual for Greg."

"Did you hear what the president just did?" Indignation poured off Mr. Perkins. He gave me a quick little sympathetic smile that made me cringe, then went back to being indignant. In all the years he'd been coming in, I don't think there'd been a president he liked. Today, though, I couldn't be certain whether he wanted to dump his take on the latest political goings-on on a new audience or whether he was trying to make things easier for me by claiming Greg's attention. The latter thought made me teary with affection for the frustrating old man. I looked away and blinked until I knew I wasn't going to humiliate myself.

Greg held up a finger, a signal to Mr. Perkins to be quiet. He took a deep breath, then exhaled. He looked at me. "They found Jase Peoples."

My hand went to my heart as if to protect it from more pain. "It's bad, isn't it?"

He nodded.

"Where?" I asked, my stomach twisting.

"Floating in the bay."

"No!" Tears came now, and I made no effort to staunch them. I pictured Jase in the kitchen, steam rising around him as he worked, a smile on his lips as he responded to something Ricky had said.

"Jase is dead?" Andi stood wide-eyed by Mr. Perkins. "That can't be! How do you know? Maybe you have it wrong."

I slipped my arm around her as Greg said, "I wish I did."

"Greg's got connections." I stroked her hair. "If he says, then it's so."

I felt her shaking, and her breathing was ragged. I felt pretty fragile myself.

"He was my friend," she whispered. "He was my *friend*."

We were all quiet, even Mr. Perkins.

Andi pulled back. "I've got to call Clooney." She bolted for the kitchen.

Lindsay appeared at the pass-through. "Is Andi right? Is Jase dead?"

Greg and I nodded.

She squeezed her eyes shut and gave a great sigh. "I liked him a lot. He was a nice guy in a world where they are in short supply." She turned and went back into the kitchen.

"Such a waste." My voice caught, and I had to clear my throat before I could continue. "Do they know what happened?"

Greg's expression hardened. "Whatever it was, it wasn't an accident."

"Murder?" The word felt foreign on my lips. Murder was for mystery novels and television shows, not for people you knew.

Greg's silence told me all I needed to know. I glanced toward the kitchen and Andi. "How long ago?"

"I'd guess Saturday night, but that's just a guess. The coroner will determine time of death."

I mopped my tears and sighed. "No wonder the tweeters couldn't find him."

Lindsay reappeared in the pass-through. "Where in the bay?"

"About midway between the causeway and the Thirty-Fourth Street Bridge," Greg said. "He was caught in the marshy grasses at Turtle Island."

"Don't you wonder why, Greg?" Lindsay walked into the café proper, carrying his scrambled eggs and toast. "Doesn't something like this get your cop juices going? Don't you want to find out who did this terrible thing?"

"Oh, yeah. I wonder who and why and how." He studied his plate, made a face, and poked at his eggs with his fork.

"Not hungry?" I could understand that. Tragic news dampened the appetite.

"It's not that." He poked at the eggs some more.

I studied the eggs. They looked fine to me, light and fluffy. I might not know much about Ricky as a person except that he was allergic to cats and yearned after Lindsay, but one thing I did know: he was a good cook.

"They're fine. Fine," Greg said with a definite lack of enthusiasm. As if to prove his comment true, he took one bite and then another. "Good."

I glanced at Lindsay just as she looked at me. Somehow neither of us was convinced, especially when he took a great swig of coffee after every bite.

The café door opened, and Jem Barnes entered. Greg looked at his father in surprise.

"I wasn't expecting you today, was I, Dad?"

"I don't know." Jem slipped onto a stool. "Were you?"

I liked Greg's father. He was a tall, slim man with a snow white mustache even though his hair was still mostly brown. He had an engaging smile, the kind that made you smile back no matter how blue you were feeling. If Greg looked like him thirty years from now, he'd be a handsome man.

"I'll have one of Lindsay's sticky buns," Jem said. "There is still one left, isn't there?"

I slid open the back of the display case and selected one for him.

"Did we have plans?" Greg asked his father.

Jem shook his head. "Not that I know of."

Greg frowned. "Then why are you here?"

Interesting question since Jem lived a good twenty miles inland, too far to just drop in. Was he here to check up on Greg? He'd done that many times after Ginny and the kids died, back when Greg was drinking too much.

But Greg was doing very well now. I studied him as I filled Jem's cup. His eyes were clear and his color good, bruises notwithstanding, visible proof that he'd been sober for a long time. I knew because I kept a running calendar in my head.

Not that he'd been alcohol dependent, not in the sense of being an alcoholic. He'd used drink to dull his pain, to make life bearable when the emotional agony was overwhelming.

Back then I would work the counter when Jem and Greg sat together, and I'd hear Jem trying to reach his son.

"You can't use alcohol as a soporific to put yourself to sleep." The pain in Jem's voice as he watched his son hurt was clear, and the look on Jem's face brought tears to my eyes.

Greg always nodded, but if his reddened eyes when he came in the next time were any indication, he ignored the advice.

"Son, drinking won't solve your problems. It'll just create new ones."

"Don't you think I know that?" That day Greg lost his temper. "I've seen what it does more times than I can count. I'm a cop, remember?"

There was a sharp silence as Jem stared into his cup and Greg looked bereft.

"At least I *was* a cop." He slid off his stool and all but ran out the door.

Jem had sighed, overtipped me, and left, shoulders rounded with sorrow.

Then one Saturday about a year after Ginny and the kids died, Greg's brothers stepped in, all five of them, including the one who was a missionary in Mexico. I know because they cornered him here at the café.

"Just what I need." Greg eyed them in disgust. "What? You didn't bring Mom and Dad too?"

"Like we want them to hear us reaming you out," one brother said. "What we have to say isn't for their ears."

"Go away, all of you." Greg glowered at them. "I mean it."

"We're going," said another, "but you're coming with us whether you like it or not."

"Five against one? I can take you all."

"At the moment you're such a sorry excuse for a man, you couldn't take any of us." It was the missionary from Mexico.

They all had that don't-mess-with-us look, and it was clear they'd take him by force if they needed to. The odds were in their favor in spite of Greg's background a Marine and a cop.

They bore him off for what must have been a humdinger of a conversation. Greg hadn't touched a drop since. Life had slowly, slowly seeped back into him, and I thought he was doing well.

Now Jem studied him. "Which one of your tenants popped you?"

Greg lifted a gentle hand to his shiner. "You didn't read about it on Twitter?"

"I don't tweet. My life isn't worth the minute examination it requires."

"There was this guy named Chaz," Mr. Perkins began and gave his version of the incident. Since he wasn't there, it was a bit skewed but by and large accurate.

Jem looked impressed. "Anything else going on around here I should know about, Mr. Perkins?"

Mr. Perkins launched into the tale of Jase.

"I heard about the murder on the news as I was driving here," Jem said. "I didn't realize there was a Carrie's connection."

"It makes me so sad!" My throat went tight, and I had to swallow.

Everyone nodded agreement. Then Mr. Perkins waved his spoon, dripping coffee on the counter. "The big question is what happened to him between when Bill decked him and he floated to the top. And a second biggie—did Bill do it?"

"Mr. Perkins! What an awful thing to say!" Andi glared at him as she came to the counter. "Bill would never do something so terrible."

"He already did something terrible," Mr. Perkins, ever the diplomat, was quick to point out. "He knocked Jase unconscious."

Andi made a brushing-away gesture. "That wasn't anything. He thought he was protecting me. He's just too nice to do something really mean."

Just moderately mean. I sighed. She was ignoring the still-purple skin about her wrist.

"Besides he was with me," she said. "How could he hurt Jase if he was with me?"

Greg studied her. "He was with you all night?"

She squirmed. "Well, no. Clooney makes me come home by midnight on weekends. I keep telling him how lame that is, but he's like a rock that can't be moved." She made a disgusted noise.

"You're lucky to have someone who cares." I couldn't resist saying it. When I was her age, I was already on my own with a ten-year-old to care for, scared to death but determined. I'd have loved a caring family, even one as removed as a great-uncle.

"Remember how Jase had come home very recently after being gone for several years?" Greg said. "My sources tell me he'd been in The Pathway."

If he was trying to divert the attention from Andi, he failed. She sucked in a breath and blurted, "They know Jase was in The Pathway?"

"The Pathway?" Lindsay looked appalled as she brought a platter of freshly baked, saucer-sized sugar cookies for the display case. "Michael the Archangel?"

"They're all nuts," Mr. Perkins said.

"Maybe." Greg pushed away the plate with the largely uneaten eggs he tried to hide beneath his napkin. "For sure they're different. I'll have one of those cookies."

Lindsay slid one onto a plate for him.

"How old was he?" Mr. Perkins asked. "He looked about ten."

I assumed he meant Jase, not Michael.

"Twenty-five, according to the paper," Greg said. "He took off at eighteen, was gone for seven years, and was with The Pathway for most of those years."

"That group's a cult, if you want my opinion," Mr. Perkins said.

This time I tended to agree with him. Everything I'd read about The Pathway sounded bogus, from the claims of their leader, Michael the Archangel, to their reclusive, secretive, "God-ordained" way of life in their isolated desert compound.

"Any man who advertises himself as the modern incarnation of the archangel Michael, the field commander of the Lord's army, has to be either quite strange or knowingly committing a fraud." Greg took a bite of his cookie and sighed with pleasure. "Either way he's dangerous."

"Are they polygamous like that FLDS group in West Texas?" Jem asked. "I can't remember."

"They are," Greg said.

Mr. Perkins made a disgusted sound. "Perverts. I hope they all land in jail."

I patted his hand. "Easy there."

"I'm going to take a few minutes, okay, Carrie?" Andi looked pale and sounded breathless. She wouldn't meet my eyes. She reached under the counter and retrieved the Sudoku book she kept stashed there. "I'll be in the booth in the back."

There was only one party in the place besides Greg, Jem, and Mr. Perkins. "Are they okay?" I cocked my head in the direction of the man and woman deep in conversation at booth one.

"They're just talking over coffee. They have their bill and said they didn't want anything more."

I nodded. "Tell Ricky what you want to eat."

"I-I don't want anything."

Another lost appetite. "Will Bill be in for breakfast?"

"I-I'm not sure."

I studied the girl, thinking she looked off balance somehow. Greg was looking at her too. Was it Jase's death? He'd been a friend, and his loss was bound to upset her. It certainly upset me. Or were things not going well in paradise in spite of her defense of Bill a few minutes ago? Perhaps Jase's murder was making her wary of him, or perhaps the bruised wrist was having a warning-off effect after all.

"Go sit," I said, feeling sad for her. "I'll have Ricky make you some of your favorite chocolate-chip pancakes and bring them when they're ready."

With a weak smile, she turned and walked to the last booth, where she settled with her back to the door.

Poor kid. I might not know her problem, but I knew the empty-stomach feel of your world spinning out of control.

16

The Pathway! Andi felt a chill deep in her bones. She kept her head down so no one would see what she feared was a panicked expression. When she'd assumed that Jase was a victim of random violence, she'd been okay. Real sad for him, of course, because she liked him and felt sorry for him, but not scared. After all, in life bad stuff happened, as she knew all too well.

But the cops knew of Jase's connection to The Pathway. If they learned that about him, would they learn the same thing about her? How would she stay safe if people knew? She was only sixteen. They might have the law on their side and make her go back. The thought made her break out in a cold sweat.

She'd die first. She would!

So the scary question was, did Jase die *because* of his connection to The Pathway?

If that were the case, then she was dead too—if they found her.

She shivered. Somehow they found him. Well, they would have his old address, the one right here where he had lived with his parents until he ran away. Jase used to talk about how much he missed the ocean, stuck as they were in the arid Southwest.

"Sometimes I dream of diving under a wave," he'd tell her and her best friend, Jennie. "And then I wake up here." And he'd look with resignation at the barren landscape.

"Do you ever think of going home?" Andi had asked, because she thought of going home all the time. And the idea of going down the shore was enough to make the saliva pool in her mouth.

Jase would smile at Jennie. "Not really. Something more important than the Atlantic is here."

But he had gone home, and they'd found him. And he was dead.

They would find her. She could almost feel them breathing down her back.

Of course, he'd made it easy, coming home to Mommy. She'd thought she was so clever going to Clooney, her great-uncle on her mother's side, even though she knew Jase lived mere miles from Clooney. But she wasn't afraid of Jase, and where else could she go?

Clooney had always fascinated her. Her mother called him "my weird uncle," and he wasn't typical, that was for sure. But he was interesting. And fun. When she was a kid and they came to Seaside for vacation, they always spent a day with Clooney. He'd take her and Becca digging for treasure. When they got tall enough, he let them use the metal detector.

"Swing it back and forth, Andi. Nice and easy. You have to go slow and take your time."

And then it would *ping*, and he'd hand one of them the red plastic spade, and they'd dig up something, usually change. He always let them keep whatever they found. The year she was eight, Andi found enough money to buy a Seaside T-shirt. She'd worn it for the rest of the week, only taking it off when she was in the water.

But no one in The Pathway knew about Clooney. Except Becca and Dad, but they wouldn't tell, would they? Tears filled her eyes as she thought of them. Like she could trust either one.

She put her hand on her stomach to still its rumbling. She felt all jittery, like she'd throw up.

Maybe she was overreacting. She didn't even know if they'd done any-thing to Jase. Of course, if they didn't, who did? She stared at her bruised wrist and shivered.

God, are You there? Can You hear me? I am so scared!

It was all Michael's fault. Michael, God's commander. God's warrior. Ha! Satan's soldier was more like it.

She hated him. Hated him!

She first heard of The Pathway when then seventeen-year-old Becca became intrigued by the group. Somehow she had stumbled on to their Web site, and next thing Andi knew, Becca was mouthing their lame phi-losophy to anyone who was unlucky enough to be around.

"You mean they're the only guys in the whole world who have it right?" Andi asked. She might have been just thirteen at the time, but she knew a ridiculous position when she heard one. "What about all the other Chris-tians through the ages? They were all wrong? And all the other religions? They're wrong too? Only Michael and his little band are right? Don't make me laugh."

"You just don't understand," Becca told her in a condescending manner.

True enough. She didn't. Still, the most astonishing thing wasn't Bec-ca's gullibility. What Andi could not believe was her parents' interest in this strange group. Soon all she heard was, "Michael said this" or "Michael said that." It was enough to ruin every meal as she gagged on their words.

They began watching Michael's videos on YouTube.

"Andi, come watch this!"

"Andi, you'll love what Michael says here."

"Oh, Andi, isn't Michael amazing?"

Granted he looked good—tall and powerful and authoritative. He had long black hair to his shoulders and brilliant, piercing blue eyes she thought weren't the result of nature but contacts. He had presence, and as a result what he said sounded right—if you didn't think about it too much.

"Love one another," Becca said dreamily after one slick bit of video manipulation. "It doesn't get any better than that."

Andi frowned at her sister. "I think Jesus said that first. You can't go wrong stealing your lines from Him."

Becca looked shocked at Andi's blasphemy. "You are so lost!"

"Maybe, but just because a guy has the same name as an angel doesn't mean he is one or that he can save me. I've got two Michaels in my class, and they can't save me either."

"You are so going straight to hell." Becca stormed away.

"Hey," Andi called after her. "What happened to 'love one another'?"

As she endured the not-very-subtle efforts to convert her, Andi thought all her family had gone more-than-slightly insane. She couldn't wait for the phase to pass as quickly and as completely as Becca's infatuation with Justin Bieber.

"I wish we could move to The Pathway's compound," Becca said almost every day.

"It sounds wonderful, doesn't it?" Mom said, her voice wistful. "No more troublesome neighbors or demanding bosses or living in fear of lawbreakers."

You'd have thought criminals stopped by every night to rob them.

"No more income taxes," Dad said with a smile.

Which had to be wrong somehow. Everybody had to pay taxes. Even she knew that.

"It would be wonderful to be part of such a loving community." Mom smiled at Dad.

Andi stared at her mother in disbelief. Was she crazy? Didn't she realize that The Pathway wasn't just 'love one another'? It was also *share* one another. Was Mom really willing to share Dad with other wives?

"They're polygamous, Mom!"

"Only if you choose that way," Mom said.

Andi looked at Dad, who nodded. He took Mom's hand. "You mustn't let that little detail keep you from appreciating the whole, Andi."

Little detail? Who was he kidding?

"It would be heaven on earth to live there," Becca said.

It would be worse than any prison in the world to live there! Thank goodness Dad had his job and they had the house. They couldn't go anywhere.

Then came the day that Dad didn't go to work.

"Girls," he said as he sat at the breakfast table with them. "You're not going to school today."

Andi stared. Something was wrong. Dad was fanatical about their schoolwork.

"Are you sick?" Fear twined around her heart. A brain tumor. That had to be it. That would explain both his presence on a workday and his enthrallment with The Pathway.

"I'm fine. In fact, I'm wonderful."

Andi had to admit he looked more relaxed and rested than she'd ever seen him. "Then why aren't you at work?"

"I gave notice a month ago and finished yesterday. I am now free to follow my rightful destiny. We are all free to follow after God." He grinned at Mom, winked at Becca, and patted Andi's hand.

"You quit your job?" Andi couldn't believe it. How would they pay their bills? How would they eat? How could she talk him into getting her a new cell phone, a wonderful pink one with all kinds of apps? And one of those cool iPods?

"And yesterday your mother and I signed the papers on the sale of the house. We're moving to southern Arizona."

Andi stared at him. "You sold our house?" He couldn't do that without telling her and Becca, could he? It was their house too. But he had. "Mom?"

She just smiled, obviously happy with the news. Of course it wasn't news to her. She'd known about everything for a long time and not said a word either.

Andi felt nothing so much as betrayed by those she thought she could trust. She was dizzy with their disregard for her life and feelings, her wants and needs.

She'd never lived anywhere but here, and she didn't want to. The place might be a little old, but it had a great yard with big trees, and she and Becca each had their own room. And friends. They had friends. Yes, Becca's were lame, but hers were great. She didn't want to leave them or lose them! Eighth grade was hard enough when you knew everybody, but if you had to change schools and start all over?

And southern Arizona? Why southern Arizona?

The answer struck her like a blow to the face. The Pathway! Why it took her so long to figure out when she had lived with the hysterical rhetoric for weeks she didn't know. The dizziness intensified, and she had to blink several times to clear her vision.

Andi began to cry. "We can't go there! We can't! Mom, tell him we can't!"

But Mom just smiled, already looking like the mindless women who smiled vacantly on The Pathway's Web site.

Becca grabbed Dad in a great bear hug. "Oh, Daddy, this is wonderful!"

"We're leaving after lunch," Dad announced. "You've got the whole morning to pack what you need. You can take one suitcase each. Remember we're going to hot weather, and remember the dress code."

Andi stared at her father in horror. The dress code! Ugly, shapeless dresses. Stupid, flat tie shoes. Hair in awful knots at the back of the head. No jeans ever, at least for the women. The boys and men all wore jeans. They looked like normal people, though Andi doubted they were. If they were, they wouldn't be living on The Pathway's compound.

"We're leaving today?" She was going to hyperventilate and pass out. She knew it. "What's the rush?"

"There's no rush," Dad said with an unruffled calm that was eerie and frightening. "We've been thinking about this for a long time."

Mom nodded like the little marionette she was fast becoming.

"But I haven't! I haven't been thinking of it at all." Tears slid down Andi's cheeks, and her throat hurt so bad she could hardly get her words out. "I'm not going." She folded her arms and narrowed her eyes. "You can't make me."

Dad's expression turned stern. "You are only thirteen. I can and will make you."

She stared at him. Was he right? Could he make her? With a terrible sinking feeling, she knew he was right. She might be feisty, but she wasn't stupid. She couldn't take care of herself, and the law wouldn't even let her try. Not yet. But the minute she could, she was leaving that place. She didn't know where she'd go, but she would not stay at that compound a minute longer than she had to.

"How am I going to say good-bye to Heather and Joss?" Her voice rose to a squeak as she realized she couldn't even call them because they were at school like normal people.

"You're going to make wonderful new friends," Mom said, so zoned out on happiness that Andi wanted to puke.

"I don't want new friends! I like my old ones just fine."

"Go pack, Andi." Dad's voice was firm.

"One suitcase?" How could she pack a whole room in one suitcase?

"One suitcase. We don't want to be encumbered with the world."

Encumbered with the world? Those were Michael's words; they had to be. "I like my encumbrances," she said defiantly.

"Things get in the way of life," Dad said. "Michael tells us they are like terrible chains binding us, weighing us down. We don't want them or need them."

I want them! I need them!

"We want to be free!" He threw his arms wide, and Mom, laughing at his joy, ducked as one of his hands sailed past her face.

While the three of them rejoiced and celebrated, Andi shriveled inside.

God, how can You let this happen? Don't expect to hear from me anymore if You don't fix things fast.

As they drove from the Philadelphia suburbs to The Pathway's compound in the middle of nowhere, her parents and Becca talked nonstop about how wonderful their lives would now become. They would be part of a larger family, part of God's blessed ones.

But Andi knew better.

17

When Ricky called that Andi's pancakes were up, I carried them to her. I found her staring at her Sudoku book as it lay open before her. She grunted thanks as I put the plate down. Without looking at me, she began slathering butter on her food, then drenching it with maple syrup.

I grinned as she licked her lips as she worked. She might say she wasn't hungry, but she still had an unconscious olfactory response to the enticing scent of the chocolate-laced food. One of the best parts of having the café was seeing the delight people experienced as they enjoyed good food.

But she didn't take that first bite. She just sat there as the pancakes cooled.

I slid onto the bench across from her. "What is it, Andi? What's wrong?"

She finally looked at me, her eyes wide and uncertain. "I don't know what you mean. I'm fine."

"I don't know what I mean either." I'd have felt better about that "I'm fine" if her voice hadn't quivered. "Are you feeling sick?"

"Of course not. I'm fine. I never get sick." After a second's hesitation she said, "It's just that Jase is dead."

I nodded. Was that it? Did she care enough about Jase to be bothered to the point of not eating? She'd only known him for a couple of weeks. Or was it another guy, big and burly and sometimes violent, who concerned her?

"Are you worried about Bill?"

She gave me what looked like a forced smile. She cut off a bite of pancake. "Bill's okay. I'm not the least worried about him." Seeing my skepticism, she repeated herself. "Bill's okay."

I wasn't convinced, and I didn't think she was either. "Well, if something's wrong, you know you can always talk to me about it, right?"

"I know, and I will," she lied, all false sincerity. "Thanks."

She was never going to seek me out, and I couldn't force her to. It seemed I didn't have Mary P's magic when it came to needy sixteen-year-olds.

I rose and left Andi to her food as the café's door opened and a stranger came in. He had brown hair and eyes and was solid looking rather than handsome, more workhorse than racing thoroughbred.

"Fred." Greg stood and held out his hand. "Carrie, we're going to take a booth, okay?"

"Sure. What can I get you, Fred?"

"Are those homemade sticky buns I see?" Fred eyed the display counter where the calorie-laden, scrumptious pastry lay.

"They are," I said. "Want one grilled?"

"They slice them in half," Greg said, "then butter and grill them. Delicious."

Fred practically drooled in anticipation. "I'll take one and coffee."

"Give me one too," Greg said.

To fill the holes left by not eating his eggs? I'd have thought the sugar cookie would have done that. "Coming right up."

The door opened again, and Bill Lindemuth strolled in, cocky as ever.

Mr. Perkins pointed his index finger at Bill before anyone had a chance to say hello. "You know they found Jase? The guy you punched out?"

"Mr. Perkins," I said. "Easy there."

Bill frowned and looked uncomfortable.

"They found him floating in the bay. Dead." Mr. Perkins glared.

Bill paled and looked around. "Where's Andi?"

I waved toward the back of the café as I moved to the cash register to take the money of the man and woman who had been talking in Andi's service area.

"Come again." I smiled and handed them their receipt. They nodded and left.

"Grilled sticky buns up," Ricky called.

On my way to pick up Greg's and Fred's orders, I passed Bill, sitting at the counter as far from Mr. Perkins as he could.

"Where's Andi?" he demanded again, as if his inability to see her was my fault.

Trying not to let my irritation show, I nodded toward the booth at the rear of the cafe. "She's eating back there."

"No, she's not."

"Yes, she is. I served her food myself."

I grabbed the warm sticky buns, all buttery and cinnamony, and took them to Greg and his friend. When I set the fragrant food in front of the men, they both took a deep breath and gave soft groans.

"Lindsay's the best baker in South Jersey," I said, proud of my little sister. I left them to their enjoyment and their business and returned to the counter to find Bill still slumped on his stool.

"She's not there," he said. "Her pancakes are, but she's not."

"Then she's probably in the ladies' room."

"Well, how am I supposed to know that?"

What would have been a legitimate question asked in another tone of voice made me wonder if the guy went out of his way to be aggravating or if it came naturally. I started for the kitchen to get away from him.

"Hey, don't walk away. I want to order."

I turned and forced a pleasant expression. "Yes?"

"I'll have a couple of fried eggs, bacon, hash browns, and whatever it is those guys have that smells so great," he told me without bothering to look at me. "And a cup of coffee."

"That'll be about ten dollars." He might as well know that I was not feeding him gratis every day. "Plus tip."

He had the nerve to look offended. "Fine. Whatever."

As I turned to give his order to the kitchen, I decided I definitely had to talk to Andi about what made a man worth her time. It wasn't petulance and entitlement, which Bill had in abundance, and cockiness and conceit were not the same as self-confidence.

It had taken me quite some time, years in fact, before I was willing to admit any man was worth a woman's time. All my pre-escape experience was with men of the lowest character and standards. I thought that was all men.

Sure, I'd seen movies and television shows with decent male characters, but those guys were fictional. They were what writers wished men could be, not what I knew they were.

Mary P's Warren was the first decent man Lindsay and I had close contact with. Linds took to him right away, sitting in the kitchen at the Surfside and talking with him whenever he had a minute. It took cynical me more than a year before I was willing to consider that he might be the sweet man he appeared. It took several more years before I was willing to admit there were many fine men out there, men of character, men of integrity. Men like Greg, Jem, and Pastor Paul, even Clooney in his own cock-eyed way.

Bill accepted his breakfast with a grunt and dove in. Literally. He leaned so far into his plate he was practically lying in his food. Hadn't anyone ever told him you brought your food to your mouth, not your mouth to your food?

I looked around for Andi, since the booth the man and woman had been sitting in needed to be cleared, but she was still in the ladies' room. I wandered back that way to make certain she was all right. If she wanted to stay in there until Bill left, I wouldn't out her, but I wanted to make sure she hadn't gotten sick or something.

The ladies' room was empty.

Andi still hadn't reappeared when Bill slapped down his money with a put-upon air and sneered his way out of the café. Did he honestly think people responded to that kind of attitude? Well, they did respond, come to think of it, or at least I did. With dislike. As I cleared his dishes, I noticed without surprise that he hadn't left a tip.

With a brief wave, Greg left, followed by his friend. Mr. Perkins finally detached himself from his stool and wandered away, and I made certain the menus had the information about the day's specials.

When Andi didn't surface for lunch, I was more than a little miffed. Avoiding Bill was one thing. Leaving me short-handed was another.

When Greg came back to the café just before closing, I was too irritated at Andi to have the energy for my usual pleasure at the sight of him. Besides, what was the use? "Didn't expect to see you again today."

Greg raised an eyebrow at my abrupt tone. "Hello to you too."

I flushed. "Sorry. I'm worried about Andi. She hasn't been here since before lunch."

He nodded. "No wonder you're mad."

"I am not mad. I do not do mad."

He grinned, his face crinkling, his eyes twinkling. "Right. You are always mellow."

I raised my chin. "I am."

"Uh-huh. May I have a Coke? Please?"

I turned and drew one for him and another for myself. I pulled the last piece of Lindsay's red velvet cake from the display case and set it on a plate.

I put it on the counter between us and got out two forks. We took turns eating, silent and, to my mind, amazingly comfortable with each other. I guessed that when I understood I didn't have a chance with him, the tension disappeared. I felt a shaft of pain over how pleasant it would have been to share cake with this man forever.

Lest he discern my thoughts, I reverted to our previous topic. "I'm worried, Greg. Where did the girl go?"

Well, they found Jason's body, that clever little weasel. It had been only a matter of time, he knew that, but he wished it had taken the cops longer. He'd been hoping that when the remains were found, ID'ing him would take a few days, what with the fish and sea creatures feasting on the body. He supposed it was dental records that did the trick. The sea snackers couldn't eat teeth.

To think it had all gone south over a girl. How trite. How common. How ridiculous.

Not that he didn't like girls as well as the next man. He grinned. His favorites were the young ones with bouncy ponytails and cute figures. It was one of the wonders of the world that there seemed an endless supply to choose from.

But when he chose, the girl was marked. She might not have his name tattooed on her forehead, but anyone with any intelligence would recognize she was now his woman.

With as much anger as regret, he hated the fact that Jason wasn't perceptive. It was sad, really. All the guy'd had to do was step back and leave her alone.

Greg reveled in the wash of peace that stole over him here at the café. His time with Fred hadn't gone badly in spite of a last-minute glitch over paperwork, and he hadn't even realized he was feeling tense—until he came in here.

"So your settlement went well?" Carrie asked, Lindsay's cake making her as mellow as he'd teased her about.

"Sort of." He paused to savor the buttery taste of the icing. "One of the papers needed was missing, an oversight on the part of the Realtor, and we have to reconvene tomorrow, but it's no big deal. Josh, my boss for at least another day, managed to keep his temper, and Fred didn't seem upset. He's staying for a few days anyway. I think he's going deep sea fishing with some friends."

"How'd he like your hole in the wall at the Sand and Sea?" Carrie gave him a wicked grin.

Greg laughed. "He was better with it than I expected. He just shook his head and muttered about strange people. He made noises about applying for a loan to underwrite the repairs and some other upgrading he wants done on several of the properties. I'm to oversee the projects, hire the contractors, etcetera."

"That's good news. It'd be terrible to lose your job."

Greg shrugged. "I wouldn't miss it. It's not like property managing is my life's goal. God just didn't wire me that way."

"Then why are you doing it?"

Talk about to the point. "Good question." He studied the tines of his fork. "All I know is that after Ginny and the kids died, I knew I couldn't handle the pressure of being a cop, so I left the force before I made some mistake that either injured or killed someone or got me fired. I was offered this job and took it more to make Pastor Paul happy than anything. Every time he looked at me back then, he was so worried."

"He wasn't the only one," Carrie said. "The whole church was concerned. I barely knew you and Ginny, but what happened was so terrible, we all hurt for you. We prayed for you for weeks, months."

"And I felt the prayers. You all saved my sanity."

Carrie licked the last of the icing off her fork and laid it across the plate, tines down. She studied the counter with a slight scowl. "You still miss them."

He nodded, hearing the wistfulness in her voice. Over *Ginny*? Or because no one had ever loved her as he'd loved his family? Runaways ran away for a reason, and a warm loving family wasn't it. His heart ached for her, and he found he wanted to know all the particulars of her life, both then and now, all her struggles. How had she gotten from waif to café owner? Was she raised with money or with none? Rich kids ran from bad situations just as poor ones did. Where were her parents today?

It was a funny thing, now that he thought about it. He'd been coming into this café almost every day for three years and occasionally before that, but Carrie had just been part of the surroundings. Then, in less than a day, she had become the heart and soul of the place, the light that penetrated and dispelled his darkness.

Or was it that sudden? Had she been creeping up on him all along and he'd been too dumb to notice?

"I'll always miss Ginny and the kids." He took care with his words. He didn't want a repeat of her misunderstanding yesterday. "They shouldn't have died. In a better world the kids would be three years older, learning to get along with new teachers, studying new subjects, maybe playing soccer or doing gymnastics. Ginny'd be teaching her women's Bible study for another year and trying out recipes that didn't work more often than did." He gave a rueful smile. "She was a terrible cook, but that never stopped her from trying."

Carrie looked at him briefly, then returned to her study of the counter. "Do you realize that's the first time you've ever told me anything about Ginny?"

Greg was surprised at that since his wife and kids filled so much of his thoughts. "Maybe I've gotten to the point that memories don't bring pain."

She looked at him, her dark eyes earnest and hopeful. "Maybe you've let the guilt go?"

A spot-on question that personal should make him angry. Even as recently as last week, he'd have pokered right up and left as soon as he could. It was his guilt, he'd earned it, and he should be allowed to wallow in it as long as he wanted. Yet today he felt she had the right to ask, and he had the responsibility to answer.

"I don't know about the guilt being gone or ever being gone. It is, after all, the gift that keeps on giving."

She looked at him with understanding. "My issue is lack of trust, not guilt. It's too dangerous to trust. I've always thought people who do so are naive and foolish. They're asking for the knife in the back. Smart people like me know everyone has an angle. Everyone wants something from you. No one's safe."

"You don't seem lacking in trust to me. You're very caring and interested in people."

She traced a vein in the pink marble. "I'm much better. I know that. But it's taken years. I used to dream of a quick fix, of a knight in shining armor riding to my rescue and carrying me away from Mom and her men. From my life in general. He never had a face, but I knew he was handsome and strong and good and kind. Then I met Mary P and Warren. They might not have been handsome, but they were strong and good and kind, so very kind. God gave me what I yearned for. Rescue just didn't look like I thought it would."

Greg thought of his family, his mother and father so strong and dependable, his brothers all grown to fine, trustworthy men. "It breaks my heart things were so rough for you, tiger."

She made a face. "You should be glad you didn't know me back then. When I met Mary P and Warren, I doubted them. Mary P and Warren! I wore my lack of trust like a Kevlar jacket protecting me from their unending potshots of love and kindness. The greatest gift they gave me was waiting me out. It couldn't have been easy for them because they were so open and accepting and I was spitting in their faces."

"Figuratively speaking, I presume." He grinned at her.

She grinned back. "Figuratively speaking. Lindsay trusted them from the first, but every time they were nice to me, I looked for the catch. It was so wearing because they were always nice, not just to me but to everyone. No one I knew before I came here—except Linds of course—was nice just to be nice. Everyone had an agenda."

"What changed you?" he asked. If she could ask personal questions, so could he.

"Time. Genuine people. Reliable people. And the Lord."

"But you did change. That's what counts." He had to admire her for that.

"It's taken seventeen years and people who cared enough to stick with me through it all." She took a pull from her nearly empty glass and flinched when the straw gave its all-gone *blat*. "Warren would take me aside and say things like, 'Not everyone's lying to take advantage, Carrie. When I tell you you did a good job, I want nothing from you except to see you light up.' Or Mary P would say, 'Trust me, Carrie. I will not cheat you out of any of your tips added to the bill electronically. I have to ask, have I ever done anything to make you doubt me?' And of course she hadn't."

"You know the ridiculous thing I get angry about because of my guilt?" He couldn't believe he was going to say his darkest thought out loud, but she'd shared her heart, giving him the courage and freedom to share his. "I get mad at Ginny for not making me move my car so she could get to hers. If she'd done that, she and the kids would be alive and I wouldn't feel their deaths were my fault."

"But you'd be dead."

He shrugged. "There were many times I wished I was." He glanced at her. "But I don't anymore."

Their eyes locked, hers widening. He thought she understood the words he wasn't saying though he couldn't be one hundred percent certain. She blinked and looked away first.

"Anyway." She straightened and gave the counter a gentle slap. "The learning to deal, whatever the issue, can't be hurried, can it? It can be helped and eased by those who care, and the Lord changes attitudes and heals hearts when we seek Him, but it still takes time. It's just a good thing God walks that healing road with us."

She picked up the dirty cake dishes and silverware, all business now, Carrie of Carrie's Café. "Excuse me, will you? I've got to call Andi yet again and see if she's answering. Every time I tried earlier, all I got was voice mail."

"She sure took off lickety-split this morning." He slid his empty Coke glass toward her.

She frowned. "You saw her leave?"

Greg nodded. "She glanced up, saw Bill, and got a horrified look. She slouched way down in the booth, slid out, and almost crawled to the back door so she wouldn't be seen."

Carrie went rigid. "She *is* afraid of him. She told me she wasn't, but she is. I knew it!"

Greg shrugged. "I think it's more not being so enamored anymore and not wanting to talk to him."

Carrie didn't seem to hear. "Do you think he's harassing her or something when she's not here? Has he hurt her? More than when he grabbed her yesterday, I mean. Do you think he hit her like he hit Jase?"

Physical abuse definitely in her background, he thought. She was projecting her experiences onto Andi. "There's no doubt Bill has anger management issues, but we may be jumping to conclusions here."

She frowned and took a deep breath. After a short pause during which it seemed she was trying to collect her thoughts, she said, "You're right. It's my lack of trust issues. I'm getting carried away." She made a face. "Probably. Maybe. But maybe not. Greg, the guy's a loose cannon. And he doesn't leave tips!"

Greg laughed at her indignation and without thinking laid a hand over hers. "Easy, tiger."

She froze, and he thought she might take exception to his touch. Instead she turned red and couldn't look at him. Very interesting response. He gave her hand a light squeeze, then released her. "When you talk with her, you'll get a better idea of what's going on. See what she has to say, and we'll go from there."

She nodded and pulled her phone free from its waist clip. He listened to her side of the conversation, and she didn't seem to mind.

"Then you're all right? You'll be here tomorrow morning?" she said. "I'm counting on you."

Andi must have answered in the affirmative because Carrie said, "Fine. Good. Just don't run out like that again. If Bill's bothering you, I won't let him in the café, okay?"

"All's well?" Greg asked as Carrie closed her phone.

"She assures me that Bill isn't a problem." Carrie's skeptical look was a mirror of his own.

"I think I'll mention to Clooney about her running when Bill appeared," Greg said. "Make sure he's aware."

"Would you?" Her relieved smile was lovely. "I'd feel so much better."

"Done. Do you fish?"

She looked startled at the abrupt change of subject. "Uh, no, never tried it."

"You live at the shore and you don't fish?"

"I know lots of people who live at the shore and don't fish."

"Name two."

"Lindsay and Mary P."

"Huh. Well, Warren loved to fish."

"He did," Carrie agreed. "Off-season they closed on Sunday and Monday, and he'd often get up early and go out on the bay in this little boat with a twenty horsepower motor. We'd have great freshly caught flounder for dinner. Mary P would make homemade French fries and coleslaw. We'd all eat like pigs. Even Bess Meyerson, our landlady, would come." Her eyes softened with memories. "I still miss Warren."

"Let me take you fishing." It would be fun to introduce her to one of his favorite pastimes.

Several emotions flashed across her face: disbelief, uncertainty, longing. "I've never fished in my life. City girl here, remember?"

"So I'll teach you. It's not hard."

"I just hang the line in the water, right?"

"A slight oversimplification, but that's the general idea."

"Do you promise to clean anything I catch?"

"The Barnes rule has always been that you clean what you catch."

She shook her head. "You're telling me that Ginny cleaned her own fish?"

"Ginny didn't fish."

She looked surprised and a tiny bit pleased. Because he was doing something with her that he hadn't done with Ginny? For some reason that touch of one-upmanship on her part warmed him.

"It was a great shock to me when I found out. We started dating in the late fall, and by the time spring and fishing rolled around and I learned the terrible truth, it was too late to turn back."

"A hard lesson in how tricky assumptions can be."

"Tell me about it. In my defense, I came by mine naturally because my mom is a great fisherman. It doesn't matter whether it's fresh water or the bay or deep sea. She loves fishing."

"You're telling me your mom cleans her own fish?"

He nodded. "Always."

"Well, I make no promises. Does she put on the worms too?"

"If that's what she needs."

"Worms are slimy."

"We won't be using worms. We'll be using squid."

At her horrified expression, he laughed. "If you're too chicken to bait your own hook, I'll do it for you, at least at first. Just say you'll come."

She studied him a moment, then nodded. "I'll go fishing with you. If you want."

If she only knew.

20

When Andi ran home in a panic, Clooney had been at the beach, practicing the fine art of retrieval as only he could. She had been so tense as she walked into the house, expecting a well-deserved lecture for running out on Carrie, that her knees went weak with relief when she found herself alone. She went to her room and fell back on her bed. As she stared at the ceiling, she took deep calming breaths. She was safe here. She was safe.

If she said it enough, she might believe it.

She'd thought she was doing so well—her heart no longer raced any time she saw a dark-haired man; it just sort of speed walked—but all it took this morning was one look and she'd panicked.

"What's wrong?" Clooney demanded when he came home and found her all pale and shaky.

"Nothing." Like there was a ghost of a chance he'd believe that.

He took her by the shoulders and forced her to face him. "Andi darlin', this is Uncle Clooney. You can't fool me. What's wrong?"

She thought for the briefest moment about stonewalling, but Clooney was not some idiot from The Pathway's compound who believed whatever he was told. In fact, except for herself, she'd never met a more skeptical, cynical person. She told him the truth, just not all of it.

"They were talking at the café about The Pathway. Jase was found dead this morning, and he belonged." She let her fear show.

"I heard about Jase on the news. I'm sorry. And you knew him from there, from The Pathway?"

She nodded. When she'd first seen him at Carrie's, she had been both glad and scared. Thanks to Jennie, he'd been one of the few normal people at the compound, so she was happy to see him, just surprised that he was alive.

"You're looking good," she had said the first time they were alone in the kitchen. "For a dead man."

"So it worked." He looked pleased with himself. "I couldn't very well hang around to see."

"It worked." She thought back to the shock of his "death." "They found the burned-up car and said the fire was so intense you were completely incinerated."

"Good. I was afraid the cops would say a body never completely burns, and they'd have doubts about my 'death.' I kept thinking I needed a body double."

"They gave you a very nice memorial service. Michael's comments were most inspiring."

"Oh, I just bet." Jase studied her. "You were so much smarter than me. You saw them for the phonies they are from day one. It took me a long time."

"It took Jennie." Even thinking about what happened made Andi feel sick. "I'm so sorry about what happened to her. I don't think I got a chance to tell you."

He was quiet for a moment, like the pain still sliced deep. He smiled sadly at her. "You must miss her too. She was your best friend."

"My only friend. She was the one who made life bearable for me." After a minute she added, "She loved you so much."

He took a deep breath and held up a hand. "Enough or I'll start to cry, not acceptable behavior at work. Distract me by telling me how you got from Arizona to New Jersey. I want to know how you escaped. If there was anyone they kept an eye on, it was you. You were at the top of their trouble-maker list."

"I hitched a ride with some motorcycle guys."

"What?"

"Not as dramatic as a torched car but not too shabby either, right?"

Jase laughed. "How did you ever meet motorcycle guys? You were con-fined to the compound."

Her jaw went rigid with fury as she thought about how constrained her life had been. "I looked for an escape for years without success. Then there it was, just like that, a few weeks before I turned sixteen. Some of the little kids got really sick, dehydrated and all. We thought they were going to die. They had to go to the hospital.

"I grabbed one of the little girls and climbed into the van. I made sure I had the seat in the far back corner. Everyone was so intent on saving the kids that no one thought about me being along. It was so confusing with parents and kids and crying and vomiting. I just walked out of the ER when everyone was distracted."

"But motorcycles?"

"Two bikers were in the ER because Stu had fallen and gotten brush burns and scrapes all up his side, and he thought he might have broken his wrist. When they left, I followed them out and asked for a ride. They took one look at me and my clothes and my desperation and told me to climb behind James. They were on their way to Yellowstone, and they took me along. We stopped at the Grand Canyon and Monument Valley and the Tetons and other neat places on the way. They were great, so normal, just regular guys looking for a fun vacation. They treated me like their little sister and bought me real clothes and fed me. After we visited Yellowstone, they even bankrolled my flight east. I'm living with my great-uncle."

"So you're vacationing around the country while I'm sneaking home by a roundabout route in case they didn't believe I was dead. I bet you had more fun than me."

Jase smiled, something she'd never have seen back at the compound. There he was so intense, so committed to doing Michael's will that he was like a robot. She'd always thought it a wonder his voice wasn't a tinny monotone.

Not that she'd ever said that aloud. Too many people were already too happy to report her failings to Michael, even stupid ones like saying someone had a robot voice.

In Carrie's kitchen that first day, Andi found herself smiling back at Jase in spite of the unwanted memories he represented. She noticed how sad his eyes were, and her heart ached. She understood the sadness.

Could she trust him? She'd love to have someone she could talk to and know that he understood. But she had to go slow and be sure. What if he had been sent to find her?

Improbable but not impossible.

But now Jase was dead.

And people were talking about The Pathway.

She shivered. She no longer felt safe in Seaside.

21

I ran upstairs to change, telling myself not to read more into Greg's invitation to go fishing than was there. He'd asked me because the day had turned unexpectedly warm. He wanted to fish, but he didn't want to go alone. His brothers and his friends were all at work—or in Mexico in the case of the missionary. I was available, and in a moment of desperation, he turned to me.

But I was grinning like an idiot, and my heart was hammering, and it wasn't from the exertion of climbing the steps.

"Well, don't you look like the cat who swallowed the canary," Linds said when she saw me.

"Can't stop to talk." I rushed past her to my room. I didn't want to share my happy buzz even with her.

I heard a disgruntled *huh* as I closed the door. I got rid of the khaki slacks I wore as part of the café uniform and pulled on jeans. My Carrie's Café shirt went in the hamper, and I yanked on a long-sleeved blue knit shirt that made my eyes seem bluer than they were. I grabbed the navy fleece jacket Greg had suggested I bring and was out of there.

"Where are you going?" Lindsay called after me.

"Fishing."

"Fishing? You don't know how to fish!"

I stopped at the door and grinned at her. "And your point is?"

Greg drove us to the creatively named Twelfth Street Marina at Twelfth and Bay. In all the years I'd lived in Seaside, I'd never been to a marina. I don't know what I expected, maybe yachts and superposh vessels, but most of the boats moored in the slips were practical bay boats like Greg's proved to be. I did see a couple of white, sleek yachts, and though I knew they were by no means the largest there were, I was still impressed. On one, an extremely handsome man with short dark hair sunned himself as he talked to a shorter, stockier man standing almost at attention. Who, I wondered as I followed Greg through the maze of floating docks, had decided yachts should be white?

Greg's boat was blue and white and obviously well enjoyed. It was neat and tidy in spite of its dings and scratches, and somehow the yachts now looked effete and phony. Here was a real boat owned by a real person, not a boy toy owned by some rich guy with a fake tan.

The real boat rocked when I stepped on. Why that surprised me, I don't know. I'd seen enough movies with rocking boats. I gave a little bleat and grabbed a seat back.

Greg swallowed a laugh, not disguising it very well as a cough. I fake glared as he handed me a couple of poles and some other equipment. When the boat rolled under him as he stepped on, I made sure I didn't even flinch.

"Sit here." He indicated the seat next to the driver's seat. I sat. He turned the key, the engine roared, and off we went.

"How big?" I yelled over the motor's noise.

"Eighteen foot I/O."

I nodded like I understood.

He grinned. "Inboard/outboard."

He stopped at a spot in the bay that looked just like every other spot to me. The sun beat down, and I thought my jacket superfluous. I squinted even with my sunglasses.

"Let's get you set." Greg handed me a pole that felt big in my hands.

Then he opened the small cooler he had brought and pulled out a chunk of flesh. I must have looked as *ick-ick* as I felt because he reached for my hook without a word.

I swallowed. "I'll do it. Just tell me how."

"You sure?"

His doubts about my heartiness straightened my somewhat spaghetti spine. "I can do it."

"Sure you can. It's just squid. People eat squid all the time."

"I don't." I took the strip of bait he handed me. "Calling it calamari doesn't fool me one bit." I looked at the wicked barbs on the hook and thought about impaled fingers.

"Fold the bait in half and push it on."

I did as I was told and felt a surge of satisfaction as the squid got pierced and my digits didn't.

"Just drop it over the side," he said. "When you feel something take it, wait a second, then give a tug to set the hook."

I stuck the end of the pole over the side and the line dropped into the water, dragged down by the weight of the bait and sinker. I tried to follow my squid visually, but it was swallowed by the opaque depths. I thought for a moment about all the water beneath me and all the strange and unknown creatures swimming in it, and gulped. Then I pushed that thought aside for a more appropriate time to think on it, like in a nightmare or something.

Greg fixed his own line and threw it in. He sat on the back of one of the seats and began whistling softly. If it was a specific tune, I'd never heard it.

I tried not to squirm, but being with him in this boat felt almost as claustrophobic as had the cab of his truck. I was nervous, excited, a breath away from hyperventilating. Alone with him twice in two days. Yikes!

"Are you allowed to talk while you fish?" I needed to know if I was going to break some unwritten fishing rule and make him mad when my nerves got the best of me and I gushed with all the discipline of a volcano spitting lava. "I mean, can they hear you and then they stay away?"

"You can talk quietly."

I took a deep breath because I was going to tell him something I hadn't even mentioned to Lindsay. "I think Andi has something to do with The Pathway."

He looked at me sharply. "Why do you say that?"

"When you were talking about Jase and The Pathway at the café, I was watching her. She turned pale."

"Maybe that was her reaction to learning a guy she knew was dead."

A reasonable possibility. "Somehow I don't see her as that sensitive to something that doesn't involve her, if you know what I mean."

"Sixteen-year-old self-involvement."

"Right. And then she went to that back booth and just stared into space."

"Again it could be a reaction to Jase's death."

I made a "maybe" face.

"How would she know about The Pathway in any personal way?" he asked.

"I don't know, but she appeared in Seaside out of nowhere, and she never mentions any family except Clooney."

He raised an eyebrow at me.

"Yeah, I know. Sounds like me at that age. I got creative and made up a mother in the military."

"You didn't."

"I did. At the time I thought I was quite clever."

"And Mary Prudence bought it?"

"I don't think so. But she never made an issue of it. I mean, there have to be lots of kids left when their mothers are deployed. It could have been true."

"Sure, but a left-behind kid isn't usually alone in a new town with a little sister in tow."

I watched a pair of sea gulls wheeling and diving, squabbling over something one of them had in its beak. The gull with the food opened his mouth to tell the marauder off, and whatever he was holding tumbled toward the water. A third gull that had been floating beside us took off, caught the falling food just before it hit the water, and flew away before the other two even realized what was happening. With outraged screams, they followed.

Greg stood suddenly, completely focused on his pole. Its tip was bending.

I jumped to my feet. "You've got something!"

He didn't respond, too intent on reeling in his catch. Up came a weird-looking fish, all horizontal instead of vertical like the pictures of fish I'd seen.

"What in the world?"

"Flounder."

"Really? They're sideways, sort of like a pancake." All I ever saw when Warren went fishing were the filets. I stared at the sideways flounder. "Amazing."

Greg pulled him in and measured him. With a look of disgust he said, "Too small. We've got to throw him back."

My rod moved in my hand. "I've got something!"

"Start reeling." Greg struggled to remove the hook from the flounder's jaw.

I reeled. Greg had just dropped his flounder back in the water when mine broke the surface. I pulled it into the boat.

"He's bigger than yours!" I couldn't stop grinning. My first fishing trip and I caught something. I was a natural at this. "He's bigger than yours!"

I knew bragging wasn't the best way to impress a guy, but I couldn't help it.

"He sure is. Congratulations!" Without even asking, he pulled the hook from my flounder's mouth with a pair of needle-nose pliers. He measured and weighed my catch and put it in a cooler of ice. "That'll make a nice supper."

I saw Warren laying his fillets on the sink for us to admire, which we did, following Mary P's example. Who'd have ever imagined I'd bring home a catch for others to admire?

Greg and I impaled fresh bait and dropped our lines back overboard. Almost at once he caught another flounder, a keeper. Then we sat for almost an hour before there was any more action. He told me funny stories about growing up in a house full of boys. I told him unfunny stories about life with Mom. I laughed at his stories and he sympathized with mine. I wasn't surprised when his stories turned to his kids.

"I used to love taking the kids fishing. Not that I had time to do much more than bait hooks and untangle line. But they loved being on the water almost as much as I do."

"Why do you love it so?"

He shrugged. "When I was a kid, it was just what we Barneses did. You fished and you loved it because everyone else did. As an adult it was wonderful because it was so far from the tension and chaos of being a cop. And now it's totally removed from how barren my life's become. It's like visiting the good parts of my life, the great memories."

He grinned. "Like the one time I was out here with just Greggie. He leaned over the side too far and in he went. He must have been about four. I watched him sink and waited. Sure enough, he popped to the surface right where he'd gone in. I grabbed his life jacket and pulled him out. We had to stay out long enough for him to dry or his mother would have had a heart attack."

I had an image of a little boy popping up and looking to his father for rescue. I could imagine them laughing as they waited for the boy to dry off, maybe draping his shirt over a seat back and his shorts over the windshield. I could see them conspiring against Ginny with great glee, not in a nasty way but a loving one. A father-son secret and a story they'd have undoubtedly told her when Greggie was older.

I smiled in spite of the hollow feeling in my middle. Just because I didn't have good memories shouldn't mean I couldn't enjoy those of others.

"Did it bother you that Ginny didn't fish?" I thought of Mary P and Warren, the only example of a strong marriage I'd seen up close and personal. They did everything together from running a business to holding hands in church—everything except fishing.

"No more than it bothered her that I didn't like stamping or scrapbooking. In many ways we were what Billy and Ruth Graham called 'happily incompatible.' Ginny was a stay-at-home mom who was very involved at church. I was a cop who met all kinds of unsavory characters every day. She was sunshine and laughter, and I was often withdrawn. She lived easily with disorder, and I liked everything in its place. Opposites."

I'd never heard the phrase *happily incompatible* before, and I found it fascinating. "Then why did it work?" Because it had, and very well, to hear him talk.

He thought for a minute, fiddling with his line as he did. "I think it was a combination of love and respect for each other on the one hand and commitment on the other. People are different, and those differences should be celebrated and encouraged. Of course you need to have common ground, which we had in our values and belief system as well as our kids and home, but you also need space to be who God made you. We were committed to the idea that the only thing that would rip us apart would be death, not differences."

We fell silent, and I wondered again at the fact that even death hadn't broken the bond between Ginny and him.

Oh, Lord, will it ever be my time?

A pull on my pole broke my melancholy. With a delighted shout, I started to reel in, and whatever was on my line was far heavier than the flounder. I reeled and reeled while my catch tried to swim away. My arms began to ache at the struggle. Then the fish broke the surface, and I found myself staring at the ugly, rounded snout of a sand shark.

Even though he was nowhere near the size of Bruce, the mechanical great white from *Jaws,* and didn't have that double row of razor teeth, a shark is a shark. I gave a squeak and backed up fast. I bumped into the seats on the far side and sat abruptly. I almost dropped my pole. The shark splashed back into the water and started to swim off.

"Come on, Carrie!" Greg called. "It's just a little guy. Bring it close to the boat."

I wasn't anxious to share my space with a shark no matter what size it was, but I reeled some more until the beast was swimming alongside. There wasn't much of an option since I couldn't very well let him swim off trailing Greg's pole.

22

Greg peered over the side at the fish and bit back a smile. "It's just a baby."

"Baby, my eye." Carrie looked appalled. "It's huge!"

"They get up to a hundred and fifty pounds. This guy can't be more than a couple of feet long, maybe thirty or forty pounds."

"It feels like a hundred and fifty." Carrie strained to hold it beside the boat. "Besides, babies are cute and this guy is ug-ly!"

He grabbed a pair of heavy scissors and bent over the side.

"What are you going to do?" She sounded concerned for him. He liked that.

"I'm going to cut it free."

"Be careful! He might bite!"

"These guys aren't man-eaters." He leaned as close as he dared, wary that it might decide to jump and bite out of fear, man-eater or not. He pulled the line taut, lifting the flat head out of the water. In one quick move, he clipped the heavy line as near the hook as he dared. The shark dropped with a soft splash and disappeared into the depths.

With all the weight suddenly gone, Carrie lost her balance and fell back onto a seat. She sat there, rod in hand, hookless line dangling. "My arms will never be the same."

He eased the rod from her hand and put it in one of the holders mounted in the back of the boat. He sat across from her. "You did great, tiger."

She grinned at him, her eyes bright. "I did, didn't I?"

He reached into another small cooler, grabbed a Coke, and passed it to her. She took a long drink.

"Why is it called a sand shark?" she asked. "Because it lives on the sandy bottom?"

"Maybe. Or maybe because of its skin. Brush it one way, and it's nice and sleek. Brush it the other way, and it's coarse like sandpaper."

She eyed him. "And you know this how?"

"With a family of boys, dares were a way of life."

"And they dared you to touch one? How old were you?"

"Ten or so. Gary was about fourteen and Logan about twelve. It was one of the first times we fished by ourselves."

"It could have taken off your hand."

"Nah. They gaffed his tail and held him sideways so I only touched him where it was safe."

She looked unconvinced and motioned in the direction her shark disappeared. "He's still got the hook in his jaw."

"He does. Did you want to take it out?"

"Are you kidding? I was just making an observation."

"Just another example of how life is messy sometimes. For people and for sharks. But he's alive and free, and the hook will work itself out in time."

A drop of rain struck him on the back of the neck. He looked up. A dark cloud had moved in while they were preoccupied with the shark. In seconds a soft but steady rain fell, and the temperature dropped significantly.

Carrie yanked on her fleece pullover, and he slipped into a nylon windbreaker. The chill rain slid down his neck as he turned on the motor and hurried toward the marina. He squinted as the rain slapped him in the face. They were soaked through by the time they tied up in his slip.

As they ran toward his truck, poles and ice chests clutched in cold hands, the rain stopped and the sun blazed a lovely pink and purple as it sank into the horizon.

Carrie laughed. "Wouldn't you know!"

That laugh charmed him. Much as he loved Ginny, she'd have fretted over being wet, having her hair messed up, being cold.

They tossed their things in the bed and fell into the truck. Greg turned on the heater as soon as the motor caught. In no time, the windshield was fogged over. He hit the defrost, and gradually the window cleared.

When he could see, he drove toward Carrie's. "Why don't you run in and change into something dry, and then we'll go to my place and eat our catch?"

He'd caught her in the middle of pulling her jacket off over her head. She let it settle back on her shoulders, half on, half off, and studied him with those amazing blue eyes. Her slow smile made his breath catch in his chest.

"I'd like that." Her head disappeared into her pullover.

When it reappeared, she looked thoughtful. "Do you think Andi should get a restraining order against Bill?"

He blinked. Where had that come from? "Don't you think that's a bit extreme?"

"I don't know. That's the whole problem. I don't know. It could be I'm speaking out of my own background again."

"You had to get a restraining order?" But she'd been just sixteen. Or younger!

"I didn't know about them or I could have, I guess."

His blood chilled. "Against who? Not your mother. Your father? A boyfriend?"

She shrugged. "Not Mom. She was weak and so flawed. I think in her own way she loved us, but she left us vulnerable. And I never knew my dad.

Neither did Lindsay. Know hers, I mean. But there was any number of guys we had to protect ourselves from. My mother's bad taste in men knew no end."

He wanted to take her in his arms and hold her, offer her his strength and protection even though it was many years too late. Instead he drove to her place. She ran inside, returning a few minutes later in dry jeans and a white knit shirt under a red fleece big shirt. She had a grocery bag in her arms.

"What's that?"

"Salad makings. My contribution."

"You've already contributed a flounder."

She grinned. "I'm trying not to be too proud about that. 'Pride goes before destruction, a haughty spirit before a fall.'"

He grinned. He loved the way she could laugh at herself.

They drove to his place, a three-bedroom rancher he'd bought two years ago after he sold the old Victorian he'd shared with Ginny and the kids. At the time he'd felt he had to get away from the painful memories and make new ones. Now as he unlocked the front door and ushered Carrie inside, he realized that this place had no memories. None. It was as if he hadn't had a life since he moved here.

"You're the first person besides my parents who's been here since I bought this place," he said, appalled at the realization of how desolate he'd let his life get. Two years and he'd not even had his brothers here or a buddy, let alone a woman.

Carrie looked around with interest. "Well, you're very tidy for a guy living alone."

And that was the best that could be said for the place. Talk about sterile. He'd never tried to add any of the homey touches Ginny always had. No plants, no pictures, no decorator stuff. In fact he'd never bothered to unpack most of the boxes.

It was past time to get a life.

In the kitchen he left Carrie looking for whatever she needed to make her salad while he got into dry clothes. Then he cleaned and prepared the fish. As he did so, he went back to their earlier discussion about Carrie's past.

"Did any of your mother's boyfriends molest you?" He held his breath as he waited for the answer.

She gave a tight smile. "Fortunately when I was young, none of Mom's men were interested in little girls. By the time I caught the eye of one man, I was smart enough to protect myself."

He hated asking, but he had to know. "How did you do that?"

"I went to the old man across the hall, a drunk who was very nice on the rare occasions he was sober, and got him to put a strong lock on my bedroom door. I bought it with money I stole from one of Mom's guys when he was passed out on our sofa. I figured I deserved it."

He thought of his home growing up, the love, the laughter, the rough-housing with brothers, the encouragement of his parents. He'd learned how blessed he was when he was a cop and saw the terrible things parents some-times did to their kids. It always hurt him, but because this was Carrie talk-ing, the barb of horror pierced deeper.

"At night I pushed the bureau in front of the locked door." She said it as if every kid fought off molesters and perverts by moving furniture in the dark. "And I had a nasty-looking knife I'd stolen from the grocery store. I hid it under a floorboard during the day and slept with it under my pillow. I only had to threaten with it and the guy would back off—if he managed to get into the room."

"Geez, Carrie!" How had she turned out so together, so kind, so *whole*?

She shrugged. "It could have been a lot worse."

Yeah, it could have been. He'd seen worse far too many times. But this was Carrie, his Carrie, and it broke his heart that she'd been forced to live through such trauma. "Didn't you tell anyone at school?"

She shook her head as she set the brimming salad bowl on the table. "They would have put us in foster care, and I was terrified of being separated from Lindsay. Protecting her and staying together became my reasons for living."

"I am in awe of you and your strength," he said, meaning every word.

She waved his comment away. "I used to ask God, if He was up there, to help us. I wanted Him to make Mom wake up one morning all better. Then she'd find a nice guy who would be a loving daddy." She gave a sad little laugh. "That didn't happen, but He sent us to Mary P and Warren." She smiled. "That's about as good as it gets."

He thought of how strong she'd been in dealing with the blows life had rained on her and how wimpy he'd been about his own pain. He resolved to stand tall and be worthy of her. *Lord, by Your grace and in Your strength!*

"Anyway," she continued, "I think where I come from is why I worry so about Andi. I don't want her to have to live in fear."

"Has she told you she's afraid of Bill?"

Carrie shook her head. "But you've seen the bruise on her wrist. You saw him give it to her."

He reached out and caught her wrist. "I could bruise you without even meaning to if I held you tightly enough."

She nodded. "He's just such a jerk."

"You'll get no argument from me." He dropped her hand and turned his attention to lifting the flounder from the pan and draining it on paper towels. He laid the fish on a plate and carried it to the table, where they sat across from each other. He said grace for them.

"This is delicious!" she said around a mouthful. "Better even than Warren's."

"That's because you caught it yourself."

"And you filleted it and cooked it." She closed her eyes as she took another mouthful, savoring it. "I could get used to this."

So could he, he thought as he stuck his fork into the salad. So could he.

23

K nowing that Mr. and Mrs. Peoples had to leave the house sometime, Harl Evans sat in his car down the street and waited, his fingers beating the steering wheel in time with the rap he was enjoying without Mike present to sneer at his choice.

After Harl's backside was asleep from waiting so long and his head ached from the slant of the blinding sun, they left, a defeated pair with stooped shoulders and sad faces. Maybe they were going to the undertakers' to make arrangements. Or maybe they were going to the grocery store to get milk. Who cared? They were gone.

As soon as their car turned the corner, Harl moved. He wore a uniform with *Joe* sewn on the pocket in case someone saw him, but it was a cul-de-sac where hedges divided the small, well-maintained properties and no one appeared to be home in any of the houses he passed. He was inside Jason's in minutes.

The house was a split level with three bedrooms and two baths, one off the master bedroom. If he were a regular thief, he wouldn't find anything of value in this place except the fifty-four-inch television in the lower level. Trouble was, you couldn't carry something that size off under your arm.

Jason's room was obvious with its few clothes and a neatness he'd learned at the compound. Harl went through it from floor to ceiling, looking in every drawer, on every shelf, yanking clothes off every hanger, checking pockets and linings. He pulled the bed apart, sliding the mattress off the box springs to be certain nothing was hidden between the two or in the mattress cover. He looked under the rug for loose floorboards.

He found some stray cash and Jason's laptop stashed on the top shelf of his closet under a sweater. The fact that it was hidden, however poorly, piqued Harl's curiosity. He hadn't found what he was looking for, but maybe the laptop would be just as good.

Then he tackled the rest of the house, going through it as thoroughly as he'd searched Jason's room, but he found nothing more of interest. He clutched the laptop as he left. At least it would be something to show Mike.

"What do you mean, you couldn't find it?" Michael hissed when Harl stood before him, heels together, shoulders back, head high. Harl had a rule that he never let Michael see his fear. His submission, yes; his fear, no.

Harl sometimes resented Mike almost as much as he used to resent his father, though he was careful to never let it show. It was Mike's I-know-it-all-and-you're-too-stupid-for-words attitude that the man didn't bother to hide unless he was in front of his flock or on camera. It was quite evident now, like it was Harl's fault the object of his search wasn't in the house.

"I looked in every drawer, under every mattress. I tore the place apart! And I found this hidden in Jason's closet." Harl held out the laptop.

Mike eyed it, then him. "Have you opened it?"

Harl shook his head, unfazed by the lie. When it came to ethics, what was a lie after all the other questionable or outright illegal things the two of them had done and probably would continue to do? "I knew you'd want to be the one to look at it first."

Mike nodded, flipped up the lid, and pushed the On button. The screen came to life. Mike's eyes flicked in surprise. He turned the laptop. "Look!"

Harl made his eyes widen. "That's home."

He made the spartan furnace of the southern Arizona wasteland sound like it was the best place in the world. Sometimes he wondered why he stayed and chose to be uncomfortable when all he wanted was a Big Mac, a soft breeze, and a softer mattress. And trees instead of cacti. Sometimes he yearned for green with a physical ache. He thought it was from all those evergreens in his youth.

But he stayed, and for good reasons. Power. Control. Sex. Freedom from legal restraint. As Mike's second in command in their little world, he had it all. And he had all the warm temperatures he could long for.

Mike studied the icons on Jason's screen as all around them Harl heard little motors kick on, putt, purr, then zoom off.

You want the file called TP, Harl wanted to tell Mike. *For The Pathway. It's an exposé, and it contains enough dynamite to blow you out of the water. Me too. It's a good thing the man is dead is all I can say.*

He forced himself to wait quietly for Mike to provide the next clue to how he should act or react. While he waited, he pondered a question that bothered him mightily. Had Jason posted any of this material on the Internet? The answer seemed obvious. He couldn't have, or the feds and cops would have been all over the compound.

But if he hadn't, why not?

Maybe he was saving everything for one big splash, like a book deal with appearances on *Today* and *Good Morning America* and all the other talk shows. He doubtless envisioned cozy chats with Bill O'Reilly and Anderson Cooper, maybe Charlie Rose. Too bad he'd miss Oprah.

The book would be a bestseller, no question. Even if Jason's writing was lousy, several publishers would pay megabig bucks for a book that exposed Mike and hire someone to make it read right.

Jason Peoples on *The New York Times* bestseller list. Harl laughed to himself. Even the thought of that would give Mike a coronary! If the cost wouldn't be equally as high for Harl himself, he'd enjoy seeing his leader swinging in the wind.

Harl returned to the present with a thud when Mike swore, surprised not only by the volume but the choice of words. Mike'd worked hard to rid himself of any vestige of his street days. He was now a spiritual man of impeccable behavior and unimpeachable standards—don't make me laugh. Coarse language was forbidden to all at the compound.

"He's writing an insider's look at The Pathway." Mike was outraged.

Well, what did Mike expect? "What? That's awful!" Harl knew it was worse than awful. He'd read what was there, and just thinking about it made him break out in a cold sweat.

For the briefest moment Mike looked uncertain. "What made him turn on me, Harl? On us? I don't understand it. After all I did for him!"

Harl shrugged, careful to keep his face neutral while he marveled at Mike's stupidity, at least about Jason's motives. Any fool could see that Jennie was Jason's backbreaking straw, and reading the chapter about her confirmed that. If Mike hadn't refused Jason's request to marry her, the guy'd still be alive, a happy camper, and that incendiary missing item wouldn't be missing.

Harl waited while Mike scrolled through chapter headings.

"Jennie?" Mike looked at Harl, then opened the file and began to read.

It wasn't pretty, Harl knew. In it Jason accused Mike of the rape of a young follower. He accused him of being responsible for Jennie's death, even going so far as to call it murder.

"I did not murder her!" Mike's face turned red with fury. "She fell. She had an attack of some kind."

Harl nodded, but he remembered the situation more as Jason did. After all, Harl had seen everything from his position in the video room where he controlled the three cameras that recorded the initiation ceremonies of all The Pathway brides-to-be. The two of them often joked that Harl had almost as much fun as Mike on these prewedding nights.

Sometimes he saw the night Jennie died in his dreams, heard Jennie's pleas, her screams, her sobs. He heard Mike order her to shut up and submit. He heard Jennie's defiance and her fear.

"Please, please don't make me marry the man you selected! Let me marry the man I love. Please!"

He saw the slaps and then the fist to the jaw. He saw her fall, saw Mike fall on her, saw her violation, saw Mike's hand over her mouth and nose to stifle her screams, saw Jennie's deathly stillness.

When Mike rose and Jennie didn't, Mike had panicked. He yelled for Harl, knowing he'd seen what happened.

Harl raced to Mike's bedroom where the two of them stared down at the dead girl. When their shock receded, they came up with the story of Jennie's seizure and fall. Who knew epilepsy could just appear like that? They cleaned her up and dressed her, arranged her on the floor in the sitting area of the bedroom as if she'd fallen there. The bed was made as immaculately as if Marty, wife number one and a saint if ever there was one, had done it.

In their haste to cover up the crime, manslaughter at the very least, though Harl thought a good case could be made for murder, they both forgot the camera that kept recording everything on a DVD. When Harl went to retrieve the DVD several hours later, it was gone.

For two days they waited for the sky to fall, but nothing happened. Harl found himself wanting to believe the missing disc was a case of cosmic intervention to preserve Mike and The Pathway. And him.

Then came Jennie's funeral followed a day later by Jason's disappearance. Oh, Jason tried to cover his flight with the phony accident that fooled no one. The police contacted The Pathway about the burned car because the license plate led them to the organization. The sign-out sheet indicating who was using one of The Pathway's cars then led them to Jason.

Once Harl's heart started to beat regularly after the fear-based rush of adrenaline at the cops' appearance, he got a kick out of Jason's daring attempt at vanishing.

"There was no one in the car when it burned," the cops said. "Nothing burns completely. There would be some indication if someone had been trapped."

Jason, Jennie, a stolen DVD—it didn't take a genius to figure it out.

Mike told the followers that Jason was killed in the fiery crash. They even had a memorial service for him at which Mike eulogized Jason in a voice that shook with emotion. Harl smirked in the back row. Anger could make the voice quiver much like sorrow.

"He must be found," Mike raged to Harl in the privacy of his office. "He's too dangerous to be allowed to live. Find him! Get that DVD at all costs."

Harl began his quest locally, showing Jason's picture at airports, train stations, and bus depots. Nothing. He broadened his search to used car dealers and car rental agencies. He checked newspapers for individuals who were selling cars privately.

The whole time he searched, he kept coming back to the issue of money. How could Jason buy a car or a ticket without money? Any time he was sent to town for supplies, he used The Pathway's credit card. Careful checking of records showed he hadn't been foolish enough to use the card for his escape.

So where had he gotten the necessary money?

On a whim Harl hired a private investigator in New Jersey to check out Jason's parents. He couldn't believe Jason would be foolish enough to go someplace so obvious, but he might have talked them into wiring him funds.

Bingo! Three weeks after he disappeared, Jason was spotted in Seaside. Harl found it strange that Jason seemed to be leading a normal life, going to college and working at some restaurant. What was he waiting for? What did he hope to gain by keeping the DVD secret? Blackmail? The thought chilled Harl's blood.

"We're going to Seaside," Mike had announced as they sat once again in his luxurious office, relaxed in the wake of the private investigator's report. Mike was leaning back in his leather executive chair, feet resting on his desk, while Harl sat on the plush sofa along the wall. Harl often wondered what would happen if the women living in those sterile dorms across the compound could see how well Mike lived.

"You want to go to Seaside?" Was he nuts? "Come on, Mike. You can't go flying off to New Jersey. You can't be anywhere near Jason. We'll stay here and use the same PI to find the DVD."

Mike stood and walked across the room, his footsteps muffled by the deep pile of the rug. He poured himself two fingers of scotch. He rolled it on his tongue, then swallowed. "No one but the two of us must ever know about that DVD, Harl. No one. *We* have to find it."

Harl hated it when Mike's arguments made sense. What if the private investigator looked at the thing? Disaster.

Mike poured himself another glass. "We need to make several videos that can be posted to YouTube while we're gone so everyone thinks we're here. And for the followers here, we'll make a big deal of going to the retreat house to commune with God."

Mike smiled that arrogant, smug smile Harl hated. "We'll find the DVD and go fishing. Maybe do some other business while we're at it. Check for good deals." And he walked out.

If he wouldn't be brought as low as Mike, Harl would wish the DVD went viral on YouTube. It was exactly what Mike deserved.

24

I set my coffee cup down on Greg's table. I still found it hard to believe that I had actually caught some of our golden brown, crunchy, and delicious dinner. I decided I liked fishing. Talk about a good ROI—return on investment.

Conversation during the meal had been general—what television shows we liked and why, what channel had the best newscasts, who were our favorite actors. I allowed him a slight crush on Gwyneth Paltrow and he ignored my swoon over Ewan McGregor.

Earlier I had been much more open than usual about my growing-up years, but I'd wanted Greg to realize the worst about me. If who I was and where I came from were too much for him, we both needed to know that before we became any more involved.

Of course my emotions were seriously engaged already. I thought of the old saying about it being as easy to fall in love with a rich man as a poor man, and I disagreed. Falling in love seemed to be something beyond a person's control, at least this person's.

One individual called out to you on some elemental level, and something in you responded. Why a melancholy ex-cop/widower who disliked his current career appealed to me I didn't know. He came with so much emotional baggage, baggage I wasn't certain he'd ever jettison. That scared me, but it didn't stop the pull he exerted on me. He was the magnet, and I was the iron filings; he was the moon, and I was the tide. Clichés, and corny ones at that, but true nonetheless.

Greg placed his knife and fork across his plate and leaned back in his chair. "I've got a question for you, Carrie. It's highly personal, but I hope you'll answer because it's part of my crusade to learn all about you."

I could feel his intensity rolling across the table, and I shivered. My stomach lurched. Maybe the fried fish wasn't that great after all.

"Go ahead," I said, wary. My hands gripped each other in my lap.

"How's your mom doing today?"

I sighed. "I was afraid you were going to ask me something about her."

"Hurtful topic."

"You have no idea."

It would have been nice if he'd said something about seeing that his question upset me so he was changing the subject, but he didn't. He sat watching me, face grave, waiting.

I hunched my shoulders, knowing I might well be killing any good thoughts he had about me. "I have no idea how she is."

I also had no idea where she was or whether she still lived at the last address we'd shared. Given her record for nonpayment of rent, she'd probably skipped in the middle of the night for a new place to lease and not pay on.

Greg stood and took his dish to the sink. He was frowning as he scraped the crumbs into the garbage disposal. He turned to me. "When was the last time you saw her?"

I couldn't look at him, and I had to force the words out. "Seventeen years ago."

It was clear my answers to his questions about Mom troubled him. They troubled my counselor and my pastor too, and I found myself getting defensive with Greg just as I had with them. After all, what did he with his loving family know about mothers like mine? Nothing!

"That's a long time," he said, voice mild. "Do you even know if she's alive?"

I watched him return to his seat. "No, I don't." And I don't care!

I knew he didn't understand, maybe even thought I was terrible, but he didn't know what it had been like. Protecting myself and Lindsay from Mom's men was only part of the story. There were constantly things, like the time I'd saved money from my job sweeping the floors and straightening the shelves for the mom-and-pop grocery down the street. I was saving to buy the cleated shoes, leg guards, and a hockey stick I needed so I could be on the junior high field-hockey team when school started in the fall. The day I got the final amount needed, I hurried home, excited to be able to buy something I needed and wanted. I opened my bureau drawer to get the envelope I hid the money in, but I found only the envelope, empty and torn.

"Oh, I borrowed it," Mom said when I questioned her. She and her guy du jour were pulling bottles of Grey Goose and Absolut from paper bags. "I needed it because we're going to have a tasting contest to see which of these is best at getting you drunk fast." She held up the vodka bottles. "Have some, and you can vote too."

I was thirteen.

There was the time in third grade I got up the nerve to invite home a friend from school and we found Mom and her boyfriend on the living room floor, half dressed and wholly toasted. My friend was never allowed at my house again.

Or the time she swore a blue streak at my teacher when the concerned woman called to talk about my belligerent attitude.

Or the time she came to school so drunk she swayed as she talked to the principal.

Or the time she offered to find me a guy to introduce me to the mysteries of sex.

So I didn't care where she was or even *if* she was, but I was aware how my attitude made me look to others. Most of the time I ignored the fact that the few who knew how I felt about Mom thought me cold and unfeeling, but Greg was different. I wanted his good opinion, and I wanted it badly. But I also wanted him to give it in spite of who I was. I would be honest with him and hope he could accept me as I was and forgive my intransigence.

"Shouldn't you try to make some effort to rebuild bridges here?" he asked. "Isn't that what everyone says is the emotionally healthy thing to do?"

I nodded. "Everyone tells me I have to go see her. My counselor, Pastor Paul, Mary P. The only one who doesn't is Lindsay." I pushed back my chair and got to my feet. I carried my dishes to the sink, where, dishes still in hand, I stood staring out the window at the black night. The color of my soul where Mom was concerned? "But I can't!"

"Why not?"

Was there anything worse than a reasonable man when you're feeling anguished and threatened? "Because!"

"Because why?"

"Because I'm afraid." I slapped a hand over my mouth and looked at him with appalled eyes. I'd voiced something I rarely acknowledged to myself.

He stood, took my plate from me, and placed it in the sink. He reached for my now-empty hand and brought it to his chest where he held it over his heart.

"But from what you've told me about her, Carrie, she's not going to hurt you, at least not physically. And you're an adult now. You don't have to be afraid. Even if she's got some guy with her, you'll be okay."

I blinked back tears at his gentle manner. I deserved for him to lecture me about how a good Christian should honor her mother, care about her and for her, not reject her. Forgive her.

"I'm not afraid physically." Could I make him understand something I had difficulty understanding myself? "I'm afraid emotionally."

He thought for a moment and nodded.

I swallowed the tears burning the back of my throat. "As long as I'm away from her, I can handle what happened. I can say I've forgiven her for exposing us to all the garbage we faced, and I can even mean it. Distance is what makes forgiveness possible."

"But is that forgiveness?"

It was a fair question. "Probably not. But it's as good as it gets for me."

He ran a hand over my hair. "She did a number on you, didn't she?"

I gave a sad little smile. "Understatement." And I'd thought he had a lot of unresolved baggage.

"What do you think would happen if you saw her? To you and to her?"

"To her, nothing. She barely noticed we existed when we were there, so I doubt she's ever missed us. As for me, I'm afraid all the resentment and anger I can control from a distance is going to overwhelm me."

"But if you've forgiven her—"

"I know, I know. If I've forgiven her, it should be all finished. Forgiveness is supposed to be once for all, like Christ's forgiveness of us." I sighed. I hated this part of myself, this fist that held tight to my right to be angry and bitter. "But it's not that simple. There are the memories of all those nights of fear, the days of want and hunger, the humiliation of everyone knowing what she was like and looking at Lindsay and me like we were bound to be as bad. And then there's the knowledge that I stole because of her and the guilt over that behavior."

His thumb made sweet circles on the back of my hand. "What if I went to Atlanta with you?" he asked as if he were asking about going down the block to the convenience store on the corner for a quart of milk.

My heart jumped and I stared, flabbergasted. "You'd do that for me?"

"I think I'd do most anything for you."

He said it so simply my insides melted. "Oh, Greg, I'm such a bad risk. Ginny was so wonderful. I'm such a mess."

"Not in my book. I think you're brave and amazing. You're even strong enough to tell the truth."

I started to cry. He wrapped his arms around me and held me while I wept all over his shirt. When I started to calm down, he kissed me on the temple. I turned my face up, and our lips met.

25

As night closed in, Harl Evans sat back and watched Mike as he continued to read from Jason's laptop. The set of the man's jaw and the narrowing of his eyes told Harl that if Jason wasn't already dead, he would be soon. He'd seen Mike angry before, but never like this.

"How *dare* he!" Mike looked up and glared at Harl. "You won't believe what he's written. About me!"

Harl fought to keep his expression neutral, swallowing his incredulity at Mike's naiveté. Of course Jason hated him. Who wouldn't after what Mike had done? The man had begun to believe his own press releases, statements he'd made up himself:

"Michael the Archangel, the messenger God has sent to give you abundant life!"

"Listen to the anointed words of Michael, God's archangel, and find life!"

"Let Michael the Archangel pray for you, and God will rain blessings beyond belief."

Harl had always liked that one with all the *b* words at the end. So did Mike. "Blessings beyond belief" had become one of his favorite lines, as in, "Send your gifts, and I will give you blessings beyond belief!"

Not God; Mike.

For a charlatan as sharp as Mike at shearing the sheep, it was amazing how he craved the approval and adoration of the shivering and newly poor lambs. Why one lamb might turn into a snarling wolf was a mystery to him.

"All I ever showed him was kindness."

Harl's stomach turned. His noble leader sounded like a thwarted, whiny child.

"And this is how he planned to repay me?"

Looked like one too with his lip pushed out in an angry pout.

Mike went back to reading. There were lots of disastrous things about The Pathway and about Mike's misuse of the organization's finances, but Jennie's chapter was the *pièce de résistance*. With great emotion Jason told how he loved Jennie and wanted to marry her. He wrote of her sweet spirit and gentle heart. According to Jason, her desire to marry him was as strong as his to marry her—if you could believe him, and Harl did. He'd seen both Jason and Jennie plead with Mike. And anyone who read the book would believe too.

Mike saw Jason's request to marry Jennie as a challenge to his authority, especially when the kid asked that Mike do away with the premarriage night. Mike refused the request, choosing one of the older men for her as a mark of his position of unquestioned and unquestionable leader. And the premarriage night was to go on as always.

"Allow one couple the right of selection," he complained to Harl, "and before you know it, others will demand the same privilege. The beginning of the end."

When three of Mike's lieutenants went for Jennie the night before her marriage, Jason followed them to Mike's quarters in spite of Mike's direct order that Jason be confined to his room. Jason forced his way into Mike's garish bedroom with the huge bed draped in red gauzy material and topped with the velvet quilt that Marty had made, all red and beige and white.

Harl couldn't understand that quilt. Polygamy, okay. Great, in fact. But making the covering for the bed where your husband took one young woman after another? Marty was sicker than Mike, who was only doing what came naturally as the ultimate male authority figure.

Harl watched from the video room as Jason pleaded and Jennie begged and Mike became ever more furious with them both. Harl watched the lieutenants drag Jason off by force. Then he'd watched Mike take the hysterical Jennie against her will.

She was buried in the compound cemetery.

Now, miles and weeks away in Seaside, Harl looked up as rain began to beat on the windows, pulling him from memories of that unbelievable night.

"What if Jason wasn't the one who took your missing disc, Mike?" As Harl had gone over that night just now, he realized Jason couldn't have gotten to the video room. He'd been dragged away and locked up. All three of the men who dragged him off said he was never out of their sight the rest of that night.

Mike looked startled. "If it wasn't him, who?"

"What if it was Andrea?" After all, she went missing too. And she was a thorn in everyone's side, a rebel through and through.

Mike scowled. "Don't be ridiculous. She's a kid, and a girl at that."

"She escaped when no one escapes. And she's managed to stay hidden for several weeks. Of course, she didn't have a family to rush home to like Peoples. And we didn't try to find her. We were all better off without her. Even her father agreed."

"Say it was Andrea, which I can't believe. How would she even know about the disc?"

"I don't know," Harl admitted. "But Jason was never alone all that night."

Mike rubbed his forehead, his anger gone. For the first time, Harl saw doubt in him. "Are we running out of time, Harl? Is it time to cut and run?"

Yes! "Let me finish what I have to do, and then we can fade away. Just a couple of days more."

"It's going smoothly?"

"Very. It'll provide a nice tidy income." To join the income from all the other deals he'd worked with The Pathway's funds, all funneled neatly through untraceable offshore accounts.

Mike nodded. "Good. Now if we only knew where to find Andrea, we could tie up that loose end."

Harl smiled. Much as he couldn't believe it, he had found that particular needle in the haystack. The odds had to be a million to one against, like walking down the street in New York City and bumping into your first grade teacher from San Francisco or like winning the one hundred million dollar lottery.

But she was here, and he'd found her.

26

Andi's head felt too heavy for her shoulders, the result of a restless night filled with dreams of Michael, barbed wire, and snakes writhing at her feet, rattles shaking, her terrified cries for help eerily silent.

A shower helped clear the Wednesday morning fuzziness, but she still felt fragile, like an expensive vase, the kind pronounced with a short *a*, one that might shatter with any pressure. She put on a rose-colored Carrie's Café shirt, thinking its soft reflection on her face might disguise her pallor and the cheery color might make her feel better.

"I'm coming to the café with you," Clooney said as she came into the kitchen.

"You don't have to." He'd already done so much, risked so much for her. He could have gotten in lots of trouble with the law for harboring her—if someone had cared enough to find her and make an issue of things. He even homeschooled her so she wouldn't have to face questions at the local school about who she was and where she came from. Oh, and so she could catch up on her education. The Pathway wasn't big on teaching much besides Michael's warped thinking.

Clooney held up a hand. "I'm coming. Not open to discussion."

She knew she could manage without him—she'd managed without him before—but it would feel good to have him beside her. Nobody had cared for so long. Not that she had any hope of dissuading him. He was like some giant guard dog, a German shepherd maybe or a Doberman, ready to protect his "person" from all things unpleasant or dangerous.

He studied her drawn face. "What do you plan to tell Carrie?"

"That I got sick?" She couldn't say she got scared and ran. Too humiliating. Too revealing.

"I suggest you just say you're sorry and assure her it won't happen again."

If he doesn't show up again. *Oh, God, please don't let him show up again.*

She frowned. She was talking to God too much. It's what came of listening to Carrie and Lindsay talk about Him as if He helped run the café. But someone had to help her, someone bigger than herself, bigger even than Clooney, and He seemed the sole possibility.

Clooney took her hand and squeezed. "I'll hang around this morning just to be sure you're okay."

Andi felt tears and blinked against them as she gave him a quick hug. Clooney was her example of "love one another," not Michael. Clooney let her see that he cared. He worried about her. Maybe he even loved her. He and she were their own little family, maybe a weird one, but one nonetheless.

Andi's hands were shaking when she arrived at the café with Clooney in tow. Would Carrie and the others accept her apology without pushing too hard to learn the reason she took off? She didn't want anyone to know she'd known Jase before she came to live here. She didn't want anyone but Clooney to know about her connection to The Pathway. And she didn't want them to know she feared *him*.

Her voice caught as she hesitated outside the back door. "Do you think Jase told Michael or someone that he saw me? Will they come after me?"

"Ah, Andi." He pulled her into a comforting hug. "I won't let them hurt you."

She wasn't sure she believed him, but his hug and his words were so soothing. She held on for a few minutes and felt temporarily safe.

Funny how he was the one people always considered a deadbeat because he refused to get a nine-to-five job, and here he was, rock solid at her side.

"He digs in the sand!" the aunts and uncles always said in scandalized voices at family gatherings—which he never attended.

"It was the war," others said in quiet tones of pseudounderstanding. "Posttraumatic stress, you know."

When she needed a place to stay, she figured he was enough counter-culture, enough antiestablishment, that he wouldn't feel compelled to either send her back or turn her over to the authorities. She'd figured right, and she loved him for his open arms.

She drew back from his embrace and made herself stand alone. After all, she'd been on her own for more than three years. The minute she, Becca, Mom, and Dad drove through the gate of The Pathway's compound, her family ceased to exist. She and Becca were given bunks in a large dorm for the unmarried teenage girls, a mirror of the large dorm across the compound where the unmarried boys lived. Mom was sent to the large building that housed the women and preteen children. Dad was given his own room in the beautiful lodge where the married men lived.

It didn't take Andi long to realize that Becca was the oldest in their dorm. And it didn't take Michael long to arrange for her marriage.

"He's trying to control you," Andi told Becca when the news of the impending nuptials was announced. "Tie you to this place."

"No, no, Andi. He's thinking only of my happiness."

"But you don't even know the man he's picked! You don't love him. You can't."

"Michael has selected him for me." Becca smiled sweetly. "I have no doubt I will be very happy."

"But he already has a wife."

"He has three," said Jennie, the girl with the bunk next to Andi. "He's been married to Abby for ten years, to Patricia for six, and to Irene for five."

Andi grabbed her sister's hand. "We'll run away. You don't have to do this."

"But I want to," Becca said. "Michael has said it, and it shall be so."

Despair threatened to drown Andi. "I'll never see you. You'll be put in the house of the married women. I won't have anyone."

"Oh, Andi." Becca frowned, but it was a gentle frown, a "poor you" frown. "Can't you see that your attitude is selfish? We are a community. We have to trust our leader."

But Andi did not, could not, would not trust Michael, especially when she realized that every bride spent the night before her marriage in Michael's bed. The thought that she might someday be required to go to him brought bile up her throat in a rush. She'd rather die.

Andi soon realized every girl was married the Saturday after her sixteenth birthday. Becca had been an older bride because she arrived at the compound two months short of nineteen. Andi, on the other hand, would be expected to marry at the appropriate time and to gladly accept the man chosen for her.

Those who were raised here seemed to think such a situation was normal, except for Jennie, who had a secret boyfriend and wanted to marry him when it was time. She was as upset over Michael's initiation process as Andi.

"But we should be able to marry who we want, when we want," Andi said out loud before she learned the folly of being outspoken. "I want to live a bit before I marry. I want to go to college, have a job, make some money, be independent."

Everyone frowned at her heresy. Even Jennie thought all those plans were ungodly because they were what Michael spoke against.

"For the sake of the community we need to marry and have children," Jennie told her. "The Bible says to be fruitful and replenish the earth."

"But at sixteen?"

She was called before Michael for her sacrilegious ideas and assigned to Marty, his chief wife, for training in "correct thinking." The one thing she learned was to keep her mouth closed.

For almost three years she endured, hating every moment, planning, plotting, knowing she must escape before she became a zombie too. During that time her father took three brides, one each year, girls his daughters' ages. The thought made her ill. How did her mother stand it? Yet every time she saw Mom, she looked peaceful. Paler, thinner, but peaceful. Or was the right word *lobotomized*?

The year she was fifteen, Andi looked with desperation and despair for any possible means to get away. The compound was twenty miles from the nearest town, out in a dry barren area where nothing but cacti, lizards, scorpions, and snakes lived. Chain-link fencing with barbed wire curling evilly at its top ringed the compound. Andi knew that no matter what Michael said, it wasn't to keep thieves out; it was to keep people in.

When Stu and James appeared at the emergency room like a pair of scruffy angels the night of the rush to save the little kids, she bolted, knowing she'd never have a better opportunity. She'd been hiding with Clooney, convinced she was safe and secure here in Seaside. She'd even begun to relax and enjoy life. Until—

Taking a deep breath and squaring her shoulders, she walked into the café. Carrie looked up from readying the cash register.

"Are you all right?" She walked right up to Andi and gave her a hug.

Andi had been steeling herself for anger or a lecture, and she had to blink back tears at Carrie's warmth. "I'm sorry, Carrie. It won't happen again. I promise."

Carrie looked at her, then at Clooney standing behind her. "I hope not, sweetie. I need to know I can depend on you." She gave a little smile.

Even this lecture was kind. "You can, Carrie. You can."

Carrie nodded. "Okay. Take the booths this morning. I'll take the tables."

Andi felt herself sag with relief. The booths were the busiest seating and meant more tips. In giving them to Andi, Carrie was showing she had forgiven her. Andi looked over her shoulder at Clooney and grinned.

He laid a weathered hand on her shoulder and squeezed. "Good girl. I'm proud of you." The words were so soft she almost didn't hear them. She flushed with pleasure.

Lindsay and Ricky waved to her from the kitchen.

"Welcome back, kiddo." Ricky blew her a kiss. "I'm glad you're here. I was afraid they were going to make me wait tables."

Everyone laughed at the absurdity, and just like that, life was back to normal. Or at least as normal as Andi's life got these days.

27

I watched Andi for the first half hour, but she seemed to be okay after whatever had set her off yesterday. Soon I was busy with my own tables, and I noticed the girl only peripherally. It was a busy morning, what with the glorious Indian summer weather drawing people to the shore for their last hurrah of the year. The chill that had come with last evening's rain was burning off under the sun's golden warmth, and while the ocean might have become a tad cold for most, the beach would be wonderful for walking and tossing a Frisbee and flying kites. I envied Clooney his metal detector and shovel and promised myself a walk in the sand after work.

Greg wandered in around nine thirty, a bit early for him, and I did my usual happy dance at the sight of him. I still couldn't believe he'd kissed me last night, and I knew I must be smiling like an idiot.

His eyes sought me out as soon as he walked in, and he winked at me. I grinned back with all the maturity of a smitten puppy. The cloak of despair he'd worn for the past three years seemed to have disappeared, and it was because of me! I bit my lip to keep from bursting into song.

"Here, Greg," Clooney stood. He'd hung around longer than I expected, I guessed to make certain Andi was fine. "I've been sitting on your stool. I've got to get going. There's gold in them thar beaches, and it's calling to me."

"It's a great day for digging." Greg slid onto the vacated stool.

I waved good-bye to Clooney and hurried to give Greg his coffee. "The usual?"

Greg nodded. "Sure."

I was turning to enter his order when he laid a hand on my arm.

"I've changed my mind. I'd like a bowl of cereal. You've got those little boxes, don't you?"

"Frosted Flakes, cornflakes, Raisin Bran, and Froot Loops." I had a terrible thought as I recited the choices. If he started eating cereal, he wouldn't need the café. He could pour a bowl at home, and I wouldn't see him every day.

"Frosted Flakes." He nodded for emphasis. "It's a milestone."

"Okay." A milestone? "Coming right up."

Andi sailed past with breakfast for the twosome at booth three. "Uh, Carrie, your quartet at table five is ready to jump up and down to get your attention. Maybe you should hold hands after hours." She grinned.

I looked down and sure enough, Greg held my hand in his. I'd been so rattled at the thought of not seeing him daily that I hadn't felt him slide his hand down my arm and take hold.

Heat flooded my face as I hurried to table five, which wanted some more butter for their pancakes. I kept busy for the next hour, hoping I'd have some free time before Greg had to leave. As I walked back and forth to enter orders and then to pick them up, I heard snippets of his discussion about crime and punishment with Mr. Perkins. One bit caught my attention, and I stopped on my way to pick up an order.

"That guy who tried to run you over," Mr. Perkins said. "I bet he's out on bail."

Greg nodded. "He is. In fact he and the furniture rental company are coming to the Sand and Sea Friday afternoon to reclaim their belongings."

Mr. Perkins harrumphed. "He should have forfeited them after his behavior."

I hadn't thought about Chaz Rudolph for the last couple of days. "He's still in Seaside?"

"He can't leave until after his trial," Greg said.

"Where's he staying?" Mr. Perkins asked the question that had just occurred to me.

"Backseat of his Hummer?" I suggested as I picked up an order of fried eggs over easy with hash browns and sausage and a side of whole wheat toast.

"It was repossessed by the car dealership," Greg said.

Mr. Perkins all but purred. "Some justice in the world after all."

"I can't quite bring myself to feel sorry for him." I set one of Lindsay's giant bran muffins laced with raisins and peaches on a plate for the wife of the fried eggs.

"Excuse me. I'm here about the sign in the window?"

I turned and saw a young woman about my age. "You're here about a job?" I was afraid to blink in case she'd disappear like a mirage.

She nodded.

Yes! "I'm Carrie. Let me serve this food, and we can talk."

Her name was Lou Reynolds and, be still my heart, she had experience as a waitress though she hadn't worked in several years because of her kids.

"We want to buy a house," she said, "and I have to work if we're ever going to make it happen."

Their problem was providing care for their three children, six, seven, and nine.

"My husband can get the kids off to school in the morning, but we don't want them coming home to an empty house in the afternoon. They're too young. With the café's hours, I can be home for them."

She looked so hopeful I almost laughed. She might think I was an answer to her problems, but I knew she was an answer to my prayers. With a second server I could spend my time on the business side of things, assessing the past season and preparing for next. And since the spate of Twitter notes about Carrie's as well as the great weather, we'd had more traffic than usual for this time of year.

Lou and I talked some more, and I sent her to the kitchen to meet Lindsay. I didn't want to hire anyone without input from my sister. The upshot was that Lou'd be in tomorrow morning at six fifteen to start work.

She left with a cheery smile, and I felt the same smile sitting on my face. I pulled the Help Wanted sign out of the window with a thank-you prayer and a request prayer that Lou turn out to be as good as she seemed.

My smile dimmed significantly when the door opened and Chaz Rudolph strolled in. When he spotted Greg, he gave a little sneer. Greg ignored him.

I waylaid Chaz. "What are you here for?" I asked with a deplorable lack of hospitality.

"Breakfast. What else?"

What else indeed. I seated him at one of the tables and took his order.

"You can pay for this, right?"

He glared at me. "Do you ask all your customers that?"

"No." I waited. Bill was bad enough. I wasn't feeding another jerk for free.

Chaz sighed as though offended and pulled a twenty out of his wallet. He put it on the table and secured it with the pepper shaker. "Satisfied?"

I nodded and left to give his order to Ricky.

On the dot of ten thirty, as the last of the customers except Chaz, Greg, and Mr. Perkins left, Bill Lindemuth strolled in.

Andi saw him as she bused an armful of dishes from one of her booths. She smiled tentatively, and he walked to her. I tried to hear what he said, but I couldn't. They were too far away, and he spoke too quietly. Sigh. I hated not knowing how she truly felt about him.

He wandered to the back booth where they had eaten before and slid onto the bench. Andi passed me as she took the dishes to the kitchen.

"I'm going to take my break, okay?"

I nodded. "Okay. Just remember, Bill pays."

She gave me a sour look. "Yes, ma'am."

I rolled my eyes. Where had the sweet penitent of the early morning gone? A few minutes later she went by with two loaded dishes, one of pancakes, the other a huge omelet with cheese and ham melting out the ends. A container of low-fat yogurt made a bump in her apron pocket. It didn't take much imagination to guess who was eating what.

I was wiping down the last of my tables when Andi sailed past again, this time returning to the kitchen. I trailed her to the counter.

"How's Bill doing today?"

Andi glared. "Because of you, he's been questioned by the police."

"Good." I refused to flinch under her anger. "Maybe his information can help find Jase's killer."

"He said they want to talk to me too."

Greg studied Andi. "Why do you have such negative feelings about talking to them? You haven't done anything wrong, have you?"

She frowned and grabbed her Sudoku book. She waved it at me. "I'm teaching Bill how to play." She said it with all the suppressed ire of a guard dog being held at "stay" when he quivered to sink his teeth into the intruder, Greg and me being the intruder.

Bill didn't strike me as someone with the patience to work out the puzzle. "Does he enjoy it?"

She ignored me and stalked back to her booth.

"I think she heard your skepticism," Mr. Perkins said, ever helpful.

Before I could reply, the door opened and SweetCilla motored in, bright orange flag flying above her chair. Fred Durning followed on her heels. I nodded at Fred but didn't approach him. I figured he was here to see Greg. Instead I went to move a chair so Cilla could belly up to a table.

She waved my efforts away and drove up to Greg, who had risen when he saw Fred.

"I just wanted to tell you I think it's disgraceful that that man was given bail and is free to walk around town." She scowled fiercely. "After what he tried to do to you."

Greg looked bemused and shot a glance at Chaz, who was busy reading the sports section of the restaurant's copy of *USA Today* as he lingered over coffee. "Thank you."

Mr. Perkins seemed to see Cilla for the first time. "I think you're absolutely right." He leaned down and whispered in a voice sure to be heard clear to the boardwalk, "That's him over there." He nodded in Chaz's direction.

Fred blinked. "That's the guy who rammed the apartment building?" He studied Chaz. "Unimpressive."

How true.

Cilla looked at the unaware Chaz in astonishment. "You are wonderful people to allow him in here. I certainly wouldn't."

Mr. Perkins slid off his stool. "Want a grilled sticky bun, Cilla? You'll love it."

She studied his wrinkled face for a moment, then gave him a warm smile. "Thank you. I believe I will have one if you'll split it with me." She motored to the table farthest from Chaz and sat with her back to him. Mr. Perkins followed her, his step jaunty.

Greg and I looked away to hide our smiles.

"I'll take a grilled sticky bun too." Fred took the stool next to Greg.

Greg grinned and settled back in his seat. "I see Lindsay's got another fan."

"I was sitting around waiting for it to be time to go sign that last elusive paper on the sale and I got to thinking about how good the sticky bun was yesterday." Fred patted his flat stomach. "I couldn't resist."

"Want to split one, Carrie?" Greg asked, as if our sharing was the most natural thing in the world. I nodded, thinking that just yesterday I'd thought I'd never share with him again, and now here we were. How cool was that!

I got the last three sticky buns from the display case. I passed them through the serving window to Ricky. I could smell Lindsay's French onion soup, one of my favorites. She made it with such a rich broth that the onions themselves were almost superfluous.

"We've also got ham and bean," she said as if reading my mind. "And there's vegetable beef too. The sandwich special is a tuna melt on an open-faced bagel topped with tomato and the cheese of your choice."

I knew this, of course, since we set menus days in advance so we had time to order all the necessary food stuffs. In the glass-fronted refrigerator unit I saw a lemon meringue pie so high it almost touched the bottom of the shelf above, a coconut custard pie, and a chocolate raspberry torte just waiting for diners to enjoy.

As I waited for Ricky to grill the buns, Lindsay slid a tray of chocolate chip cookies from the oven.

"You guys are amazing back here," I said. "I love you both, and I especially love the goodies you turn out."

"Yeah, yeah," Ricky answered, his eyes bright under the bill of his baseball cap. He flipped the sticky buns deftly. "That's what they all say." But I could see he was pleased.

He turned to Lindsay. "Do you think this is a good time to ask for a raise?"

"Sure, you can ask," I said. "But don't hold your breath."

With a laugh, Ricky brought the grilled buns to the serving window. I took them and set them in front of those who had ordered them. I made certain everyone's beverages were topped off and that all had forks and napkins and extra butter. Then I leaned on the counter across from Greg and dug in.

All was silent for a couple of minutes as we savored Lindsay's genius.

Then Fred sighed. "Ambrosia."

The rest of us said, "Umm."

"She's gone again."

I blinked my way out of my cinnamon-and-sugar trance and looked at the unhappy Bill, standing in front of me. "What?"

"Andi's gone." He scowled at me as if it were my fault.

I looked back at the booth where she'd been sitting with him. Sure enough, it was empty.

"She said she was going to the ladies' room." Bill's scowl intensified. "She never came out."

I straightened, concerned. "I'll go check."

I hurried to the back of the café and pushed open the cream-colored door with *Women* stenciled on it in Caribbean blue. There were two stalls and a sink along one sidewall. The other was blank except for a mural of a beach with lapping waves, oversized seashells, a jetty, and colorful beach umbrellas.

Across from the entry door was a window usually covered with a Caribbean blue curtain. The sash was kept closed in deference to the air conditioning in summer and the heating the rest of the year. Now the curtain was pushed aside and the window was wide open, the screen pushed free.

I stood for a moment, hand to my head as if the pressure from my fingers could hold at bay the headache I felt brewing behind my eyes. Not again!

28

I was more than grateful when Mary P answered my SOS and served lunch in Andi's place.

"Just so you know, this isn't to be a regular thing," she said as she tied her apron around her ample middle. "I'm happy to help on occasion, but I'm a retired lady."

I kissed her cheek. "You've saved me twice in one week. No wonder I love you."

Mary P lit up at my words. "Back at you, kid." And she bustled off.

I forced myself to smile at all the nice customers, knowing that in the hospitality business nothing mattered quite as much as attitude, not even the food. A warm smile could cover a multitude of serving mistakes, from spilled iced tea to grilled cheese too browned.

But I was fuming inside. I was very aware of the phenomenon of teenage girls and irrational behavior. After all, I'd once been sixteen and I'd lived with Lindsay when she was sixteen. Moodiness went with the territory.

But Andi'd promised! Had she stood right there and with knowledge aforethought lied? Surely not. Andi might be volatile at times and have terrible taste in men, but I would never have thought her a bald-faced liar.

Even Clooney had believed her. He stood with her as she gave her word, and he told her he was proud of her. Had she just been repentant because he demanded it of her? I'd witnessed that don't-mess-with-me aspect of his personality when he'd come down on Bill for daring to act too familiarly. Had he exerted that same force on Andi and made her apologize? Then she'd fled at her first opportunity?

That line of thought didn't make sense to me. Clooney was her family. She never spoke of parents, not even to say they were dead. It was as if her life began when she came to live with Clooney, and if his home was now hers, she couldn't afford to alienate him.

So what had happened? What made her go out the window? People didn't climb out windows unless under great pressure to escape.

But escape what? Was she that frightened of Bill? She'd been sitting with him just before she ran. Had he said something that upset her? Had he threatened her somehow?

If that was the case, why didn't she just say he scared her? A word to Clooney, and Bill would be history. It took a stronger personality than that of any has-been high school athlete to stand up to that man. And there was always the possibility of a restraining order if needed.

As I waited for a tuna melt and a grilled cheese and tomato, I placed a quick call to Clooney. He needed to know what had happened, and I needed to know if Andi'd gone home. All I got was his answering machine. He was undoubtedly out digging treasures from the sand with his little red spade.

"Clooney," I told the machine. "She's gone again. Is she at home? Andi, are you there? Pick up! Let me help. Clooney, do you know what's going on with her? Call me."

Both Greg and Fred left with worry clear on their faces. I thought it kind of Fred to be concerned over a girl he didn't even know. If the people he represented were as nice as he was, Greg would like his new employers more than his last.

Cilla left with Mr. Perkins, and I got the impression he was walking her home. In spite of my worry over Andi, I had to smile at the thought of a golden-years romance.

At two thirty, when we were down to two tables finishing up their lunches, Greg came back.

"How's it going?" He stood across the pink marble from me.

I was so weary both physically and emotionally that all I wanted to do was lay my head on his shoulder and absorb some of his strength. "We managed. Mary P came in and took Andi's booths, so we got everyone fed."

He nodded with sympathy. "I've got the perfect antidote for your tension."

"A hot bath and a coupon for a full body massage?"

He laughed. "Better. Surf fishing."

What? "You mean the kind where you stand on the beach and dare the fish to swim in and get caught?"

"You fish from the beach, yes, but it's not quite that hopeless. The stripers are running, and it's great fun trying to get one."

I didn't think it sounded as relaxing as my longed-for massage, but it was with Greg, so it had to be fun even if it turned out to be terrible. "Will the surf be too rough what with the higher-than-normal seas caused by the hurricane passing out at sea?"

"If anything, it'll be more fun."

I eyed him, my skepticism clear. "If you say so. What time?"

He thought a moment. "I need to fix a couple of minor problems at the property at Sixteenth and the boardwalk. You need to finish up here. How about four?"

"It's a date." I heard myself and colored. What if it wasn't? What if it was just a desire not to fish alone? What if last night's kiss was just some freaky sort of accident? Though how it could be an accident was more than I could understand. "It is a date, isn't it?" I had difficulty forcing out the *d* word, and I hated feeling so insecure.

Lindsay and Ricky, sitting at the counter eating their late lunch, looked at each other and smiled. So glad my dating ineptitude brought joy to their world.

Greg cleared his throat. "I haven't done this in years, but if I remember right, then yes, it's a date."

My smile felt as if it would split my face. "Cool." No way could Snoopy move his feet fast enough to keep up with my tap-dancing heart.

"Very." His smile mirrored mine.

Yippee, Lord! It's finally my time! I think.

We walked toward the front door. I moved behind the register, where I picked up Andi's Sudoku book left lying on the counter. I looked at it quizzically.

Mary P glided past with the last of her dirty dishes. She cocked her head toward the book. "She left that on her table when she ran."

"I hope that means she's coming back." I set the book on the shelf under the register, and it fell open to the page that had a pencil stuck in it.

I glanced at the puzzle she had been working and saw a bunch of numbers running along the side of the page like a numerical sentence. Absent-minded doodles? Certainly they had nothing to do with solving the Sudoku.

I set the book on the counter between Greg and me. "This was the last thing she was doing before she left."

Greg studied the page. "The last thing?" He turned the book so he could read the string of figures. "Then these numbers have got to be important."

I studied the now upside-down-to-me page. "You think this is a message of some kind?" Surely not. "A secret code to open a treasure chest or a safe where we find a note written in invisible ink telling us what's going on?"

"Cute." He was caught in the numbers and the questions they raised. "There has to be something here. Otherwise why did she write them?"

We stared at the numbers on the page. 2912 11912 10. 49424.

"She told me once she used to send coded messages as a kid." I began to get excited. "She subbed numbers for letters. When she was young, it was numbers for vowels, but as she got older, it was numbers for all the letters. You know, 1 equals A, 2 is B. Like that."

"So 2912 is a word? 2 is B, 9 is I, then A and B. B-I-A-B?"

Disappointment bit deep. "There's no such word. Unless the 1 and 2 are 12. B-I-L. Bill?"

Greg nodded "Then line two is either 1-19-12 or 11-9-12. A-S-L or K-I-L."

I felt a chill. "B-I-L K-I-L. Bill kill?"

"Bill Kill 10." He worked his fingers, counting off letters. "Bill Kill J."

"Greg! Is she telling us that Bill killed Jase?"

"Don't know. 4-9-4-2-4. D-I-D-B-D."

I glared at the letters. "They don't make sense."

I could feel excitement snap through Greg. "They do if the last 4 stays a 4 and doesn't become a D. Did B4."

"Bill killed Jase. Did before." Before? He'd killed someone before?

Greg, looking incredibly serious, picked up the book. "I'll take this to the police. They've got to find Bill, and fast." He leaned in and gave me a quick kiss on the cheek, as if it were the most natural thing in the world. "I'll be back as close to four as I can make it." And he was gone.

My head reeled at the thought that I had served a killer and thought his worst fault was not tipping. For want of an idea about how to fix things for Andi, I went back to work. I was filling a needy saltshaker at one of the back booths when the door opened again. I grimaced. I'd forgotten to lock it in the distraction of Andi's Sudoku clue. I turned to tell the newcomer that we had stopped serving.

My breath caught, and I felt the blood drain from my face, leaving me lightheaded.

My mother stood in my restaurant.

It was all about timing, wasn't it?

Act at the right time and you succeeded. Think the stock market.

Be at the right place at the right time and you met the right people. Think business contacts, networking.

Go to the doctor's at the right time and you lived. Think early detection.

Make sure you were seen by the right people at the critical time. Think alibi.

He excelled at doing things right, at timing everything.

It was enough to make him shake his head in wonder, not just at his own abilities but at everyone else's idiocy. People were such fools, so easily manipulated. So gullible.

Having the right name was also an asset. The right name got you respect. The right name opened doors. The right name even offered protection from the law.

He had the right name. And the perfect sense of timing.

Chaos might reign around him, but his life was ordered, timed, and controlled. All you had to do was look at him, and you knew: He was head and shoulders above everyone else.

M y mother!

After a moment of shocked immobility, I turned my back and fought for calm.

She looked good, better than I ever remembered seeing her. Her skin was a healthy pink instead of the dead gray it had been when all her nutrition came from a bottle. Her hair was a shining cap of curls, and while her figure was slightly thickened, she looked healthy and vibrant. She wore a red V-neck sweater over a white shirt, jeans, and white sneakers. She was somewhere around fifty, though the abuse she'd heaped upon herself should have made her look eighty. Instead she looked wonderful.

There was no justice in this world.

I saw all this in the moment of shock before I turned away, and as I digested it, I began to shake, feeling as stable as the biblical house built upon the sand.

A handsome man was with her. He wasn't as tall as Greg, but he held himself with authority. He had sandy brown hair that had turned gray at the temples, and he had his arm around my mother's shoulders as if he were protecting her, though from what I couldn't imagine. Right now I was the one who needed protecting.

What was she doing here? Was she looking for me? For Lindsay? No, that was impossible. There was no way she could have found us, not after all these years.

Under the guise of picking up a piece of paper from the floor, I sneaked

another glance. My first impression had been accurate. She looked wonderful. Where had the sloppy drunk gone?

Mary P spoke as she came out from behind the counter. "I'm sorry.
We've stopped serving for the day."

"I realize that," my mother said with a smile. "I saw your hours in the
window." Her voice was soft but clear, not slurred from some substance
she'd ingested. "I just had to step in for a moment. The name drew me. You
see, I used to have a daughter named Carrie, but I lost her."

There was a moment of silence at that amazing comment. Then I
wanted to turn and scream, "You lost me? *You lost me?* You threw me away,
me and Lindsay."

Oh no! Lindsay! Where was she? I looked toward the kitchen and saw
her through the serving window deep in conversation with Ricky, a list in
her hand.

Stay there, Linds. Stay there! Oh, Lord, keep her there!

"This is a lovely place," Mom said. "Warm and seashore-y with the
blues and creams, though that pink counter is something else." I heard the
smile in her voice.

"It used to be the registration desk in a hotel that was once on this
property."

"How lovely to have rescued it."

Right. Lovely.

"If you're staying in Seaside," Mary P said in her warm, inviting way,
"perhaps you could stop in tomorrow for breakfast or lunch."

"What do you think, Luke?" Mom said.

I heard the deep rumble of Luke's voice, but I couldn't make out his
words.

"I'm Mary Prudence Hastings," I heard Mary P say. "This used to be
my place before Carrie took over. Now I work for her."

"I'm Sue Fletcher. This is my husband, Luke."

Again came Luke's rumble. If I turned, I'd doubtless see the three of them shaking hands like new best friends. And what was with the "Fletcher"? When had she acquired a husband? She didn't deserve one.

"So Carrie's has a real Carrie," Mom said. "I'd love to meet her."

There was a pause during which I felt Mary P's eyes boring into my back. I held my breath, clutching the saltshaker so hard it's a wonder it didn't implode in my hand. I waited for her to give me away.

"Our Carrie isn't available at the moment," Mary P finally said. "Maybe tomorrow."

And I knew Mary P knew she was speaking with my mother.

"That'd be nice," Mom said.

"Where are you staying?" Mary P asked.

"We're renting a house at the south end of town. We're here for a couple of weeks. I used to come to Seaside when I was a kid living in Camden and loved it. I talked so much about it, Luke decided we should come for a visit."

"Where did you come from?"

Good grief, Mary P, why not just ask for their résumés? Get rid of them!

"We live in Atlanta, in Buckhead," Mom said.

Buckhead! Was she kidding? Ritzy, rich, toney Buckhead? Don't make me laugh!

"What do you do, Luke?" Mary P asked.

"I'm a lawyer," Luke said, his words clear as a bell this time. "Business law."

"And you?" Mary P asked Mom.

"I'm a writer, a novelist. Maybe I'll set a book in Seaside." Again I heard a smile in her voice.

I wanted to scream. When I knew her, she couldn't even write me notes for school. I learned to forge her signature and wrote all correspondence for both Lindsay and me. Otherwise we'd never have had an excused absence for illness or gone on a school trip or had our report cards signed. Now she wrote novels? I wanted to puke.

"We'd better go, sweetheart," Luke said, and my stomach turned at his gentle manner.

"Yes, of course. It was so nice to meet you, Mrs. Hastings."

"Please, call me Mary Prudence. I feel like we've known each other for a long time."

"Oh," Mom said, disconcerted. "How nice."

Nice, my eye! The whole situation was terrible, from Mary P, the turncoat, to Mom, the unwelcome Ghost of Christmas and every other day Past.

God, this isn't fair! She looks good. She sounds good. She's married to a man who seems to care about her and makes lots of money. She writes books, for heaven's sake! Not fair! So very not fair!

As Mom and Luke—my stepfather? Good grief!—walked out the front door, I bolted for the back door. The last thing I wanted was to talk to Mary P.

I raced up the steps to the apartment, ignoring the wind and scudding clouds. I ran into my bedroom and fell on my bed feeling cold all over. I pulled the quilt up, tucking it around my shoulders. I lay there shivering, staring at the ceiling.

My mother was in Seaside, in my restaurant!

I can't deal, Lord! I can't! And I don't want to. Make her go away! Please!

I imagined her wanting to help run the café or trying to give us advice about life and love or telling us how naive we were to live like we loved Jesus. I imagined her trying to cut Mary P out of our lives or criticizing Greg or putting down our little business.

And Lindsay! She was going to hurt Lindsay. She was going to pretend she loved her, draw Lindsay in, and then she was going to disappear or fall into her bottle again, leaving Linds bruised and bleeding.

At least Lindsay was an adult now, grounded in the Lord, with a career of her own. She didn't need Mom as she had when we were still at home. But that didn't mean Mom couldn't still hurt her deeply with abandonment, indifference, and invective.

Make her go away, Lord! I don't want her here.

I closed my eyes as I heard myself. I felt miserable and guilty about my terrible attitude.

I told You this would happen. I told You that if I was near her, all the old hurt and bitterness would spew out. I told You! I don't like myself like this.

The bed moved as Oreo jumped up. She walked up to my face and looked down at me with her great green eyes as if to say, "What are you doing here in the daytime?"

"Hey, baby," I whispered.

She lowered her black head and ran her raspy tongue over my cheek. I gave her a weak smile.

She stepped onto my pillow and began turning circles. When she was satisfied in that feline way that never quite clicked with humans, she collapsed, curling into a furry ball beside my head. Then she reached out and gently laid a paw on my cheek.

Well, somebody loves me!

And I began to cry.

31

At ten before four, I pulled myself from bed and got ready to meet Greg. I felt so very tired, the emotional toll of Mom draining me. *Just like she always did, Lord!* I also felt angry and resentful at both God and Mom for making me feel so confused and weepy.

Poor Greg. I wouldn't be a great date, but at least the stripers wouldn't mind if I cried.

Lindsay stuck her head in my room. "Greg's here." She grinned and wiggled her eyebrows.

I nodded morosely, and she gave me a "what's up with you?" look. I forced a smile. If she only knew. She frowned at me and left.

I looked in the mirror to comb my hair and saw the sick smile I'd directed at my sister. No wonder she looked startled. It was Halloween-mask grotesque. I sighed. In my current frame of mind there was no way I could conjure up a genuine happy face, not even for Greg.

My melancholy will probably kill our budding romance, Lord. What guy wants to spend time with a downer of a date? Leave it to Mom to ruin another thing for me.

Greg was waiting in the kitchen, and I managed a weak smile in which he seemed to see nothing amiss.

"If we're lucky, you can join us for a fresh fish dinner," Greg told Lindsay.

She grinned. "Then you'd better be lucky. I'll look up striper recipes and be ready when you bring your catch home."

Her happy enthusiasm made me feel even worse, something I wouldn't have thought possible. The idea that I had to tell her about Mom made my stomach curdle. How would she react? Because she had been so young when we left, she didn't harbor any of the negative memories I did, or at least not as many. And she had a more forgiving nature than I.

What if she were eager to accept Mom, to reestablish a relationship? What if I lost Lindsay to Mom? I swallowed the bile that threatened to gag me.

I was silent during the ride to Twentieth and Ocean. Greg kept looking at me with concern.

"Okay," he said after he parked the pickup at the foot of the boardwalk ramp. "Give. What happened between when I last saw you and now?"

"What do you mean?" I didn't want to tell him because it would show all too clearly my petty and spiritually immature nature.

"Don't give me that." He studied me through narrowed eyes. "As a rule you're pretty perky, and you've lost all your perk."

Perky? I was so not perky. Ever. Cheerleaders were perky. Ingénues were perky. I was—well, not perky.

"I'm fine."

"Liar."

I glared at him and he smiled back, his eyes full of sympathy. "Come on. Give."

A tear slid down my cheek. He reached out and caught it with his index finger.

"Trust me, Carrie."

That was all he said, and I started talking, words hemorrhaging without the moderating effect of an emotional tourniquet. "She's here…lost me!…looks beautiful…has money…handsome husband…novels…not fair! Greg, it's so not fair!"

"No, it's not. But who said life was fair?"

Just because what he said was true didn't mean I wanted to hear it. I wanted to wrap my blue funk around me like a hair shirt and suffer. I didn't want veracity. I wanted sympathy and poor me.

"Remember I told you I couldn't handle being near her? That it would make me into this awful person I didn't want to be? Well, that was when I thought she was still the unreliable drunk I knew." I drew a shuddering breath. "Being near her like she is now, when she's—she's—"

"Everything you'd want a mother to be?" he suggested.

"But never was. Never!"

"But never was." He nodded.

"It's awful!" I dropped my face to my hands. "I'm awful! The one who's good is her!"

He gently pushed some hair back from my forehead and pulled my hands down.

"I look blotchy, don't I? I always look blotchy when I cry. Lindsay cries pretty, but I don't."

"Your nose is red." He leaned over and kissed it, surprising me. "It's cute."

Cute. And perky. Who was this fictitious person Greg thought I was?

Then he leaned over and kissed me on the lips. It was a kiss that held so much promise my throat ached. When he pulled back, I sat with my eyes closed for a few moments more, holding the beauty of him close while ignoring the truth of me. Then I looked at him, letting my pain and anger show so he'd see the real me, the ugly me.

"Oh, Greg, I feel so terrible. I hate her. I hate what she does to me. I hate me." Tears fell again.

He didn't seem fazed. "You know, what you're suffering is a kind of posttraumatic stress thing."

Oh, great. More rational thinking.

"Seeing her has set off all the hurtful memories. It's sucking you back."

That was certainly true. "But I'm not sixteen anymore. I'm thirty-three! I should be able to do better. Be better."

"Like being thirty-three means you shouldn't have flashback fever? I'm older than you, and I get it."

Of course he did. Who wouldn't with stuff like he'd suffered? "She writes novels, for Pete's sake."

"And this is bad how?"

"I don't know!"

He took my hand in his across the distance between our seats. "Well, I'm not sure what a counselor or Pastor Paul would say, but I suspect they'd tell you that you have to talk to her for your own emotional and spiritual health. Now me, I'm going to tell you that you don't have to do it this very minute. Give yourself time to get used to the idea of her being here. For now let's go fish and let the ocean breezes clear your head. And, Lord, teach Carrie what to do and when." The last was a prayer.

Somehow his giving me permission to take my time and his prayer for the Lord's help eased the iron bands constricting my chest. I took a deep breath and thought how wonderful the timing was between us. Even three days ago I wouldn't have been able to confide in him no matter how much I longed to.

"No guy's ever prayed for me before." If guys knew what it did to a girl, it'd be in all the how-to-date books as the number one way to a girl's heart.

He gave my hand a gentle squeeze. "I hope I get the chance to pray for you for a long time to come."

Really? I studied his face and asked *the* question. "Greg, why did you say Ginny's name the other day?"

He blinked and looked out the window toward the beach. My stomach lurched. I should have kept my mouth shut.

"It's going to sound so strange. It sounds weird, even to me." He cleared his throat. "Ginny spoke to me. Or at least it sure sounded like her."

Whatever I'd expected, this wasn't it. "She spoke to you? You heard an audible voice?"

"Yes and no." He looked thoroughly discomfited.

I waited, knowing that somehow what he had to say would make or break whatever it was we had growing between us. What if I found my un-wanted mother and lost the very-much-wanted Greg, all on the same day?

Greg cleared his throat again, a sure sign he wasn't certain of my reac-tion to what was coming. "I was sitting at your kitchen table wondering how long I'd been aware on some subconscious level of how special you were and questioning my intelligence because I'd been too dumb to realize it sooner. Then I wondered if it made me somehow unfaithful to Ginny—which I knew was ridiculous even as I thought it. That's when it sounded like she spoke. Not out loud, of course, but in my head or heart or wherever."

I remembered my stomach falling when I heard his soft whisper of her name. Right now it felt like oceans of acid were forming a giant whirlpool down there. "And what did she say?"

Greg gave me a lopsided smile. "She said, *I like her. I do.* Meaning you."

I stared at him, my mouth probably hanging open.

"Then she said, *Go for it, Greg. With my blessing. It's time.*"

"You heard Ginny's blessing?" My voice cracked, but my abdominal whirlpool began to settle.

He nodded. "Weird, huh?"

I watched him, hope and uncertainty battling it out inside. "Unusual at the very least."

He reached out and ran a knuckle down my cheek. "Even before I heard that voice, I'd already decided to pursue things with you. I just hadn't acted on my decision yet. It's important you realize that. Maybe the voice—

which, by the way, I've decided was the Holy Spirit prompting me—made me act more quickly, but I already knew deep inside."

"You did?" The whirlpool had become a placid, sun-splashed sea.

He nodded with a smile that curled my toes. "I finally figured out the reason I loved coming to the café. For a long time I was stupid enough to think it was the café itself, but it's just a building. It was the woman inside who was sharing her warmth and calm. You gave me a peace and ease I couldn't find anywhere else, completing my healing."

I stared at him, struck dumb.

"You're a wonder, Carrie Carter."

No! No, I wasn't. At least not in the wonderful way Greg made me sound. "But I'm a mess, Greg."

He shrugged. "At the moment maybe. But you cared when I was a mess. Now I'll return the favor. And hopefully someday we'll both be fine at the same time. Now let's go get us some stripers."

32

This surf fishing was a lot more complicated than fishing out of Greg's boat. First there was the size of the poles. Then there was the problem of casting into the incoming tide without getting all wet or getting your line snagged on the nearby jetty because you were a lousy caster. Stripers followed the smaller fish that came in with the tide and the hurricane residue. For some reason the middle of the beach between Twentieth and Twenty-First was a great place to catch the big silver and black fish. Made as much sense to me as stopping at a particular spot in the bay had, but then, I'm neither a fish nor a real fisherman.

I was standing there, rod in hand, trying to tell myself my arms weren't heavy enough to fall off when Greg stuck two cylindrical tubes into the sand.

"Drop the rod in here until something happens. It's too heavy for you to hold."

"Thank you!" I slid my rod into the holder and shook my arms to release the tension of holding the rod so tightly. "So we just stand here and wait?"

He nodded. "But with any luck not for long."

The sky was gray, which might or might not mean rain, and the wind off the ocean was strong and humid, though not particularly chill. The water was agitated, the waves more pronounced than usual, and high tide would creep farther up the beach than usual. The massive Hurricane Marcel was hundreds of miles out to sea, but its reach was long.

I sat on the dry sand and prepared to be bored. I was a doer, and sitting for too long was hard for me. At the moment the last thing I wanted was downtime in which to think.

I watched a pair of boys about ten years old playing catch farther up the beach and wondered if they'd like a third. Then Greg sat beside me, and I decided I wasn't bored after all, especially when he slid an arm around my waist.

Clooney appeared in the distance, red spade and bucket in one hand, metal detector in the other. He stopped for a moment to talk to the boys, and he reached in his bucket twice and pulled out something for each boy. They studied what he'd given them as he started toward Greg and me.

"Thanks," one of the boys yelled after him, belatedly remembering his manners.

"Yeah, thanks!" echoed the other.

He gave them a little wave over his shoulder and continued toward us, his ponytail blowing out behind him.

"Well, look who's trying her luck," he called as he neared.

"You ever do this?" I called back, pushing away hair that had blown into my mouth.

"Not me. Too much like work."

At that moment Greg got a strike. He jumped up, grabbed his rod, and began to reel in. Whatever was on the hook fought valiantly while he labored to bring it home as Clooney and I cheered him on. So did the ball-playing boys, who were excited over the battle between man and denizen of the deep.

"I've never had quite this much trouble with a striper," Greg managed between pulls on his pole and the quick winding of his reel. Then he pulled the rod high again and wound quickly as he lowered his bowed pole toward the water. Pull, lower and wind, pull, lower and wind.

"Maybe it's not a striper," one boy yelled.

Seemed an obvious possibility to me, but what did I know about stripers?

"It's a great white," called the other and was then booed down by his buddy because there was no dorsal fin showing above the waves.

Greg's catch broke the surface, and both kid one and I were right. It wasn't a striper. It was a ray.

"Eee-yew," shouted the boys. "Ugly!" They waded into the water to get a closer look.

Clooney laughed. "No wonder you had trouble. Imagine all the drag from those wings."

With mutters and head shakes, Greg dragged the skate the rest of the way in, pulled the hook, and released it while the boys cheered. He grabbed another strip of squid and baited his hook. He cast over the foaming breakers and grinned at me.

"Never caught one of them before." He lowered his pole into a holder.

The excitement over, the boys went back to playing ball, and it was just the three of us.

"Here," Clooney said to me. "I've got a present for you." He reached into his bucket and pulled out a sandy woman's watch. He held it out to me, and I took it.

I examined the piece, delicate, feminine, gold with black numbers on a white face. Its band was more like a bangle than the usual stretch style of the numerous inexpensive watches I'd had through the years.

"This is not a Timex," I said. "This is a very good watch, and it's studded with what I bet are real diamonds."

"You're right. Those aren't cubic zirconias, not on a Piaget."

"I bet someone misses it." I could imagine a distraught woman coming back to the beach—this past summer? Last year? Whenever she realized she'd lost the watch? She'd spend time searching where she thought she'd been sitting when she took it off so she could go in the water. Maybe she cried when she couldn't find it because it had been a special gift and its loss hurt.

With gentle fingers I brushed off some of the sand that still clung to it. "Will it ever work again?"

"Only a jeweler can tell you that. Regardless, it's yours because of the symbolism."

I looked at him, uncertain what he meant.

"There's a time to every purpose under heaven." He looked at Greg, who was studying the watch over my shoulder.

My face warmed. "Clooney!"

"It's all good," he said. "And it is about time. For both of you."

I made believe I wasn't embarrassed. "So says a lifelong bachelor." I closed my hand around the watch. "Thank you."

He shrugged. "What would I do with a woman's watch?"

I smiled to myself. Heaven forbid I think him a nice man. It went against his long-established image, an image everyone who knew him at all saw through.

"By the way." I hated to bring up a painful topic, but I had to. "I left a voice mail for you. Andi took off again."

Clooney swore.

"I think she's hiding from Bill."

He shrugged. "He's a jerk, but I don't think he'd hurt her."

"She left a note indicating that he killed Jase."

"She said Bill killed him?" Clooney seemed genuinely surprised.

"B-I-L-K-I-L-J. Greg took it to the police."

Greg nodded. "They're taking it seriously. They want to talk to him again, press him."

Clooney snorted. "Bill's many things—arrogant, insensitive, stupid—

but I doubt homicidal. He's not the problem where Andi's concerned. I mean, he is a problem, but not like you're suggesting. The real issue is that cult, I'll bet anything."

"What cult?" How'd we get from Andi's running to talking about a cult? "You think she took off to join one?"

Clooney tossed his shovel in frustration. It flipped once and landed blade down in the sand, handle quivering. "Of course not. She's running *from* The Pathway, not to it. She's been upset ever since it came out that Jase was a member."

Greg's pole began to sing as the line played out. He raced to it, lifting it out of its holder and beginning the struggle with whatever he'd hooked.

I stayed with Clooney. "I'm missing something here. Why should it upset Andi so much that a guy she didn't know all that well was a member of a cult in Arizona?"

"Because her parents are members."

"Yikes!"

"Tell me about it." He looked disgusted. "They suddenly got religion and forced Andi and her sister, Becca, to join with them."

My mind was zipping around corners and arriving at a destination that unsettled me. "She came to you after she ran away from The Pathway?"

He nodded. "She's such a brave little thing, but all this Jase business has brought back too many memories."

Another posttraumatic stress victim.

He pulled his baseball cap off and slapped it back on, pulling his ponytail through the back opening. "I'd like to string up her parents. First off, they weren't some green kids who got taken in. They were in their forties. Andi's mom might be my niece, but she's got a lot to answer for as far as I'm concerned."

I couldn't help but wonder which was worse: having my mother or having Andi's.

"Take it from me, Carrie." His voice was fierce. "Religion is the bane of civilization, whether it's those Muslim extremists or the megachurch guys in this country or a cult like The Pathway. It's all about power. And money."

Oh, boy. How should I respond to that comment? "You could call me religious if you wanted, and I'm not that bad, am I?" Except where Mom was concerned.

But he was on a roll and ignored me. "Terrible things have been done all through history in the name of God, from Cain killing Abel to the Crusades and the Inquisition to the fanatical bombers today." His strong emotions were reflected in his tense expression. "Religion, all religion, should be banned! All it does is divide people and make con men rich."

I'd heard all this before on television talk shows and read it in books. It had been easy to discount in those circumstances. I could even feel smug because I knew those pundits were wrong. But this was Clooney, whom I liked a lot. What I said and how I said it mattered.

I looked at Greg. *Help!* But he was busy fighting whatever was on his line.

"You're right that terrible things have been done in the name of God," I said. "But that doesn't mean that He approved. Come on, Clooney. I bet you know plenty of wonderful Christians."

"I do?"

"Me and Greg and Lindsay and Mary P for starters."

Clooney made a little snorting noise. "I've got to go find Andi." He turned and walked off with a careless flick of his hand, grabbing his shovel as he passed it.

I watched him stride away, his pail and shovel dangling incongruously from one large hand, his detector slung over a shoulder. Why, smart as he was, didn't he see the difference between a faith that hurt and a faith that helped? Didn't he understand that believing in Jesus and living for Him should make a person better, kinder, wiser? Didn't he get that it gave purpose to life and the strength to make right choices?

But faith was invisible. It was about believing in things hoped for, in things not seen. Faith was about being conformed to the likeness of Christ in one's actions, not about screaming on street corners or from pulpits or in grainy videos with one's face hidden behind a mask. Faith, an accurate faith, was about making the hard decisions to do what was right when what was wrong was by far the easier way.

I thought of my recent meltdown and my heart gave a little hitch. I'd never convince Clooney of all these thoughts if he'd seen me weeping up a storm in Greg's car just a little bit ago.

And I knew deep inside that Greg was right. I would have to talk to my mother. I would have to forgive her for both then and now. If I ever wanted to represent a valid faith to Clooney, I would have to make the hard but right choice.

But not yet. Lord, not yet.

E ventually everyone became a liability, even people you liked. The only thing you could do in such a situation was get rid of them.

Friends always felt betrayed when the tie was broken. They never saw themselves as weights pulling you down. They saw themselves as your equal when your superiority was so obvious to anyone who looked without prejudice.

But supremacy and leadership required the tough decisions, and that meant severing ties that were no longer an asset. Look at Jason. He became a liability. He had to go. And he was gone. No regrets. Merely a matter of the survival of the fittest.

No one was indispensible. No one. Not even your closest confidant. The spoils went to the victor, and he was the victor. He always had been, and he always would be.

He breathed deeply, energy and excitement zinging through his veins. It was time for another to go. He'd seen it coming for some time. The big question was how total the disconnect would be. Another Jase?

He smiled at his reflection in the tiny mirror. Probably.

I turned back to Greg just in time to see him land a good-sized striper. "He's got to be at least twenty-eight inches." He pulled out a plastic ruler much like a dressmaker might use. "Twenty-nine inches! Lindsay will have to use her recipe tonight." He radiated pleasure.

My reel started to hum as the line played out. I grabbed hold of the rod without taking it out of the holder.

"Reel in!" Greg called.

I clutched the handle or whatever you call it and tried to reel in, but whatever was on my line didn't want to be caught. "Help!"

Greg abandoned his rod to the holder and came behind me. He reached around me and helped hold the rod.

"Here, you take it all." I tried to hand everything off to him and duck under his arm.

"Oh no. This is your baby."

With his strength helping control the rod and his knowledge helping me play the line, I eventually hauled in my own striped bass. It was a beauty, all silver and black, and I watched anxiously as he measured it to see if it was big enough to keep.

"It's a keeper."

I felt like I'd landed a hundred-dollar tip.

"I'll teach you how to clean it and filet it," he said.

Ack! The guy just grabbed his money back right out of my hand.

I decided to quit while I was ahead and my arms still functioned. I shook my head when he offered to rebait my pole. I walked a bit away and climbed onto the jetty.

"I'll watch you from here," I called.

I sat on a huge flat rock and watched the windblown tide advance. Greg tossed out his line, stuck the rod on the holder, and came over to join me.

I loved climbing on the jetties even though there were lots of signs that said Keep Off Jetty. Everyone ignored them, thinking they were Seaside's attempt to protect itself from lawsuits brought by those unlucky enough to fall and break a leg while climbing. Every so often a true tragedy happened on a jetty, like the seven-year-old boy who fell off one in Ocean City a couple of years ago. His body washed up a few blocks south.

But the jetties called to people in spite of their danger—or maybe because of it. I always felt like an intrepid mountain goat as I moved from boulder to boulder. I also loved the sensation of being out in the water without actually being *in* the water. And it was invigorating, being so close to the spray as it kicked up when the waves dashed themselves against the rocks—which they were doing with extra vehemence this evening.

Sharing jetty magic with Greg was like sharing one of Lindsay's grilled sticky buns with him, intimate and sweet.

"Andi's family is in The Pathway," I told him after a few moments of comfortable silence. "Clooney just told me. She ran away from their compound."

"Ah. Poor kid. I wonder if she knew Jase from there."

"Clooney didn't say."

A big wave washed right up to the edge of the boulder we were sitting on, the foam swirling inches from my feet.

"Why do people fall for the cults?" I asked. "Especially the extreme ones? In your police work, did they ever teach you that?"

"I went to a seminar on the topic as part of my continuing ed, and there was always constant information available about the cults considered dangerous or somehow skirting the law. The Pathway and Michael the Archangel were frequently in the bulletins. And there were always the Web sites that debunked the cults and kept track of their activities."

"The Pathway is illegal somehow?"

"It's hard to prove anything, but there's lots of speculation and questions because they keep to themselves like most cults do. That us-against-the-world mentality is a cornerstone of cult teachings." He looked at me. "Believe it or not, The Pathway has a very clever group of lawyers representing them. So far they've gotten them off any charge."

"Isn't the head of the Fundamentalist Latter Day Saints polygamist group in West Texas in jail?"

"Yes, but for forcing the marriage of a fourteen-year-old to her nineteen-year-old cousin and for marrying girls twelve and fourteen himself. The Pathway has been smart enough not to go that young a route."

"But they practice polygamy."

"They do, but not with girls little more than children. Sixteen is their usual age, but they get around it by having parental approval. They live on their compound in the southern Arizona desert, keep to themselves, and do whatever Michael the Archangel says."

Another wave licked at our boulder. "I just do not understand how people can turn their backs on our culture and standardized religion for something so off the wall. I mean, Michael the Archangel?"

"I have a theory about why the women join, but I *know* why the men are attracted. It's about power, money, and sex."

Pretty much what Clooney had said. "That's pretty nasty. No fine points of belief or heart?"

"I don't think so. In these cults the men have all the power, both positional and sexual. The women are pawns, taught to be submissive, not in the healthy submit-to-one-another way of the New Testament but regardless."

"They take verses out of context and push them."

"They do, another cornerstone of the cults. 'Wives, submit yourselves to your own husbands' without the balance of 'husbands, love your wives, just as Christ loved the church and gave himself up for her.'"

"Is there money in The Pathway?"

"That's the big question. When someone joins, he or she has to turn over all their finances to the leadership, which means Michael. The group claims this money is used for the care of everyone, but knowing the estimated worth of several converts and the primitive facilities at their settlement, there's a contradiction. There's hidden money somewhere, but to my knowledge no one's been able to find it."

"They want to get Michael on tax evasion like they did Al Capone." I sounded like I knew what I was talking about.

"They're trying."

We stood and moved back a boulder, and the incoming tide splashed over the place I'd just been sitting. "But the women? Why do they join? I can't imagine sharing a husband with other women. I don't think I'm particularly selfish, but if I marry, that man will be mine and mine alone for life. I'm not letting another woman near him."

He grinned at me. "Possessive, huh?"

"You know it." Our eyes held, and I thought of my new watch. A time to every purpose under heaven. My heart raced. Was what I'd longed for, prayed for, coming to pass? Was now my time?

Greg's fishing rod jerked, drawing his attention. He climbed off the jetty and hurried to it. He gave it a tug, then shook his head. "Whatever that was didn't take the hook." He climbed back beside me.

"What about the women in cults?" I asked.

"My theory is that many of the women who join come from backgrounds similar to yours. They've been abused, hurt, maybe raped. They've been made to feel worthless. They find life overwhelming. The cult offers safety and security. You'll be taken care of all your life. You have to marry, but your sister-wives take much of the sexual pressure from you. You're told what to do, so you know exactly what's expected of you. You have rules and assignments that regulate your life. Choices and the uncertainty they bring disappear. And you're part of a forever family. There is no divorce in groups like The Pathway."

I was startled by the idea that many of the women were from backgrounds like mine, though it did make sense. If your life was hard, fragmented, or frightening, security forever would look very attractive. Did women join groups like The Pathway, then leave when they felt they had control of themselves again? Or was the world forever scary? Were they even allowed to leave?

"Wouldn't Jesus be a more sensible way to deal with the pain and rejection?" He had been for me. "With Him you have security and family, but you also have freedom and room to grow as a person."

"So says a woman who is strong and independent."

We stood, preparing to move back from the relentlessly encroaching water again. I took a step as I smiled at Greg over my shoulder. I liked being thought of as strong and independent.

My athletic shoe struck a slick spot where moss grew, and before I knew what hit me, I was on my back with my leg bent at an extreme angle.

35

Carrie!" Greg was beside me in an instant. "Are you all right?"

I blinked at him. "I think so." Except for the pointy rock sticking into my back. I put out a hand to push myself upright.

And found I wasn't quite as all right as I'd thought. A shaft of pain shot up my right arm from my wrist. I yelped and pulled my arm to my chest, cradling it in my other hand. The pain dulled from a ten to a four and throbbed in time with my heart. I'd become one of the many that the Keep Off Jetty signs were written for.

"Your wrist?" Greg reached to take hold of it.

"Don't touch!" I sounded like a two-year-old yelling, "Mine!"

He blinked and pulled his hands back. "I wouldn't hurt you. I've had lots of emergency training."

I nodded, feeling foolish at my overreaction. "I must have put my hand out to catch myself when I fell." With care I extended my injured arm and studied it. Already the wrist was swelling.

"Can you move your legs?"

My legs. I tried to move, and while one leg cooperated, the other didn't. "I can't move my left leg!"

We both looked and saw the problem at the same time. When I'd fallen, my foot had kicked forward and gotten wedged between two of the jetty's boulders, toe down, heel up. Somehow when I'd landed, my leg, already caught, had been wrenched and twisted at an awkward angle. My knee was bent, and the inside of my leg lay flat on the jetty. All I could see of my foot was the thick heel of my athletic shoe.

"I can wiggle my toes without any pain, so I don't think it's broken. Just stuck."

"Well, let's get you unstuck and to the hospital to have that wrist looked at." Greg slid his hands down to my ankle and began the process of releasing me from my rock trap.

"I can't have a broken wrist!" The implications of losing the use of one hand, my right one no less, loomed large. "I've got to work! How can I wait tables with only one arm? O-o-ow! Stop! My foot doesn't bend that way." I felt it all the way up in my hip.

"Sorry." He tried again.

"Pain! Stop! Let me try." I shifted my weight, but my foot, sneaker sole caught beneath an uneven protrusion on the boulder, remained immobile. A wave washed over the rock I sat on, sliding inexorably toward me, wetting my legs and bottom. It was uncomfortably chilly, and my jeans sopped up the wet like a denim sponge. As the water receded, I realized my trapped foot was now submerged in its crevice, water gurgling around it. Time and tide were not going to wait for me to get free.

I started to get nervous. "How high will the water get where we are?"

"Uh." Greg looked around in the fast-falling dusk. We were quite a ways out on the long jetty. "Three feet maybe?"

How far was it from my bottom to my nose? How deep was three feet? I looked to my right and left to see where the tide line normally was. I tried to picture how high the water would be where I sat when the waves washed higher than usual on the beach. I began to fear I was going to become one of those wild animals who chewed off their foot to get free from a trap.

"Before you panic, let's just untie your shoe, and you can slide your foot out." Greg, the ever practical.

"Right. Good. Wonderful idea." Such a brilliant and easy solution.

But my foot was wedged upside down, and the laces were not only under water but unreachable.

A man I'd never seen ran out onto the jetty. "I saw you fall. I called 911 for you. I told them we needed an ambulance and a rescue squad."

As I tried to smile my thanks, a piece of silver plastic riding on the water bumped against my leg. Greg picked it up.

"Looks like the cover on a slide phone," the 911 guy said.

My cell phone was that color. With my good hand I reached for my belt clip. Empty. That wasn't a rock in my back when I fell but my phone, and the fall shattered it. I should have gotten that extended warranty.

As I mourned the loss of my phone, I became aware of wet dripping down my neck. I reached back with my good arm, and my hand came away sticky. "My head's bleeding!"

Greg whipped off his sweatshirt, then his T-shirt. He folded it up and slapped it gently against the back of my head. "Hold this."

I held it as he pulled his sweatshirt back on. Then he moved my hand, lifted the compress, and examined my head. His hands moved through my hair, and I thought how I'd dreamed he'd do this but under slightly different circumstances and for slightly different reasons.

I could feel 911 Man peering over Greg's shoulder as another wave washed over me. By now I was sitting in sea water, very chilly sea water. Stripers might like it cold, but I didn't.

"How soon do you get hypothermia?" I asked.

Greg put the compress back in place and held it there. "I think you're safe for a while," he said with a smile in his voice.

I heard a rumbling noise, and a strobe light began playing across the water, turning the foam red and blue by turns.

"Oh, good," 911 Man said. "The cops."

I looked over my shoulder. The cop car had driven right up on the boardwalk. Close on its heels came an ambulance, lights flashing.

I didn't rate a siren from either.

People poured out of both vehicles, and the jetty became crowded. Now 911 Man had his smartphone in hand and was texting away. He was very unhappy when he was sent back to the boardwalk to watch the action from afar.

"But I called it in," he protested, as if that gave him the right to take up precious space on the jetty.

"And we appreciate it," Maureen Trevelyan said. "You can help us, sir, by keeping everyone away from the area."

Slightly mollified, he left, doubtless to regale the small crowd gathering with what was going on when he wasn't texting the Twitter world.

I crooked a finger at Greg, and he bent to me. "Are they all Twittering about me back there?"

"Probably. Does it bother you?"

I shrugged. "Twice in one week. I'll be famous. Though come to think of it, they don't know it's me. Ouch!"

I glared at Maureen, who had tried to free my foot.

"How did it get wedged?" she asked, as if people caught in a jetty were all in a day's work—which they undoubtedly were.

"I slipped and fell, and it was stuck."

"I think she's broken her wrist," Greg said. "And she has a cut on the back of her head, but I don't think it's serious. More an abrasion than a laceration."

Maureen moved behind me and shined her flashlight on my head. Greg removed the compress he'd been holding in place.

"I don't think it's even bleeding anymore," Maureen said.

One of the EMTs dropped to his knees beside me. "Hi, Carrie. I'm

Ryan and that's my partner, Amy." He pointed behind me, and I craned my neck to see who he was pointing to. Amy and I smiled at each other, well-mannered even in catastrophe. "Can you tell me if you hit your head hard?"

"I didn't. I don't remember hitting it at all. It's my wrist." I held out my arm and winced at the sight. Instead of being indented at the base of my hand, my wrist was the size of an Easter ham and just as pink in the flashlight beams.

"Let's make sure the rest of you is okay," Ryan said. "Then we'll get you to the ambulance."

"The rest of me's great. Except for my foot."

He put his hand on my knee and followed my leg to the foot. He felt around down there, his hands submerged, while I made little yips as he tried to turn it.

He frowned. "You are caught, aren't you?" He looked at the wave that rolled over us, soaking me to the waist and him partway up his thighs. He looked up at Maureen. "We need heavy rescue and fast."

"What?" I turned to Greg, on his knees across from the EMT, also soaked well up his thighs.

"Just a precaution," he said. "Don't worry."

I might have felt better if he didn't look so distressed.

Maureen, in water above her ankles, stepped away and spoke into her shoulder mike. I couldn't hear her, but I knew what she was saying.

More rumbles, more lights, more crackling radios, and the heavy-rescue truck pulled up beside the ambulance, followed by a fire truck.

"Why a fire truck?" I asked Greg as I tried not to shiver.

"Part of the first responders. It's better to send them home unneeded than to get them to an emergency too late."

A fleece blanket fell around my shoulders. Ryan's partner smiled down at me. "Let's keep you as warm as we can."

Greg tucked it close, and I smiled my appreciation.

Suddenly the jetty was bathed in bright light as the rescue team kicked into action. The light revealed the wave that was barreling toward me. It hit and I was lifted from my rock by the force of the water, floating for a few seconds. Greg and Ryan were both shifted by the surge and scrambled for balance. I put my hands out to keep from falling backward into the water and yelped as my bad wrist took some weight.

It always amazed me the small amount of water that was needed to create a dangerous situation, especially moving water. It was people who didn't comprehend this fact who stayed to ride out hurricanes and who often died. Right now I was at the waves' mercy. First came the slap and the push, then the suck and the pull.

As the wave receded, I settled back on the boulder, my free foot pressing against the same rock that held me captive, trying to keep me steady. It took me a moment to realize that my left leg wasn't bent at that unwieldy angle anymore. I reached forward. I still couldn't feel the laces on my shoe, but I could feel its side.

"My foot's shifted! Cut it off!"

The last was lost in the gurgle as I turned my head to escape a wave full in the face. I floated again, then settled, spitting out salt water. I held my breath as I reached down into the swirling foam. What if my foot had been turned back with only the heavy sole showing again?

"Cut it off! Cut it off! Quick!"

36

Greg forced himself to breathe slowly and deeply. He could do this. He could. The trick was to breathe without hyperventilating. Water swirled around him, but that was nothing compared to the emotions swirling inside. In a strange way, he felt proud he'd managed to hold it together this long.

Then Carrie yelled, "Cut it off!" and the hair on the back of his neck stood on end. He thought he'd be sick.

All around him lights strobed, radios crackled, and people moved with purpose. Memories surged, threatening to drown him more thoroughly than any of the waves rolling in. Waves he could fight. Waves he could run from. But this vivid recall? Memories lived inside, inescapable and terrible.

"Why don't you move back, Greg?" Maureen said. "Let the rescue guys in."

"Right," he mumbled. He should have gotten out of the way as soon as they showed, but he'd been paralyzed. He'd been fine when Carrie fell, when she realized her head was bleeding.

Then *they* came, and with them the noise, the lights, the panic.

He rose and made his way off the jetty onto the dry sand. He stood there, useless and jumpy. He wanted to go home, to safety and quiet. For the first time in a very long time, he thought about how comforting a few stiff drinks would be.

While he stood there, mute and useless, others came and helped. And then Carrie was free.

The rescue squad guy whose name escaped Greg held up a white athletic shoe with one side sliced from edge to sole. He held it toward Carrie. Greg saw her shake her head as she was helped to her feet and assisted off the jetty. She looked fine, upbeat and in control. He, on the other hand…

She was bundled into the ambulance. Just before they closed the door, she called, "Greg, would you call Lindsay for me?"

Somehow he managed a nod.

The bright lights illuminating the jetty blacked out, and the darkness of a fall night was extra black in contrast. The fire truck rumbled off the boardwalk, following the ambulance. The rescue truck left as soon as the lights were stowed. In what seemed the blink of an eye, he was alone except for Maureen Trevelyan and Rog Eastman.

"You okay, Greg?" Maureen asked.

"Sure," he lied. But he knew she knew it was a lie. Maureen had been one of those who responded when Ginny and the kids were killed. She was a tough cop, but she had a tender and insightful heart, and she made Greg very nervous.

"I imagine you're going to the hospital to check on Carrie after you call Lindsay."

"Right." He'd already forgotten about his promise to call Lindsay.

"Where's your car?" Maureen asked.

He pointed vaguely in its direction.

"Come on. I'll walk you."

Because he couldn't figure out how to lose her, he went with her as she walked up the stairs to the boardwalk and down the Twentieth Street ramp. Rog followed, driving their squad car down the ramp behind them. When Greg found himself hoping the cruiser's brakes held, he was somewhat cheered. That was a normal thought, right?

When they reached Greg's pickup, Rog put the poles, fishing gear, and the two stripers in the cooler in the back of the truck.

"Thanks," Greg managed. He'd forgotten all about that stuff.

Maureen looked at him with concern. "She didn't die, Greg. She's going to be fine."

But she could have! Somehow he managed a nod as he got behind the wheel. *And it would be my fault!*

"Don't forget Lindsay," Maureen said as he closed the door.

He nodded again and pulled out his phone. He had to dial 411 to get the apartment number, and he was glad for the automatic connection. He didn't think he could push the right sequence of numbers because his hands were shaking too much.

It was because he cared. He hadn't had any negative reaction to the sirens and static, the calling voices and organized chaos when he found Jase's body. Of course he'd been sad about Jase, but if he'd been upset about anything, it was that he wasn't part of the action.

He'd felt almost jealous of the team dealing with the crime. He frowned. Maybe jealous wasn't the right word, but he'd felt something strong. Displacement? Here was his world, but he was no longer part of it.

But that day there hadn't been even a touch of the fear that struck with such ferocity tonight. What if he'd lost Carrie as he'd lost Ginny and the kids?

He couldn't let himself love again. He couldn't. It was too frightening, too risky. When you thought about it, you lost everyone you loved, guaranteed, and he couldn't take any more loss. If that made him weak, then he was weak.

He was forcing himself to breathe deeply when Lindsay picked up.

"She's all right," he said several times. "She's all right."

But saying it didn't ease the constriction in his chest or relieve the paralysis in his limbs. Maureen and Rog were long gone before he managed to put the truck in drive and head for the hospital.

He had just entered the emergency room when Lindsay burst through the door, eyes wide. She saw him and ran to him, throwing her arms around his neck. He automatically returned the embrace, patting her on the back.

"I'm so glad you were with her." She gave him an extra squeeze. "No one could have been as helpful and as comforting for her as you."

The cramp in his gut intensified.

Mary P rushed in. Lindsay must have called her. "How is she?"

"She'll be fine," Greg assured her. "She's wet and cold and I think she has a broken wrist, but she's fine."

Would saying it enough still the churning?

Lindsay and Mary P went to the desk to ask if they could see Carrie. Pastor Paul arrived, and Greg felt bad that he hadn't thought to call him and glad that either Lindsay or Mary P had. Of course Carrie'd like to see him, have him pray for her. With her.

But Paul made no effort to go see Carrie. "Come sit," he said to Greg.

Great. Sympathy. Understanding. Concern. Just what he needed. Not. The man was too perceptive by half.

Greg followed him because there was no alternative short of running screaming into the night. He sank into an uncomfortable plastic chair. Recognizing the chair as uncomfortable was another good sign, wasn't it? Another normal thought.

He leaned forward, elbows on knees, and studied the floor, anything to keep from letting Paul see his eyes. They were the windows to the soul or something like that, and he didn't want anyone to know what a quivering failure he was.

It took a few minutes before he realized that Paul was resting a hand on his back, comforting him as if he were the one who was injured. He hated being so transparent.

Lindsay and Mary P came out of the patient area and joined them.

Paul stood. "Let me go see her for a minute. Then she's all yours, Greg." He disappeared down the hall.

"They took an x-ray," Lindsay reported. "The break's clean, but it'll still require surgery for pins and a plate. They're going to keep her overnight and operate tomorrow morning. Then they'll put a split cast on, whatever that is."

Lindsay looked weary but relieved that things weren't any more serious. He felt relief too, and now seemed a good time to leave while he was still holding himself together.

"She'd like to see you, Greg," Mary P said.

He must have made some sound of distress because both women turned and looked at him.

"Are you up to it?" Mary P asked.

How could he explain that it was no longer the emergency itself but the fact he'd responded so emotionally that ripped through him? He'd thought all that posttrauma stuff was behind him. He'd dared to think he was well.

How wrong that was. He was still a mess. He had been all but useless in a simple crisis, the kind of thing he had handled every day back when he was a cop. He might as well have a big *L* for *loser* plastered across his forehead.

Lindsay frowned. "He'd better be up to seeing her."

Greg held up a hand to ward off any more comments and walked back to the patient area, passing Paul on his way out. He felt like he was slogging through quicksand, and his next step might be the one that pulled him under.

Failure. Loser.

He found Carrie's curtained-off cubicle. She lay on a gurney, her head slightly raised. She was wearing a hospital gown, and her wrist was wrapped in an elastic bandage and held snug to her body by a sling. A lightweight blanket covered her. She looked tired but in good spirits.

She smiled at him. "Hey."

The wave of relief that rolled through him shook him. She really was all right.

The problem was, he wasn't.

She patted the side of her bed, and he sat near her knees.

He took her good hand in his. "So you're staying the night."

She nodded. "Surgery tomorrow morning to set this thing." She didn't seem at all apprehensive about it. "I think I'll be allowed to go home tomorrow afternoon. Pick me up?" It was clear she assumed he'd be happy to do that little favor for her.

"Sure." Who could he get to come in his place? Failures didn't deserve the prize or even the honor of being in the prize's presence.

But he stayed with her until an orderly came to take her to a room. He walked with her as she was wheeled to the elevator, still clasping her hand. Her eyes were droopy with the painkiller she'd been given, and she'd be asleep the minute she was in her bed.

"I'd better go now and let you get a good night's sleep."

She smiled at him, an intimate smile that plunged him deeper into his own personal black hole. He didn't deserve intimate. He couldn't do intimate. What in the world had he been thinking?

He kissed her on the lips, a sweet, lingering kiss he thought of as goodbye. She smiled groggily at him as she was wheeled into the elevator.

"I love you," she said.

He gave a stiff smile and watched the doors close. He turned for the exit. Lindsay and Mary P were already gone. He walked through the automatic doors into the parking lot and flipped the remote to unlock his car. And flicked it again to relock it.

He turned and hurried back into the hospital. He rode the elevator to the third floor and walked down the hall until he found Carrie. A nurse was checking her vital signs as Carrie lay in the bed nearest the door in her semi-private room.

He stood in the doorway.

Go home, idiot! She's fine.

When the nurse was finished, she clicked out the light over Carrie's bed. She did one last check to make certain the call button was in place.

"Just push if you need me."

But Carrie didn't respond. She was asleep.

The nurse paused as she passed Greg. "Don't stay long. She'll be fine. We'll take good care of her."

He nodded. He walked into the room and stood by the bed. She looked so fragile. So beautiful.

He pulled the visitor's chair as close to the bed as he could and sank into it. He reached through the bars and under the blanket for her good hand. He laced their fingers. He laid his head back and closed his eyes for a minute.

The nurse who came to check vitals at 4 a.m. woke him and made him leave.

37

B y seven in the morning I was in surgery and by eleven I was back in my room, sporting a cast split on one side to allow for the swelling that was still present. At four in the afternoon, Lindsay appeared to drive me home.

"I thought Greg was coming." I tried not to look too disappointed to see my sister.

"He asked me to come because he had some business stuff to take care of."

That made sense. "He'll probably stop by this evening. You can make us those stripers for dinner." One-day-old stripers would still taste okay, wouldn't they?

It was amazing how tired I felt after the ride home, and I snoozed on the sofa with Oreo as a blanket. When it was time to go to bed for the night, Greg still hadn't appeared.

Was it because I'd blurted out that I loved him? I could blame the surge of honesty on the drugs I'd been given, but drugs or not, what counted was the way he received the news. Did the fact he hadn't shown mean that he hadn't wanted to hear any such confession from me?

But he'd spent the night in my room. The nurse had told me so.

"Held your hand all night," she said with a smile. "He must be pretty special."

I'd just grinned.

Now I was confused.

I had a fragmented night's sleep, waking myself whenever I moved my arm, taking pain meds on my schedule, not the doctor's. When I woke Thursday feeling groggy and drained, I could sense that the apartment was empty. I glanced at the clock by the bed. Six thirty! We were about to open.

I dragged myself from bed and tried to get ready for the day with one hand. Since I wasn't supposed to take a shower and get the cast wet, I tried washing up in the sink. I couldn't wring out the washcloth except by pressing it against the sink, which was very unsatisfactory, so I dripped all over myself. I couldn't hook my bra. I could barely pull up my underwear and khaki slacks. When I wiggled the slacks in place, I was panting from the effort. Then I couldn't zip or button them. Shoes and socks were beyond me.

I did manage to brush my hair, though it still looked as if it would win a contest for the messiest rat's nest. I put on some blush and swiped some mascara over my lashes so I wouldn't look as miserable as I felt. I slid my left arm into a man's jacket that had been left at the café and held it to my right shoulder. It was large enough to hide the clothing malfunctions so I could go downstairs without feeling like a stripper. I had to give my slacks several tugs to keep them on my hips as I descended the steps.

Pull up pants, lunge for slipping jacket. Pull up pants, lunge for slipping jacket.

I eased in the café's back door and into my office. I peered out. The new server, Lou Reynolds, moved past, serving booth one. Lindsay appeared, four plates balanced in her hands. Mary P was seating a couple in booth five. I felt tears of gratitude and love as I watched my sister and my Godmother taking over my responsibilities for me.

I waited behind the door until Mary P began to turn away from the new customers. I called her name softly. She looked around, as if she was uncertain she had heard her name. I signaled to her, and she hurried to me. I shut us both in the office.

"What are you doing down here?" she scolded as she gave me a careful hug.

"Do me up. Please!" I dropped the jacket, turned my back, and hiked up my Carrie's Café shirt, this one Caribbean blue with the unoccupied sleeve flapping forlornly. She laughed and stuck the hooks and eyes of my bra together. I turned around, and she zipped and buttoned me.

I handed her my old sneaks, the good pair having been reduced to a single shoe two nights ago. She went down on a knee and slid the shoes on one at a time, making me think of a shoe salesman back when shoe salesmen still helped customers try on shoes.

"Lindsay's working tables." The import of that fact finally penetrated my foggy brain.

Mary P nodded.

"And you're here."

She nodded again.

"That means no Andi." Both anger and concern rode me. "Where is that girl?"

Mary P looked as concerned as I felt. "I don't know, and I'm getting more worried all the time."

"You think she's not just being a temperamental teen? Something is truly wrong?" There was *Bill kill* and there was The Pathway. Either could put her in a very uncomfortable place. Dangerous even. "I need to call Clooney."

Mary P patted my shoulder. "I've got to get back to work. The place is jumping. I think you'll have to write Chaz a thank-you note."

"What?"

"It's all that Internet publicity, and he's responsible."

I snorted. "Like I always thank someone who almost kills people I care for. Go save the café from being overrun while I call Clooney."

I didn't even have time to punch in his number before he stomped into the cafe, looking like Chief Thundercloud wearing an Eagles sweatshirt instead of an Indian blanket. I walked out to meet him.

"She never came home," he said without preamble. "I sat up waiting for her and fell asleep around two. I overslept. Is she here?"

Uh-oh. "I'm sorry. She's not."

"When I get my hands on that boy..."

I was glad I wasn't Bill.

"If it is that boy..." And he looked even more worried.

"I'm assuming you called Bill's home?"

"Several times. I got to speak to Billingsley Lindemuth Junior. That was a rare pleasure." He glared at me. "Why would anyone name a child Billingsley? And why would others pass it on as if it were a name to be proud of?"

Keeping him on task, I asked, "And what did Billingsley Junior say?"

"The kid was home all night. If Junior was the only one who told me that, I'd disbelieve on general principles, but when I went to the house, his wife said the same thing. She was very sweet and helpful."

"What? Moms don't lie for their kids?"

He made a frustrated sound, stalked to the counter, and took the empty stool beside the ever-present Mr. Perkins. I followed him over. He looked so upset and angry that even the garrulous Mr. P didn't try to talk to him.

"I don't know why I'm worried," he said. "It's not like she's my kid. And she got herself all the way across country from Arizona on her own."

"You love her," I said.

He snorted. "Right. I want pancakes and sausage, double syrup."

I left him in Mary P's care and went to the cash register, where I thought I could be of some service.

Wherever she is, Lord, keep her safe!

Greg didn't come in for breakfast, and I thought of him at home, eating cereal. I'd been right. He didn't need me or the café anymore. He was never coming back.

"There's a time to every purpose under heaven."

Those words Clooney had quoted to me when he gave me the watch were from Ecclesiastes, though without doubt Clooney knew them from the old folk song. They were probably written by King Solomon. I thought Ecclesiastes and its writer very melancholy and pessimistic. You try your best, he wrote, and it's all meaningless, a chasing after the wind. "All is vanity" was how the old King James Bible put it.

I'd like to find out if being in love was meaningless, if being loved was chasing after the wind. Was it heartbreak, or could it be like the romance novels said, just not quite so over the top? Real life as moonlight and roses? It was broken wrists and missing girls, that I knew. I sighed. Maybe the writer of Ecclesiastes was right.

A psalm that usually comforted me came to mind, and I all but snarled inside. It wasn't what I wanted to hear from the Lord. *"Wait for the LORD; be strong and take heart and wait for the LORD."*

Lord, I've got to tell You, I'm getting very tired of waiting.

Your times are in My hands.

I blinked. This hearing voices was getting old fast.

The café door opened, and in walked my mother and her husband.

Where were the people you could trust? You asked a simple favor or issued a straightforward order, and all you got was incompetency and questions. Had he asked for something difficult? He had not.

"Take care of it," he'd said.

"Here's my decision," he'd said.

"Find it," he'd said. "Find her."

But did his man honor his word or do as asked?

He would not live with the results of ineptness any more than he'd live with someone wrestling him for control. He was not a man who accepted halfhearted allegiance. He was the man in charge.

He was the one with the skill and intellect to lead.

He was the one who deserved the financial benefits of his leadership.

He must not be challenged.

He would not share.

He was God's archangel.

Andi huddled in the darkness of the closet and listened to her stomach growl. She'd been here two days, and it felt like forever. At least she thought it was two days and today was Friday. She was so hungry, but there was nothing in this place but beer. What kind of a diet was that? And how long before you died of starvation?

She'd brought some snacks with her—chips, a six-pack of Sprite, a small box of Cheez-Its, a couple of Hershey's chocolate bars—but they were all gone. She couldn't leave to get more until she was sure *he* was gone. Trouble was, how could she know he was gone if she stayed here? She wiped angrily at the tears.

No crying, Andi. No more crying! Just suck it up.

She had to use the bathroom, but that meant walking out into the bedroom. Sure, it was shadowy there since she'd closed the curtains, but compared to the comforting dimness of the closet, it looked like high noon on a sunny summer day.

From where she sat, she had the company of the flickering light of the muted television. It was sort of interesting trying to figure out what people were saying when she didn't dare allow any volume for fear someone might hear and come to investigate.

Watching it was what had kept her from going nuts. She'd bitten off her nails and jumped at every little sound. The rumble of her stomach was the loudest noise by far. Sometimes she slept huddled on the closet floor. It made the time pass and kept her from thinking about how hungry she was.

But now her bladder was sending *very full* signals to her brain.

You can go to the bathroom, stupid! It's safe. No one knows you're here.

She moved to the closet door and peeked out. No one was there. She knew that before she looked. She also knew she didn't have to stay in the closet. She just felt safer in there. The darkness and the small space were sort of like curling under the covers at night after a bad dream.

It was all Becca's fault, the whole awful mess. Andi struggled hard not to hate her sister, but at times like this it was a losing battle. If Becca hadn't found that stuff about The Pathway online and then been dumb enough to fall for it, they'd all be safe in their own house in the old neighborhood. She'd be sleeping in her old bed, going to school with her old friends, maybe dating.

Instead she was hiding in a closet and Becca was a mom twice over. Who knows, maybe three times by now, and she wasn't even twenty-two yet.

When the family had been driving from Philadelphia to The Pathway's compound not much more than three years ago, Andi'd still fought her parents' decision.

"Mom, this is a polygamous group! Dad's going to take other wives."

Her mother laughed. "Oh, Andi, don't be foolish. Of course he's not. I've told him that if he takes other wives, I'll take other husbands."

"That's not the way it works." Andi felt as if she alone could see past the reflection in a pane of one-way glass to perceive The Pathway for the warped and corrupt religion it was. The others saw the image Michael wanted them to see. "It's the men who have multiple partners, Mom, not the women."

Her mother and father had grinned at each other like the idea of multiple partners was ridiculous. But Andi was seated behind her father and saw his face in the rearview mirror when he looked forward. There was something in his expression, a slyness maybe, that made her know he planned to enjoy all the perks at The Pathway.

And he had. Three young wives at last count. Maybe more by now. And her mother had been devastated by his perfidy.

With each new wife, she grew paler and more despondent. By the time she was sent to the tiny infirmary where Andi worked, helping the one woman in the compound who was a registered nurse, Mom had lost her will to live.

"Mom, there's nothing wrong with you physically." Andi held her mother's limp hand and stared in disbelief at this wan creature she'd become. "You're giving up. Don't do that! Don't let them win. Don't let *him* win."

Mom gave a weak smile.

Andi took that for encouragement and leaned close so her words weren't overheard. "We'll leave here, you and me, Mom. We'll go home. We'll—"

Mom shook her head. "It's too late for me."

"Don't say that." Suppressed tears made Andi's throat ache. "Please don't say that!"

Mom patted her hand. "You were right about this place, Andi. It's evil here. It's about domination and control." She sighed. "But I'm too tired to fight it any longer." Her eyes fluttered closed as if keeping them open was too demanding a task.

"You have to fight!" How did you reach someone who was quietly but with determination committing suicide? "You have people who love you. Fight for them. For me!"

An expression of great distress contorted Mom's face. "No one loves me, Andi. I lost your father the day we drove through the gate."

The veracity of that statement made Andi want to hurt her father and hurt him badly. How dare he! She ran a gentle hand over her mother's hair.

"I lost you that day too, honey."

Andi kissed her mother's pale cheek. "You didn't lose me. You could never lose me. I love you. I always will."

Mom kept on as if she hadn't felt the kiss or heard Andi's words of affection. "Becca might live in the dorm where I live, but she's busy with her children and those of the others. I don't see her very much. I think she avoids me. I embarrass her."

"Oh, Mom." Andi's heart broke for the pain she heard, the pain of shattered dreams, of unexpected and undeserved rejection.

They sat for a few minutes, the only sound Mom's labored breathing.

"She fits here." Despair and sorrow limned Mom's words.

"I don't," Andi said fiercely.

Again that weak smile. "You don't, thank God. And I don't either. I don't do well with being alone."

"With being betrayed, you mean. Being forsaken."

Mom didn't disagree.

"Get well, Mom, and we'll figure out a way to escape. We'll go back home."

Mom shook her head. "No money. Your father gave everything we had to Michael—the money from the sale of the house, Becca's and your college funds, his 401(k). We didn't have lots, but what we did have is gone."

Andi listened in horror, not to the recitation of the money issues, which she'd figured out long ago, but to the desperate little gasps her mother made as she spoke, small little panting huffs as though even talking was too much effort.

"You though." Mom clasped Andi's hand in both her pale, cold ones. Her nails were cyanotic, as were her lips. "You're strong, honey. You can do it. You can escape."

"We," Andi said, tears now falling. "*We* can escape."

Mom shook her head again and turned to the wall. Two days later she was dead.

Now Andi rested against the back of the closet. She'd escaped, and if she hadn't tried to be so clever and taken what wasn't hers, no one would care. They'd never miss her, and no one would come looking. They'd be glad to be rid of her.

But she had stolen, and she knew they'd never stop looking.

She tensed. She heard voices, faint, but at a time of day when everyone should be out of the building. She leaned out of the closet door so she could hear better.

Someone bumped against the front door, then spoke. She recognized Greg's voice. With a feeling of alarm she understood that he was going to enter the apartment. Surely if she just hunkered down here in the closet, she'd be okay. Why would he look in a closet?

But what if he was showing the place to potential renters? They'd want to check out the closet. Alarm bloomed into pure panic.

Under the bed! She could hide there. No one looked under a bed. She stood, ready to charge across the room and dive into the dust and dirty socks Chaz had left there.

She'd taken one step when the door opened and Greg's clear voice floated down the short hall.

"I know the clothing is all yours, Chaz. Get it and leave."

"What? You don't trust me?" Chaz's whiny voice chilled her.

Greg gave a snort in answer, and a third voice said something. All she caught was the word *bed*, but it was more than enough. The rental company guy was here to reclaim his furniture. He'd take the bed apart, and if she was beneath it, there she'd be, vulnerable and exposed, as helpless as a beached whale, only skinnier.

The bathtub! No one could take that apart. It was attached to the walls.

She moved as quickly and quietly as she could, pushing the remote on the television to kill the picture as she passed. Greg wouldn't hurt her, and he wouldn't let Chaz hurt her, but he'd tell Clooney where she was. He was a straight arrow that way.

And Clooney would try something. She didn't know what, but she knew he would. She'd seen the guns he had, and it scared her to think of him going after Michael or Harl. He might still see himself as a soldier, but he was old now. Michael would hurt him, maybe kill him. Or Harl would. And then where would she be? Back at the compound under house arrest was where—if she wasn't dead too.

The shower curtain, an ugly opaque green with black mold growing halfway up it, had just settled in place when Chaz walked into the bedroom.

"Who closed the curtains?" he called. "It's like nighttime in here." She heard him pulling the cord that opened them and held her breath, waiting for him to say someone had been or was in the place.

"What?" Greg called from the living room. She heard his footfalls as he approached the bedroom.

"Nothing," Chaz mumbled, and she wilted with relief.

She could hear the drawers being wrenched open and slammed shut. She heard the hangers rattle as he pulled his few shirts free. Would someone notice that the television was warm from use? It sat on top of the bureau, and maybe Chaz would feel the heat coming off it as he grabbed the few items he had there.

She shivered and tried to think about something besides her full bladder and her overwhelming fear.

"Okay, you've got it all," Greg said. "Let's go."

"Don't rush me," Chaz answered, all smarmy and snarly. "I've gotta get my stuff in the bathroom."

Andi slapped a hand over her mouth to hold in the cry of distress that

struggled to break free. She stood frozen like a monkey-speak-no-evil cari-
cature as Chaz yanked open the medicine cabinet so hard it slammed back
against the wall. She heard him slide things across the glass shelves as he
pulled them out.

What if he had stuff in the tub? She kept her shampoo and her body
soap and scrubber in one of the corners of the tub at Clooney's. She looked,
and there sat a bottle of Pert on the back corner, the acid green bottle a sharp
contrast to the dingy white of Chaz's never-washed tub. She watched,
trapped, as his skinny hand with the dirty, ragged nails reached for it. She
watched, paralyzed, as he scanned the tub for other stuff and his gaze settled
on her. His eyes widened, then narrowed.

"Well, well, well," he said with soft menace. "Look who we have here."

She put her finger to her lips and looked at him in despair, not expecting a rotten person like him to do as she wanted but unable to resist asking.
Sometimes miracles happened, didn't they? "Please," she mouthed. "Don't
tell."

His nasty grin made her think of a hungry wolf, and she knew she was
the helpless lamb.

He surprised her when he backed away and walked out of the bathroom. "I got it all. Can I go now?"

Her knees gave way.

40

I felt trapped behind the register as I looked at my mother and her husband standing just inside the café door. I held my breath and hoped I was up to whatever happened.

I'd watched too many movies. There was no "Carrie, I can't believe I've finally found you!" There were no eager hugs, no signs of recognition as Mom's gaze brushed over me.

She did look at my sling and say, "Oh my, I bet that hurt."

I managed a nod and the word, "Jerry," but she was already scanning the room for her new best friend, Mary Prudence.

Luke smiled at me. "Breakfast for two," he said. I couldn't get my mind around the idea of his being my stepfather.

Of course he didn't know me. Why would he? I doubted Mom had a picture of me at any age to show him. Even if she did, I looked different. Back then my hair, an unappealing dishwater blond that I hacked at every so often, was pulled straight back in a ponytail. Now it was a glossy highlighted blond cut shoulder length with feathered bangs that made my eyes pop, or so my beautician told me. I had developed a figure, lost the acne and the slouch, but most important, I'd learned confidence I hadn't had as the kid everyone pitied.

I slid off my stool and picked up two menus. As I walked from behind the register counter, I had a chance to study Mom.

Her curls, a permanent I knew, were an artful chestnut, flipped back and up with the visual effect of a facelift. The puffiness that had been her chronic look courtesy of the booze was gone, replaced by a healthy glow.

Her makeup was subtle and expertly applied, a far cry from the runny mascara and heavy eyeliner that used to cake and bleed under her eyes and run down her cheeks. She wore a collared red shirt under a textured royal blue sweater flecked with the red of her blouse. She wore a loose denim jacket over the sweater. Her black jeans looked comfortable, as did her white walking shoes.

In spite of myself I wondered about her story. How had she gone from my drunk and unfit mother to this sleek, sophisticated woman I resented with an antipathy that shook me? What right did she have to this man and his money and position after what she'd put Lindsay and me through?

God, I've got to tell You, seeing her all put together and happy stinks. What would our lives have been like if she'd been this way when we were little? You should have changed her back when we needed her!

Mom was busy waving at Mary P, who was behind the counter. Mary P smiled and waved back, then glanced at me with one eyebrow raised in that you-know-what-you-must-do look.

I ignored her as I led the way to an empty booth.

"Lou will be your server," I told Luke, unable to look at my mother. I gave a little head bob and ran. I slid onto my stool behind the register, nervous sweat wrapping me like a damp beach towel.

Thankfully I didn't have much free time to worry over them. I had customers to seat, customers to take money from, and customers who wanted to know what had happened to my arm. Then Luke was in front of me with their bill.

I forced a smile, took his platinum card, and ran it. Mom walked to Mary P while Luke waited for the machine to do its work. The women talked for a brief moment; then Mom wandered back to the register.

"I'll wait outside," she said to Luke. She gave me a little nod and stepped out into the gusting wind. She lifted her face and let it sweep over her.

I breathed a huge sigh. Safe once more.

"Your baked goods are exceptionally good." Luke slipped his receipt into his wallet.

I smiled for the first time since they'd walked into the café. "My sister's the baker. She is great, isn't she?"

At that moment Lindsay walked out of the kitchen. "We're going to have to drop the minestrone and the blueberry crumb from the lunch menu, Carrie. What with serving breakfast for Andi, I didn't get a chance to make them."

I stared at Lindsay. I hadn't realized it before, but she was the image of a younger Mom, or rather Mom as she would have been if she'd been clean and sober. I didn't look much like Mom. I'd always assumed I looked like my father, whoever he was. I might have thought I was a cuckoo in the nest if I hadn't known Mom'd never have bothered to keep me if she didn't have to. However there was no doubt about parentage with Linds.

Thinking about the uncanny resemblance and not thinking about what I said, I nodded. "Thanks for letting me know, Lindsay. I'll take care of the menus."

She nodded and headed back to her domain. "Oh, by the way, Greg is at the motel with Chaz, the sheriff, and the furniture rental guys. Thought you'd like to know instead of wondering where he was." She grinned. "It's SweetCilla on Twitter. She must spend all day glued to her window, reporting every little thing she sees. She tweets that Chaz looks evil." With a ladylike hoot she disappeared through the kitchen door.

I turned and saw Luke staring after her.

"Lindsay?" he said.

With a sinking feeling, I wanted to deny it, but he'd heard me. I nodded.

He settled his gaze on me, and I thought I never wanted to be a hostile witness at any trial he was participating in. He skewered me with intense brown eyes. "And Carrie. Carrie and Lindsay Carter?"

I stared at him dumbly. With desperate hindsight I thought I should have changed our names when we came to Seaside, but Atlanta had seemed so far away. What were the odds we'd ever be found out?

"She looks just like her mother." Luke jerked his head toward the kitchen. "Does she know?"

Again I wanted to deny understanding what he was talking about, but someone like him would just laugh and start investigating us. In no time he'd discover what he was already convinced of. "Lindsay doesn't know."

"You have to tell her."

I nodded miserably. "I know."

"And you have to tell Sue."

I glanced at Mom through the picture window, her face still raised to the wind. I loved to do the same thing, to feel the power, to be invigorated.

I turned back to Luke. I had no idea what my expression revealed though I suspected panic. "You don't understand," I blurted. "You didn't know her back then."

His expression softened. "Ah, but I did." He stretched out his right hand. "Hi. I'm Luke, and I'm an alcoholic."

He knew her from AA? What was I supposed to say to that? *Hi, I'm Carrie, and I'm bitter? Hi, I'm Carrie, and I'm having a hard time forgiving?* Or, *Hi, I'm Carrie, and I resent that she looks so good?*

What I said was, "Don't tell her. Please."

"It's not my place. That honor is yours."

Honor. Now there was a laugh.

"Honor your father and your mother."

The trouble with memorizing Scripture was that the verses came back to bite you at the most inopportune times.

"You have no idea how she mourns for you two." Luke piled on the guilt. "I can't tell you the number of nights I've held her as she's cried over the mess she made of her time with you."

What about the nights I quaked with fear and held Lindsay while my little sister cried herself to sleep? What about the nights I was sure some man was going to break through the feeble barricades to my bedroom and I'd have to use my knife? What about the horror of the night I'd actually knifed Bob?

Luke laughed without mirth. "I understand her grief because I lost my family before I sobered up. At least I get to see my kids every so often and can try to make them forget the father who made their lives a living hell for so many years."

I had stepsiblings. What a strange thought. How many? Male? Female? And would they like to share horror stories?

He skewered me with another look, making me itch all over. "You know what you need to do."

And he left.

41

Harl pulled open the door to Carrie's Café. Carrie was behind the register.

"Hello," she said with a smile. "Counter or booth?"

"A booth." He glanced at the glass bakery shelves. "And I'll have two eggs over easy and one of those sticky buns grilled."

"Lou will be your server." Carrie indicated her right arm in its cast. "I'm not doing much today."

"Whoa. What happened?"

"A jetty tripped me, and I broke my wrist."

He shook his head, trying to look as if he cared. "Hope it's better soon."

He slid into the booth and, sure enough, some woman named Lou came to take his order. Where was the kid? She had worked the booths the other times he'd been in. He'd enjoyed seeing her panic when she spotted him.

"Where's the girl who usually works here?" he asked Lou. "Is it her day off or something?"

"You mean Andi?" Lou gave him a tired smile. "She didn't come in today."

He nodded as Lou left to turn in his order. He had expected to find the kid here. It was time to stop tormenting her and get down to business, to corner her or follow her or do whatever was necessary to get her to tell him what he wanted to know.

She was so different from her sister. Becca was compliance personified. She bought Mike's line completely, believed in him absolutely.

Harl laughed to himself. If she only knew.

Not that he'd ever enlighten her. He liked her fine just the way she was. She accepted that her job in life was to make him happy, and so she did everything she could to be the perfect little wife. Sometimes her attentions were a bit much, but with his three other wives to temper her time with him, it wasn't all that bad.

But Andi. She was a chronic headache. She fought the system with everything in her, stirring up constant trouble in the girls' dorm with her questions and complaints. Even her sessions with Marty, Mike's first wife, didn't stop her. If anything they agitated her further. The one place she didn't cause trouble was the infirmary, where she proved herself a more-than-competent nurse.

If she weren't such a thorn in his side, he might appreciate her grit. As it was, he'd be happy to send her to perdition. He and Mike used to laugh at the plight of whoever ended up being her husband. Some poor guy had escaped a fate worse than death when the kid ran away.

But if he was right, she was a greater danger to them now than when she'd been at the compound. They had defanged Jason permanently, but she was out there, a loose cannon if ever there was one.

It was all because she'd been best friends with Jennie.

"Hello. Mind if I join you?"

Harl looked up to see a scarecrow of a guy sliding into the booth across from him without waiting for an invitation. Everything about him from his complexion to his twitches screamed druggie.

"I been looking for you," the guy said.

"You've been looking for me?" What could this putz want with him?

"I seen you in here before."

Harl shrugged. "They have good food."

Scarecrow Guy rolled his eyes at that disclaimer. "I seen you watching the girl."

Harl went still. How could that be? He'd been so careful!

"Learned all about you and your boss online."

How did the Scarecrow know about his connection to Michael and The Pathway? No one else in town did. He frowned. Did they? Harl made himself shrug again as if he hadn't just felt a bolt of adrenaline flash through his system. "You and millions of others."

"I got lots of free time, and I been using it watching you lots."

Scarecrow Guy looked proud of his own cleverness. Harl bit back a sneer. People who so obviously thought themselves clever usually weren't.

Even Mike.

"Why would you watch me?" Harl asked. "I'm just an ordinary businessman."

"Right." Scarecrow Guy smirked. "You and the archangel."

Harl said nothing. He just stared at Scarecrow Guy as if he were something malodorous underfoot. As Harl had suspected, Scarecrow Guy couldn't stand being looked down on. He snapped back with a zinger Harl didn't see coming.

"You know that empty houseboat moored next to your miniyacht?" Scarecrow Guy smirked again. "Well, it isn't empty after all. I needed a place to stay quick-like, and I thought, *Why not the best?* After all, I deserve it, right? Off-season, the best is one of them fancy unused boats."

The hair on the back of Harl's neck rose. The Scarecrow had not only hidden mere feet away, he'd done so without either Mike or him realizing it. They survived by foreseeing and forestalling any dangers. And they'd missed a threat right under their noses.

What had the druggie seen? More to the point, what had he heard?

Harl tried to look as if a trapdoor hadn't just opened beneath him. "So you're living there without permission? The cops would find that very interesting."

Scarecrow Guy didn't so much as blink. "I don't think so."

"And why not?"

"Because, like I said, I seen you watching that girl. Because I got good hearing. And because I been connecting the dots I bet others don't even know are out there to be connected." He grinned and the yellow, rotten teeth he revealed made Harl fight the impulse to gag.

"What dots?"

Lou's arrival with Harl's sticky bun and eggs prevented Scarecrow Guy from answering.

"Hey, that smells good." Scarecrow Guy looked at Lou. "I'll have one of them sticky buns, and you can put it on his bill." He jerked a thumb at Harl.

Lou looked at Harl, and he gave a little nod. No sense riling the guy until he learned all that the guy knew. As soon as Lou left, the Scarecrow began talking again.

"You know that Jason you killed?"

What did he just say? Harl forced himself to show no reaction.

"You don't have to play dumb with me." Again the yellow teeth. "At that party last weekend, I heard Jason talking to the girl who works here, that Andi, the one you been watching."

"They must be letting anyone into parties these days," Harl said in an attempt at redirection.

Scarecrow Guy snorted. "They like me and my product. But like I was saying, I heard Andi telling him that she had something you wanted and wanted badly. I heard them plan to meet to talk about what to do with it."

Harl felt his sticky bun turn from ambrosia to alkali burning his stomach lining.

Scarecrow Guy looked very smug. "Didn't know she had it, did you? Or didn't know for sure."

Harl sucked in a deep breath and took another bite of his bun despite the fact that it had lost all its taste. He washed it down with a casual mouthful of coffee.

"And I saw you 'help' Jason when he left the party." Scarecrow Guy's grin was sly. "Drove off with him in his car, you did. Next thing you know, he's missing, then dead. Murdered, the way I heard it."

Never had Harl felt such an urge to kill, not even when he'd incinerated his father. No one this stupid deserved to live.

"Now you want the kid." The Scarecrow rested both arms on the table and leaned way too close, invading Harl's personal space with his halitosis and body odor. "I know where she is."

42

I sat with my chin in my good hand, elbow on the register counter as I waited for the last few customers to leave the café after lunch. It had been a long day, not because the work was hard but because my wrist hurt big time, my heart felt bruised, and I had way too much time to think.

My mother was in Seaside. I couldn't get over the coincidence of her coming to the café. Of course I knew that with the Lord there was no such thing as coincidence. He knew the end from the beginning, and He knew about her trek from Georgia to New Jersey.

I hope You don't think You're doing me a favor, Lord.

Actually I do. His voice was quiet but implacable, even though it wasn't a voice so much as an impression. The impression continued to talk to me.

Since you're big on it being or not being "your time," remember that there's a time to hate and a time to heal.

I sighed. *I get it. It's time to heal. I have to talk to her. I know it.*

But I did not want to face the feelings writhing like a colony of poisonous snakes in my heart. On the other hand, I knew if I didn't, I would become ever more spiritually and emotionally deformed.

You don't ask much, do You?

I had to talk to Lindsay before she heard about Mom's presence from Mary P or, heaven forbid, Mom herself. Linds had to have the opportunity to make her own peace with Mom, something I suspected she would have done years ago if she hadn't thought I'd view it as disloyalty and a knife in the back—which I was ashamed to admit I would have. She should never have to choose between me and her conscience or me and Mom. Everybody lost that way.

And right up there with the problem of Mom was Greg. He hadn't contacted me since Wednesday night, not even to ask how the surgery on my wrist went. For all he knew, I could have died on the table.

Idiot that I was, all day I'd looked up with hope every time someone came into the café. I wanted to see him with such desperation, the disappointment felt like one of the huge jetty rocks pressing on my chest, making it difficult to breathe. He was the only one I could talk to about the quandary of Mom. He already knew how terrible I was, so I couldn't make myself look worse.

So where was he?

The door opened, and there he was, tall and handsome.

And remote. No smile. My happy Snoopy dance became an old lady shuffle.

"How are you feeling?" he asked.

I looked at my wrist in its split cast and shrugged.

"Does it hurt much?"

"As a matter of fact, it does. A lot. It hurt less before the surgery."

"I'm sorry about that."

I shrugged. "That's what pain meds are for."

"Right." He looked around the café. "Did Andi show today?"

I shook my head. *Come closer. Tell me you missed me.*

"Mmm. She has me worried. Your mother?"

"She was here."

"You talk to her?"

"No, but her husband told me he's an alcoholic. They met at AA."

He nodded. "Interesting."

It was way more than interesting. It was mind-boggling.

"She doing well?" He tipped his head toward Lou.

"Very. She started yesterday morning. It's a good thing she's here, what with Andi not showing and me out of commission."

"She any good?"

Why were we talking about Lou when I felt the distance between us growing wider by the moment? "She knows what she's doing. Has good rapport with the customers. Even puts their beverages over their knives instead of at the edge of the booth."

He gave an absent half smile. "That's important, huh?"

"That's where beverages go at a properly set table." I sounded like a prim old maid.

He thought for a minute. "Yep, that's where I remember Mom and Ginny putting drinks."

He fell silent, watching Lou bid farewell to her last customers.

As the man handed me their bill, Greg went to the counter and got a cup of coffee to go. I ran the man's card and handed him the slip to sign. As he and his wife left, Greg walked up and handed me cash for the coffee. I made change, and he turned toward the door.

I grabbed his arm to hold him there. I thought I had diagnosed his problem, and it wasn't the "I love you." "It's just a broken wrist, Greg. No big deal."

He glanced at me a second, then looked away. He didn't deny knowing what I meant. In a strained voice he said, "You deserve someone who's not going to lose his nerve at the first sign of trouble."

"You didn't panic."

He didn't believe me. "As good as. Oh, I might not have run off screaming, but I was doing it inside."

"Then it's all the more impressive that you stayed with me. A sign of strength."

He brushed my comment away as he might brush a gnat. "Out there there's some nice guy who is whole and healthy, perfect for you."

I shook my head. "It doesn't work that way, Greg. I'm the one who gets to choose who's perfect for me, not you. And I choose you."

With a feeling of despair, I could see I wasn't making a dent in the wall he was building between us and around himself. I understood being paralyzed by emotions. I understood fighting against doing what needed to be done, choosing the expedient way even if it wasn't the right or the best. I'd been doing it for seventeen years. I was still doing it.

"It wasn't my fall that upset you, you know. Or my getting hurt." I hoped I didn't sound as desperate as I felt. It would be nice to keep at least a shred of pride. It might be the only thing keeping me warm at night for the rest of my life. "It was the lights and the milling people, the ambulance and fire truck, the shouted orders and the static, all the things that must have been present the day Ginny and the kids died."

He flinched, but I wasn't going to cater to his PTSD-like behavior. Acknowledge it, yes. Respect it, yes. Yield to it, no. The price was too steep.

Lord, hit him upside the head for me, please! "Tell me I'm wrong."

He said nothing for a few seconds.

"See? You can't because I'm right."

He pulled his arm free. "You're wrong," he mumbled and was gone.

43

Greg took a seat on a boardwalk bench facing the water, today serene with gently cresting waves and a receding tide. He waited for it to soothe his insides, which felt as turbulent and storm tossed as the wild waves of the other night as they slammed themselves against the jetty. Against Carrie.

He ran a hand through his hair. He'd barely slept the last two nights, and his thoughts were fuzzy as a result.

He'd been okay at first. Carrie was right about that. Then came the flashing lights, the static-y radios, the many uniforms, the solicitous emergency workers. And he'd folded. All he'd wanted to do was run.

But she was wrong about the reason. It wasn't the noise and commotion. It was because he loved her.

Which scared him most of all. He didn't want to love again. He'd thought he did, but he didn't. The potential cost was simply too high.

Somehow Carrie thought the fact that he hadn't run was something to be lauded, but he'd been a cop, a man who ran toward trouble, not away from it. He should have been able to care for her, be there for her when she needed him most. Instead he'd curled into himself like an injured animal. He hadn't even called her yesterday to see how she'd made out in surgery. He should have taken her flowers, sat with her, prayed with her.

At least he could give himself full marks for praying *for* her. But what good did that do when she needed what someone had called "Jesus with skin on."

God, what is wrong with me? Most people would consider being able to love again a wonderful gift. I should never have let myself fall for her. All I've brought her—and myself—is pain. She doesn't deserve a man like me.

Today he'd wanted to see her, to be with her with a physical ache. Because she deserved better, he made himself a bowl of cereal at home rather than go to the café. It was amazing how lonely it was sitting at the table by himself with only the ghosts of his former family to keep him company.

"Ginny," he'd muttered at one point, "I thought for a while there I'd found a new family." He sighed. "I should have known better."

He could imagine his late wife, hands on her hips, scowl on her face. "Get a grip, Greg. Wallowing isn't becoming."

At lunch he went to Burger King and got a Whopper that he couldn't eat. At least Ginny didn't scold him there. She'd never liked public scenes. When he got back in the car, he lowered the windows to release the heat that had built up from the sun and just sat.

Finally at two thirty, unable to resist any longer, he drove to Carrie's. He had to see her, see for himself that she was fine. And he had to tell her he'd changed his mind about them as a couple. He had to tell her to look for a better man, one who'd always be there for her. He was shriveling inside at the thought, but it was the right thing to do. He didn't let himself think about what he'd do tomorrow when he had no excuse to see her.

He'd parked across the street from the café, and as soon as he saw her through the front window, working the cash register, he calmed.

"She looks pale."

Greg turned and saw Cilla sitting in her chair beside his car. He nodded. "She does. She should be in bed."

"Carrie? Are you kidding? She's a doer. Staying in bed would drive her crazy."

Too true. He watched her smile at a customer as she took his money. He must have asked about her wrist because she looked at it and spoke.

"She tells them a jetty got her." Cilla smiled. "She makes it sound like a great time was had by all."

"Sounds just like her," Greg managed. And he became all the more certain that someone that brave deserved more than him.

With a wave Cilla rolled off, and Greg crossed to the café. Carrie looked up when he entered and smiled with such hope and pleasure when she saw him that it made his step falter.

He should smile back, tell her how brave she was, how strong she was, how glad he was to see her and to see her well, but did he? Not him. He pokered up, becoming all frosty and withdrawn. It was the only way he could manage what he had to say. His spirit constricted with guilt when her face fell at his cool behavior. She struggled to act naturally, but she didn't quite succeed.

Now sitting on the boardwalk bench, his stomach spit out a whole new batch of acid as he thought of how she had laid her hand on his arm and begged. Carrie, strong independent Carrie, pleading with him. For him. And what had he done? He'd pulled back again.

The crazy part was that he didn't want to push her away. He wanted to take her in his arms and tell her she was his and he was hers. He wanted to tell her he'd be there for her always, whatever the circumstances.

But he was afraid he couldn't keep that promise. She deserved a man who could. This choice he was making was for her good. The cramp in his gut was but one proof that it wasn't for his benefit.

"There's a time to every purpose under heaven."

Right. And this was the time for saying good-bye. He thought of another line in that passage that said there was a time to mourn and a time to dance. A hiccup of protest caught in his throat.

Lord, haven't I spent enough time mourning?

He wanted to dance, to take a chance and live again. Love again.

Another thought zapped through him. While he didn't know if he'd always be able to be what Carrie needed, he didn't know he wouldn't either. If he looked at this situation rationally instead of emotionally, did any man know if he'd be able to be all his woman needed or even most of what she needed? Of course not.

He hadn't been everything Ginny needed any more than she'd been everything he needed. No man or woman could fill all the holes in another's life, no matter how deep their love. Two sinners, fragile and flawed, could not make a perfect relationship. They could make life deeper and richer for each other, but that was it. It was stupidity to think otherwise.

Once, when he was fifteen, to his surprise and adolescent embarrassment, his father had grabbed his mother in a romantic clinch, and after a great smacker said, "Greg, find a woman who makes you feel more alive. She won't make life perfect, but she'll make it infinitely more interesting." He'd swatted Mom on the bottom, and she'd grinned at him. "And then love her with all that's in you."

One thing was for certain: Carrie made his life more vibrant, more alive. In fact she had brought him back from the dead. She was the woman he needed and wanted. She was smart and beautiful, and she had a heart for the Lord. She'd gone through her own personal fire and come out pure gold.

And he loved her. He'd never expected to feel this way again, to experience that bolt of joy when he saw her, that frisson of desire when he kissed her. He'd thought that life would always be sterile and lonely at worst, filled with mere companionship at best.

"I think I'm the one who gets to choose who's perfect for me. And I choose you."

No more than the sky could tell the sea to go away could he tell Carrie he didn't want her, especially when, miracle of miracles, she chose him.

He didn't hear any Ginny voices or find any encoded messages, but he knew what he had to do. He had to go back and tell her how he felt. He had to ask her forgiveness for the pain he'd caused. He would hold her and tell her how sorry he was about her wrist and his withdrawal and her mother coming, and oh, yeah, he loved her so much it hurt.

"I can't promise I'll always be your knight in shining armor," he'd say. "But I'll try. And I can promise you that I will always love you."

Please God, that would be enough.

He felt his blood fizz in anticipation and his spirits rise like a great colored balloon soaring into the sky. He stood, turned to go, and there she was.

44

Soon after Greg left the café, I went upstairs, my spirits dragging. I couldn't tell which hurt more, my wrist or my heart. Well, I might not be able to do much about the heart, at least in the short term, but I could do something about the wrist. I slugged down an oxycodone, lay on the couch, and waited for it to take effect.

I woke up about forty-five minutes later, edgy and restless, but at least the wrist wasn't throbbing as much.

Lindsay sat across the room in her favorite chair, reading her latest mystery novel. "How you feeling?"

I shrugged as I sat up. "Blurry."

She nodded. "Naps and pain pills will do that."

I stood and glanced out the window. The sun was still shining, and a brisk ocean breeze might be just what I needed to whisk the cobwebs from my head. "I think I'll take a walk."

Lindsay laid her book aside. "I'll come with you."

In spite of my heavy heart, I smiled at my sister. She was a wonder—true-blue, smart, gifted, and beautiful—even if she did look just like our mother.

"I think I'd like to go alone." I wasn't up to conversation, even with one of my favorite people in the world. "Do you mind?"

Her smile was sweet. "Not at all. I was just trying to be a good sister. I'd rather not leave my book. I'm about to find out who the bad guy is, and the hero and heroine are about to declare their undying love."

At the thought of undying love, I thought of "to everything there is a season" and Clooney's watch lying on my bureau. And I thought of "Wait for the LORD; be strong, and let your heart take courage; wait for the LORD!"

I went to the closet, grabbed my fleece jacket, pulled it over my head, and thrust my good arm in a sleeve. I walked slowly down the street. I passed Cilla's house, a three-story clapboard place where she rented the first and third floors and lived on the second.

"The ground floor'd be easier with my scooter," she told me one day at the café, "but if there's a hurricane or a nor'easter, the second floor is drier."

I thought of the lovely e-card she'd sent me yesterday, all beautiful flowers being painted by a brush that moved across the screen with no visible hand to guide it. Ah, the wonders of technology.

"Posted about you on Twitter," she wrote on the card. "You've got lots of people praying for you."

I looked up at her front window and waved. I didn't know if she was looking out or not, but it felt friendly to do so. For all I knew, she'd post about me again.

I walked by the Sand and Sea and was surprised to see that the hole Chaz had made was still boarded over with the plywood Greg and I had bought. So much had happened this week that our trip to Home Depot seemed ages ago rather than just four days. I wondered how soon someone was coming to make the repairs and if the new owners were giving Greg a hard time over the delay. Not that it was his fault, but did they realize it wasn't?

I trudged up the ramp to the boardwalk. It seemed extra steep, a sign of how depleted I was after my surgery. Never having had anesthesia before, I hadn't realized how it sapped you, even when the surgery wasn't serious. I mean, a broken wrist. What's that in comparison to cancer surgery or heart surgery or something truly life threatening? But there were still aftereffects, even for not-ill me.

Pushing myself became worth it when the ocean came into view, look-ing placid and peaceful. The westering sun burnished the foam-flocked waves with a touch of gold, and the sandpipers on their little legs were run-ning in and out of the water's edge as if they feared getting their belly feath-ers wet.

A man rose from a nearby bench, drawing my eye. For an instant I couldn't move, couldn't even draw a breath. His delighted smile when he saw me confused me. Just over an hour ago he'd rejected me and run.

He lifted a hand and beckoned. "Come here, Carrie." He reached to me, palm up, welcoming. "I need to talk to you."

Again? How much more pain did I feel like inflicting on myself today? If I turned and walked away, it would be no less than he deserved. If I went to him, it might prove to be the emotional equivalent of taking up a razor blade and cutting myself for the fun of watching the blood flow.

"Please," he said.

I took a deep breath and studied him. The glacial chill that had given me emotional frostbite seemed gone from his manner, and he appeared re-laxed, more like the old Greg. The Greg I had fallen in love with.

I slid onto the end of his bench and waited, my good hand clenched, my knuckles white. My heart thundered in my ears so loudly it didn't matter what he said. I wouldn't be able to hear it.

He caught my hand, rubbing along the knuckles until my fist opened. Then he laced our fingers. I looked at him and tried to squash the hope that insisted on stirring to life.

Be strong, Carrie. Be realistic. Hope can be so hurtful when it doesn't pan out.

"Greg, I can't deal with another go-round of attention, then withdrawal. I don't have the emotional strength. Weak heart, you know?" I managed a small half smile.

He made a noise of regret deep in his throat and slid his arm around my shoulders, pulling me against his side. I ought to push away, but he felt warm and comforting and *right*. We sat there in silence for a few minutes, both studying Tennyson's wrinkled sea with a calm we didn't feel, or at least I didn't.

"I'm an idiot," he finally said. "Can you live with that?"

I frowned at a gull flying by. What did that mean? Not the idiot part. I understood that very well and even agreed. Only an idiot would throw away what had begun between us. It was the can-you-live-with-it part that threw me. Did he mean live with it as in he and I living together as in marriage? Or was I reading my heart's yearning into his words that in actuality meant nothing more than he was going to be hanging around Carrie's and could I put up with him as a customer?

Because I didn't know what he meant, I said nothing.

He put a hand under my chin and turned my face to his. "I'm sorry, Carrie. I was wrong."

I studied his expression and saw only sincerity, but I was still afraid to believe. I stomped on my burgeoning hope, Army boots crushing a grape. "For what? About what? You mean for not calling to see how I was after my surgery?"

His face twisted and he nodded.

"That hurt a lot." I blinked against tears as I remembered the loneliness, the bewilderment.

He dropped his forehead to mine. "I'm so sorry," he whispered.

His obvious regret made me feel a little better, a little more hopeful, but I sniffed dramatically. "Or do you mean for telling me you weren't interested in me after all? 'You deserve better.'" I snorted. "Talk about a bad breakup line."

"You do deserve better."

But I didn't want better, so I pushed. "I should forget the heated looks and the amazing kisses? It was all a sham?"

"That's just the thing." He sounded almost desperate. "It wasn't a sham. It was as real as anything has ever been in my life."

I shrugged and stared at the sandpipers. Advance, retreat. Advance, retreat. I would not accept a sandpiper kind of love. I would not, could not settle. "Right. And guys brush their girls off every day."

He grabbed me by the shoulders. "But not girls they love."

I went still all over. Even my pulse paused as I took in the monumental thing he'd just said. "You love me?" I whispered. Dared I believe him?

"With all my heart."

He gave me a soft kiss, little more than a brushing of lips, but I went soft and gooey inside, not that I was ready to let him know. It wouldn't hurt him to squirm a bit after the agony he'd put me through. I was not a pushover, never would be, and he needed to know that.

Besides, petty as it was of me, I liked having the power for a change.

He leaned back and looked me in the eye. "I'm a very flawed man, Carrie."

Like this was a secret. "An idiot," I agreed solemnly, quoting his own word.

He looked a bit grumpy. "You don't have to agree."

"Why not, if you're right?"

His frown intensified as I looked blandly back. I think he must have expected a quick capitulation on my part with my immediate forgiveness and my arms thrown around his neck as I kissed him in gratitude that he'd taken me back. After all, my hurt had been obvious.

I just continued to look at him.

"What do you want me to say? That I was an idiot to think I could walk away from you? I already said that."

"Feel free to repeat," I said primly. Then I ruined my cool stance by touching a finger to the frown lines in his forehead and smoothing them away.

His eyes narrowed. "You're playing me. Making me sweat."

I tried to look innocent. "Me?"

"You." He swallowed me in a great hug.

I gave a yelp. "My arm!"

He let go so fast I almost lost my balance. His face had gone pale. "I'm so sorry! Did I hurt you a lot?"

I lowered the zipper on my jacket and looked inside as if I expected my arm to have disappeared. Everything looked fine inside the sling, and I zipped up again. "I'll be fine," I said, as brave as a pioneer woman about to have her baby on the Oregon Trail.

He looked at me as if he wasn't certain whether I was still playing him. He must have decided I was because he said, "Can I expect you to make me get on my metaphorical knees every time we have an argument?"

"Yes, if you ever try to throw me over again." I was serious now, and he was smart enough to realize it.

"Never again, Carrie. I can't promise I'll always be the man you want me to be, but I can promise I'll always try."

I put my hand against his cheek and looked right into his eyes. "I'm holding you to it, champ."

His shoulders relaxed and he grinned.

"A time for every season," I said.

"A time to dance."

"A time to laugh."

We sat cuddled close and watched the sun disappear.

45

The ringing of Greg's cell phone was an unwelcome intrusion into our private rosy world. I straightened to give him room to move and immediately missed the warmth of his embrace.

As he pulled his phone off his waist, he glanced at the caller ID readout. He made an uh-oh face, looked at his watch, and rolled his eyes. He slid the phone open.

"Hey, Josh," he said with a marked lack of enthusiasm.

Josh, his boss, or I should say former boss since Josh's properties were now owned by Fred Durning's people.

"Right, dinner." Greg looked at me with regret. "I'm on my way. Sorry for being so late. I-I got held up."

Yes, he did. I grinned at him and he grinned back.

He stood. "I've got to go, babe. Duty calls. Our final meeting. It's been on the calendar for a while."

"Go," I said, though I wanted him to stay.

"I'll stop at your place when I'm finished." He was already backing away, preparing to run.

"Don't forget." I blew him a kiss.

He paused, gave a heart-stopping smile, and came back to me in a rush. He drew me close, taking care not to squish my bad arm, and kissed me thoroughly. "I could never forget."

His voice, all hoarse and husky, gave me the shivers in a really good way. As I watched him jog down the ramp, I gave myself a one-armed hug.

Thank You, Lord! It was definitely my time. My wrist might be starting to throb again, but my heart was singing.

It had gotten almost full dark while we sat, but with the boardwalk's streetlights, I hadn't realized just how dark until I started down the ramp. Windows up and down the street threw golden ribbons of light into the night. I glanced at the Sand and Sea as I passed and saw Chaz's unit was the only one where the windows were black.

A sliver of light caught my eye. I squinted, thinking I couldn't be seeing what I saw. The slice of dull illumination gleamed at the side edge of one of the plywood sheets tacked over the hole in the building. Granted, it wasn't very bright compared to the light streaming from the occupied units, but it was still light where there should be none.

I glanced again at the windows of Chaz's unit. No light. Of course that could be because they were covered by blinds or shades or curtains, though I doubted Chaz had had something as sophisticated as window treatments. Of course the renters before him might have left some.

I crossed the parking lot to the boarded-up wall. I hadn't been mistaken. Light seeped out along the vertical edge of the horizontal sheet of plywood. I touched the wood and swallowed a little gulp of surprise as it moved under my hand.

How could that be? Greg and I had nailed the sheets, both sheets, firmly in place. One panel was on the vertical and the other horizontal because of the configuration of the hole. I pushed on the vertical sheet, but it remained just as snug as it should.

I stared at the horizontal sheet. There was no way the nails Greg had pounded into place could have popped out on their own. As I felt along the edge, sure enough, all the nails were missing. If it were light enough to see the ground, I'd probably see them lying there.

I remembered asking Greg about someone prying the plywood loose to gain access to the apartment. I smirked as I remembered he'd said there was no reason for someone to want to get into a place where there was nothing worth taking.

But what if you didn't want to take? What if you just wanted to hide? What if you were a scared, confused, and lonely sixteen-year-old?

I pushed at the plywood with my good hand, attempting to slide it sideways, wishing for a healthy second hand. I tried to be quiet, but there was a grinding, scrunching sound as one sheet slid with reluctance behind the other.

Finally I had an opening I could squeeze through sideways. With my good hand, I protected my throbbing wrist, still snug in my jacket. When I got inside, I turned back to the plywood sheet and began the tedious job of sliding it back in place. I wrapped my fingers around the edge and pulled. Since I couldn't get much purchase on the board, my hand kept slipping. If I could reach the piece's far side, I could wrap my hand over the edge and pull toward me, so much easier, but no such luck. That area was hidden between the vertical sheet and the outside of the building.

The flickering illumination inside the apartment, which I thought came from the bedroom or the bathroom, disappeared, and I was left standing in complete darkness.

Lord, I sure hope I'm right about who's in here.

"Andi," I called softly as I tugged on the plywood. "Andi, it's me. Don't be afraid."

I felt the air move behind me, heard the faintest whisper of cloth rubbing on cloth. The kitchen light flicked on, and there stood Andi, a hammer in her raised hand.

"Carrie?" It was a whisper of disbelief. She lowered her arm, and the hammer dangled against her leg.

"Yep. It's me. No need for a weapon."

She looked at the hammer. "I stole it from Clooney and used it to pry the board loose." She gestured toward the opening. "I had to wait to break in until it was late enough to be sure Cyber Cilla was in bed, or she'd have me all over Twitter."

True enough. "What did you do while you waited for night? I mean you left the café around ten."

"I went to the little store near our house and bought some food because I didn't know how long I'd have to hide. Then I hid behind the Dumpster at the store until it was safe to come here."

My heart ached to think of her crouching there, alone, terrified. "You should have told me you were so afraid of Bill. I'd have helped you. Greg would have helped you, and your uncle certainly would have."

"I'm not afraid of Bill." She looked at me as if I were slow-witted. "I keep telling you he's okay."

I frowned. "But your puzzle. Bill killed Jase."

"Not Bill. B-I-L, texting shorthand for brother-in-law. My brother-in-law killed Jase."

Her brother-in-law? How did he get involved in this puzzle?

"And he killed someone before?"

"Or at least helped with the cleanup."

I heard one hiccup, another, and Andi's face collapsed as she started to cry. "I'm s-so s-scared."

I reached for the weeping girl. "Come here, honey."

She stumbled toward me, the hammer falling to the floor with a thud. We met in a clumsy hug, her whole body shaking as she wept. Her hard embrace pressed against my wrist, and pain shot up my arm. An involuntary gasp slipped out before I could swallow it.

She pulled back. "What's wrong?"

"I broke my wrist."

"Oh, Carrie! How? When? I'm away for two days and look what happens! Oh, and I hurt you when I squeezed, didn't I? I can't do anything right." More tears.

I pulled her back into a hug, taking care she was touching the left side of my body. "Shh. I just slipped on a jetty. I'm okay." If I didn't count the throbbing pain that brought tears to my eyes. "At least now that I've found you I am. Do you have any idea how upset we've been?"

She wrapped her arms around my waist and held on. "I c-couldn't put you at risk."

Her words made no sense. "What do you mean, at risk?"

"I can't tell you." Another shuddering sob and a moment or two of silence. Then she sniffed and pulled away.

"Greg was here today." She rearranged the sweatshirt she wore over her Carrie's Café shirt. "He came with Chaz, the constable, and the rental company guy."

"And they didn't find you?"

She shook her head. "I hid in the tub behind the shower curtain."

"Clever girl."

"Chaz saw me. That's why I had the hammer. I thought you were him." She hugged herself. "I don't like him. He's mean. Slimy."

I silently agreed. There was something about the guy. When he'd come into the café today and talked with Fred, there had been something very sneaky about his whole demeanor.

"Shush, honey." I patted Andi's back. "It'll be all right. Whatever the problem is, we can work it out."

"But they might hurt him like they did Jase." Her voice shook. "Or maybe me!"

I took her hand and pulled her down to sit on the kitchen floor, leaning back against a cabinet. The apartment might be pretty much empty of furniture, but there was grit and dust galore. I reached beneath my seat and pulled out a piece of wallboard. I flipped it across the room.

Andi shivered, and I thought about her hiding in this sad-looking unit. I sat shoulder to shoulder with her, taking her painfully cold hand in my good one. She clutched at me.

"Who will they hurt, Andi? And who are they?"

"Clooney! They might kill him!"

I blinked. "Someone's going to kill Clooney?"

"And it'll be all my fault!"

"But why? Who?"

"Harl. And Michael."

Clearly I was supposed to know who these men were. "I don't—"

"Sure you do. Michael the Archangel. And my brother-in-law."

"Michael the Archangel? From The Pathway?" I might have some serious questions about the man and his cult, but I'd never thought of him as a murderer.

She nodded. "And my brother-in-law."

"I know who Michael is, but I don't know—"

"Sure you do. He comes into the café."

"He does?"

"He keeps meeting with Greg."

I frowned. "That's Fred Durning. He's buying the properties Greg manages. Or he represents the people who are."

"That's Harl. He's married to my sister, Becca. He's Michael's right hand. He's the one who got my father so mixed up in bad stuff."

"Fred is your brother-in-law Harl?"

She nodded. "They've got scams going all the time. Whenever dirty work needs to be done, Harl sees that it's done, and he uses my father lots of times. He used to use Jase too."

"What do you mean, scams?"

"I don't know exactly. I tried to spy, but they watched me all the time. I just know they are evil. They lie all the time."

"Like?"

"Like Michael and Harl are supposed to be at the retreat house for personal meditation, but I'd see Harl leave the compound with Dad or Jase. Once I saw him leave with some tall guy with short dark hair." She looked around like she expected to see someone lurking in the shadows right now. "I don't know where they went or what they did, but I know it's bad."

"You *think* it's bad."

She shook her head. "I know. Just like I know Harl's the one who murdered Jase."

"You can't know that."

"I do." Her voice was fierce. "For two reasons. One, Harl's here in Seaside. He came after Jase. Otherwise why would he be here?"

"He oversaw buying this apartment building and others."

"But he's supposed to be living an austere life for God's glory in Arizona. And believe me, if Harl is buying, it's because Michael told him to."

What she was saying was hard to believe, but her reasoning seemed sound. "I suppose the money they use for their scams is from gifts given by followers."

"My father gave them all his money. Everyone who lives there does. And people send money in response to his YouTube stuff."

I was always amazed at how gullible people were. "But, Andi, there's a huge difference between financial indiscretion and murder."

Her chin got that stubborn look, and her voice shook with both anger and sorrow. "I saw what they did to Jennie."

"Who's Jennie?"

"She was my best friend. Michael was forcing her to marry some old guy, and she wanted to marry Jase. I snuck into Michael's headquarters the night of the initiation to try to help her escape somehow."

"What's the initiation?"

"That's when Michael sleeps with all the brides the night before the wedding."

My skin crawled. "And people go along with that vile practice?"

"That's my reaction too!" She seemed excited that I understood.

"So Jennie?" I said to bring her back on topic.

"Right. So there I was, in headquarters skulking around, looking for Jennie. I didn't have a plan. I just wanted to get her out of there, or if worse came to worst, hold her while she cried afterward. Instead I stumbled into the video room and saw Harl and Michael set up the phony scene of her death."

"Jennie's dead?" I wasn't all that surprised.

"And Michael killed her! It's on the DVD. I didn't know that when I grabbed it and ran, but it's all there."

"You have a disc showing Michael committing murder?" I was appalled at the danger this girl had put herself in, if even a fraction of what she said was true. "What did you do with it?"

"At first I hid it in the infirmary until I could escape. When the little kids got sick and had to go to the hospital, I saw my chance. I taped the disc in its jewel case to my stomach and grabbed a sick kid."

I listened, amazed, to the story of the bikers who had rescued her. "How did Michael and Harl know you were the one who took the disc?"

"They didn't. I think they thought it was Jase because he left right after Jennie was buried. He tried to fake his death with a lame auto accident. But they found him. I can't prove they killed him, but I know."

"And that's why you think he was killed? Because they thought he had the DVD?"

"I *know* that's why he was killed." Her stomach growled, and she dropped her hand as if to muffle it. "And that's why they'll kill me if they find me. And they might hurt Clooney if they thought he could tell them where I was."

"You don't think he can take care of himself?"

"He's old, Carrie. He'll try to defend me, and they'll get him."

Somehow I didn't think he'd appreciate being consigned to the trash heap because he wasn't thirty anymore.

Andi's stomach growled again. Murders and stolen evidence weren't my forte, but food was. "When was the last time you ate?"

"I finished my last candy bar last night."

I climbed to my feet and held out a hand to her, pulling her up. "Come on. We'll go to the café and I'll make you a sandwich and heat some of Lindsay's soup. And we'll call the police."

Her stomach growled approval as she stood and brushed the grit off her seat.

"What did you do with the disc after you left the compound?"

"I watched it."

Not what I meant, but obviously what had affected her deeply. She clutched my hand.

"It shows Michael kill Jennie and Harl help cover it up. I don't think he meant to kill her, but he was violent with her. He wouldn't listen to her. He killed her."

Maybe not murder but involuntary manslaughter? "Why didn't you take the DVD to the police?" It's what I would have done.

"My dad. I've lost all respect for him, especially after what he did to my mom, but he's still my dad, you know? I don't want him to go to jail." She gave a broken sob.

Poor kid. I gave her a comforting squeeze. "You know you can't protect your father if he did wrong things."

She gave a sigh torn from deep down. "I know. And it's not just the scams. He married these underage girls, and I think he's done other stuff for Michael, bad stuff. Dad's a computer whiz, and who knows what he's done?"

"I'm very sorry about that for your sake, Andi, but we need to go to the authorities and give them the DVD as soon as possible. Then Michael and Fred—Harl—will be arrested, and both you and Clooney will be safe."

"You think so?" she asked, and I heard hope for the first time. "What about my dad?"

"I don't know, but if he did wrong, he needs to be held accountable."

Andi sighed. "My mom died and my sister might as well have, and Dad is all I have, though I don't really have him either. Or even want him."

Been there, kiddo. "I never knew my father, and my mother might as well have been dead." A picture of the lovely woman she now was flashed through my mind, and I pushed it ruthlessly aside. "No parents is a lonely place to be. But there are lots of people here who love you, honey. I know we don't replace family, but we care and we're here for you. And God cares. He always cares."

"If He cares, why am I in this mess?" Her question was desperate.

"Because a lot of people didn't do things His way. That always complicates life."

She gave a sad little laugh. "Complicated. Yep. That's my life."

"Well, let's go uncomplicate one part of it." I flicked off the kitchen light and moved with care toward the hole in the wall. The less dense blackness of the outside showed where I hadn't been able to pull the board back into place. "Where's the DVD now?"

"At the café."

"My café?"

"Yeah. They'd never think to look there." She sighed. "I never expected them to find me."

I reached out my good hand to push the plywood sheet out of our way, aware that the outside darkness had gotten deeper as I neared it. I frowned, trying to make sense of that fact, when my hand touched fingers reaching for a hold from the other side. I gave a squeak as the sheet rumbled aside.

A bright light struck our faces, blinding us, but I recognized the voice that said, "But we did find you, didn't we?"

46

I stared at the trio who pushed their way into the apartment: Michael, the so-called archangel, Harl, alias Fred Durning, and Chaz.

Andi hid behind me, peering at the three over my shoulder. How I wished there was someone for me to hide behind, preferably someone very tall and very wide, armed to the teeth and trained in martial arts.

Michael ignored me and spoke to Andi. "So you're the one who has the disc." He sounded as if he were speaking of something as innocuous as the weekly shopping list.

"Michael?" she said. "Where's your hair?" She looked at me, and I thought of the tall man with short dark hair she'd seen leave the compound on some past occasion.

He ran his hand over his extremely short cut. His smile was scary, filled with pride at his cleverness and scorn that she, like everyone else, had been deceived.

Andi grabbed my shoulder and held on like I had to hold her upright. I could feel her shaking. I didn't feel any too steady myself.

"Let's go get it." Michael motioned toward the opening in the wall, and for the first time I realized he had a gun in his hand. It glinted dully in the beam of the flashlight Andi's brother-in-law held.

I'd always wondered what I'd do if someone approached me at gunpoint and demanded I go with him. I'd always thought I'd be strong enough to say, "No! I will not go with you. Shoot me here if you must." After all, most dark country road murders didn't start at that location.

Michael must have sensed my reluctance. "You too, lady, or I'll shoot the girl."

Even as I heard Andi moan behind me, I took a step toward the opening. I didn't think Michael would kill Andi before he got what he wanted from her, but shooting didn't have to mean dead, at least not right away. It could mean hurt a lot.

I eyed Michael askance. This well-known, charismatic man might sound composed, but his carefully constructed house of cards would collapse around him if that disc ever saw the light of day. With so much at stake he was as dangerous as the iceberg lying in wait for the *Titanic*. Apparent calm above, desperation and determination below. If Andi was correct, murder had already been done to preserve the secrets recorded on that disc, and murder would have to be done again this night to keep Andi and me silent. Not a heartening thought.

I moved toward the opening, praying I'd find some way to save us before the disc was recovered. I tried not to dwell on the unhappy thought that if Michael became too agitated, I was the expendable one.

Andi gripped my jacket and the sweater beneath in her fist. She had to let go when I got to the opening so I could climb out. She followed so quickly she stepped on my heels. When we were standing in the fresh air, she spun me around so she was behind me again. She leeched onto my jacket with both fists this time.

Michael waved the gun in the direction of a gray sedan. "Get in. Hurry!" Anger and an unhealthy volatility shimmered around him. If I could see auras—if there was such a thing—his would be jagged with instability and as black as midnight.

I looked around as I moved toward the car, hoping against hope for someone who would save us. *Lord, where's our superhero?*

The closest thing to Superman in my life was Greg, and he was having dinner with Josh Templeton.

I'll take Cilla peering out her window, Lord. Someone. Anyone!

No one showed.

A thought swam through my fear, and I latched on to it because I liked its logic. Surely the Lord wouldn't let anything happen to me and put Greg through the death of another person he loved, would He?

Fred/Harl yanked the back car door open and pushed Andi and me inside. We tumbled over each other as he pushed his way in behind us. He had a gun too, and its little round opening was pointed right at me.

Michael took the driver's seat, and Chaz jumped in the passenger side. Michael hit the gas and roared out of the lot.

I couldn't believe my situation. I was just a woman in the hospitality industry, trying to make a living in my cozy little café I leased from Mary P, trying to establish a lasting relationship with a man I'd loved from afar for a long time. In other words, normal, ordinary. Kidnapping at gunpoint was wrong on so many planes.

Yet all around me were armed men who saw me as the enemy.

Lord, this is supposed to be my time to dance, not die!

My shaking hands hadn't even managed to click my seat belt closed before we pulled up behind the café. As Harl shoved me out, I glanced up at the apartment.

Let it be dark, Lord!

Light bled out into the night, and as Chaz slammed his car door, Lindsay moved to our back door and looked out. She held Oreo in her arms, the cat's black body obvious against Lindsay's light-colored shirt.

Michael glared at Chaz. "You think you could make any more noise?"

"Sorry," Chaz whispered, but he didn't look sorry to me. With his usual arrogance he thought himself equal to the powerbroker he was running with.

"The sister's looking at us," Harl said.

I opened my mouth to scream, "Call the cops!" or something equally helpful, but Michael grabbed Andi. She squeaked as he pushed his gun against her temple.

"One word. Just one word," he warned me.

I closed my mouth.

"Wave like everything's fine," he ordered.

I waved. Lindsay waved back, but I could see she was wondering what was going on. Michael must have seen her confusion too.

"Get the sister. Quick!" he ordered, but Harl was already at the top of the stairs.

He knocked at the door, a smile on his face.

Don't open it, Linds! Don't open it!

She opened it with a smile. "Hi, Fred. Looking for Greg? He's not here."

He laughed. "Not this time. I'm after you." He raised his gun.

Lindsay's face registered shock. As she stiffened, Oreo stirred.

"Downstairs or your sister gets it." It was the normalcy of his voice, a voice I was used to hearing ask for a sticky bun, that made the threat so chilling.

Lindsay stumbled to the steps and started down. When she reached for the handrail, Oreo jumped free. She was a black bullet streaking down and around the corner of the building. The men ignored her.

"Carrie?" Lindsay's voice quaked with fear.

"I'm okay, Linds," I assured her as she reached the bottom. "It's okay." Talk about a ridiculous statement, but it seemed to help Lindsay. She blinked away the shocked look and frowned.

"Inside, all of you." Michael gestured with his gun.

Lindsay grabbed my hand. "What's going on?" she whispered.

"Shut up." Harl poked her in the back with his gun. She jumped and shut up.

Chaz tried to open the café door. "It's locked!"

"Of course it is," I said. "The café's closed."

Harl grabbed Lindsay, jerking her against him. "Open it," he snarled at me.

"I don't have my keys."

"Then figure out another way."

I looked at the solid slab of wood with no little glass window I could break so I could reach in and pop the lock. "It's as break-in proof as they come," the salesman had told me. I never thought I'd see the day I regretted taking his advice.

"I've got the key." Lindsay pushed against Harl's grip. "Let me go, and I'll get it."

He released her at a nod from Michael. She reached into her pocket and pulled out the key.

"When I saw it was Fred on the landing, I grabbed it from the counter by the door where you dropped it, Carrie, because I thought he must have left something in the café."

"No good deed ever goes unpunished." Harl laughed at his own sorry humor.

While Lindsay unlocked the door, I stood quietly, trying to decide how I could take advantage of the alarm system we had installed a year ago. The keypad to disengage the alarm was just inside the back door, and you had to enter a code within thirty seconds after entering or they called to check on you.

Suddenly thirty seconds seemed a very long time to keep Michael, Harl, and Chaz from hearing the warning beeps.

The turn of the lock sounded loud in the quiet night, and Lindsay pushed the door open.

"Inside, all of you." Michael gave Andi a shove.

She lost her balance and crashed against me. I in turn fell against the doorjamb. My bad wrist exploded in pain.

I screamed; I couldn't help it. I hunched over, cradling my arm still tucked inside my jacket.

"I'm sorry! I'm sorry!" Andi began to weep. "He pushed me. I didn't mean—"

"Carrie, are you all right?" Lindsay cried, rushing toward me.

I sagged against the jamb and made pain noises, gagging noises. It wasn't hard to exaggerate them because the pain was real and intense. I sank to my knees in the doorway.

"Get up! Now!" Michael ordered.

"She's got a broken wrist." Lindsay went down beside me, throwing her arm around my shoulders.

"Catch me if I faint," I mumbled, raising a hand dramatically to my forehead. I could hear the alarm beeps going faster and faster. If I could stall just a few seconds more...

A hand grabbed me by my jacket collar and pulled me to my feet. Harl. "Inside!" He had Lindsay in his other hand, and the three of us stumbled into the café. Michael and Chaz followed with Andi.

By now the alarm beeps were an almost-constant thrum.

Michael strode to the keypad. "Code!" His finger was poised over the numbers.

I opened my mouth to tell him the right numbers when the alarm went silent. Almost immediately the restaurant phone rang.

"It's the alarm company," I said. "They'll want me to give them the password and key in the code."

Michael indicated the phone, and Chaz ran for it. He brought it to me. As I took it, I watched Michael raise his gun to Andi and Harl pull his from his waistband and aim it at my sister.

"Hello?"

"We have an indication of possible trouble at your place," a man's voice said.

"I just didn't get to the alarm pad in time," I said as apologetically as I could. "Everything's fine."

"What's your password?"

"Lemon chiffon pie."

"Okay. Now please key in your code to reset your system," he said.

"Sure." I handed the phone to Lindsay and walked to the keypad. I blocked it from view as much as I could. I took a deep breath and coded in four digits: 0911.

The code for a hostage situation.

I t was not going to end because of some little girl who thought she was so clever.

It was not going to end, period. At least not for him.

Those years of storing up treasure, not in heaven but offshore, were going to pay off big time. He smiled in anticipation.

Being a genius was often a trial because of all the imbeciles you had to deal with. But having the intellect to think things through carefully and plan quickly was the upside of brilliance.

And he had tonight planned. Get the disc and destroy it. He sighed at the thought of losing all those videos at the compound, but he could start a new collection at his new home. There were always willing girls, especially for a wealthy, handsome man like him.

Harl would kill the women for him tonight. The man was putty in his hands. They would then take the yacht and head for the islands. Mysterious— and unreported—disappearances at sea would take care of Harl and Chaz.

Then the good life. Money from all the properties purchased through the years would stream in, and he'd sit back in the sun and enjoy life. He'd earned it. This time tomorrow...

The waitress had just taken Greg's order when his phone vibrated against his side. He glanced at the readout and didn't recognize the number. He decided to let the call go to voice mail. He'd not even taken a drink of his iced tea when the phone vibrated again. He glanced down and saw the same number. As he debated answering, the waitress appeared with his house salad, and the call was forgotten.

For almost twenty seconds. Then as he swallowed a mouthful of salad, the telltale vibration began again.

When he saw the same number, he frowned. "I'd better take this, Josh," he said to his former boss. "It's the third call in the past couple of minutes, always from the same number."

"You're not a cop anymore, Greg. No more emergencies. No more ruined dinners." Josh took a bite of his Caesar salad.

Greg forced a smile. "Still I'd better check it. Could be a big problem at one of the properties."

Josh shrugged. "Who cares? Not my concern anymore."

"But it's still mine. I'll be right back."

As he started for the small lobby, he flipped the phone open. "Yes? This is Greg."

"Greg! You've got to help them!"

The skin on Greg's skull contracted. "Who is this?"

"It's Cilla Merkel."

"And who do I have to help?"

"Carrie. And Andi."

His heart skipped a beat. "Carrie's in trouble?"

"Three men have them."

"What do you mean, have them?" he shouted, drawing strange looks as he bolted out the door and toward his car.

"Like in kidnapping. At gunpoint."

He had to swallow to keep that lone lettuce leaf down.

"One's that Chaz," Cilla continued. "I'm not certain about the other two. It's too dark."

"How do you know this?" She was old. Maybe she'd miss-seen. He'd hang up and call Carrie, and she'd be fine. They'd laugh about Cilla's penchant for drama.

"Perk and I were coming back from dinner and had just pulled up in front of my place. We were looking at that hole in your building, thinking that the boards seemed wrong. Crooked or something. We weren't certain, you know, given the parking lot lights."

"Cilla!" Greg slammed into his car and slid the key into the ignition.

"Right. Well, we decided one of the boards had been pushed aside. While we watched, Carrie and Andi climbed out through the hole."

So that was where the kid had been hiding.

"Then three men came next. One was Chaz. The other two had guns. They made the girls get into a car."

Greg could hear Mr. Perkins yell, "Gray or silver Ford Taurus. Maybe beige."

"Did they head for the causeway?" Greg's tires squealed as he pulled onto the road. He could intercept them there.

"Don't know yet. We're following them."

More amateur sleuths. "Be careful. Guns can shoot anyone who scares the bad guys even if they weren't the original target."

"Of course we're being careful. Do you think we're nuts?"

Greg didn't say what he thought.

"They've turned into the alley behind the café."

"The café?"

"Perk has parked on the cross street at the end of the alley, and we'll keep watch until you get here. Oh no!"

Greg went cold. "What?"

"One of the—it looks like that Fred—has gotten Lindsay from upstairs."

"Fred? As in Durning?"

"Perk doesn't know his last name, but it's the guy who came to the café to see you."

Greg blew through two red lights without lessening his speed, thankful for off-season traffic. He wished he had a Kojak light.

"They're taking them in the café. Why would they do that?"

I wish I knew. "You called 911, right?"

"Oh."

"Cilla!"

"I tweeted."

Greg's knuckles turned white as he gripped the wheel. Like that would help. "Never mind." He flipped his phone shut, then open. He hit 911.

He got a busy signal.

He cut the call and tried again. When the dispatcher answered, some of his tension drained away.

"Stephanie, Greg Barnes. There's a hostage situation at Carrie's Café."

"Got it. You're my fourth call about it."

"What?"

"It's all over Twitter."

Cilla.

"The alarm company called first. Someone gave them the hostage code," Stephanie said. "Chief Gordon is assembling a team."

Greg tossed his phone onto the passenger seat. Chief Gordon was intelligent, trained, and more than competent, but it would take time for him to get his people in place, time Carrie and the others might not have.

Greg rounded a final corner and pulled up behind Cilla and Mr. Perkins. He reached into the glove compartment for his Taser and restraints, which he stuck in his pocket. He grabbed his gun and flicked off the safety. He'd asked himself a thousand times why he continued to carry these things, but he knew enough about the underbelly of mankind to want some protection. Now he thanked God that he had.

As he ran for the alley, Mr. Perkins powered his window down. "They're still inside."

Greg waved and kept moving, noting with one part of his mind how comfortable his weapon felt in his hand. Maybe handling a gun was like riding a bicycle. The muscles and memory were always there, just waiting for recall.

He stopped at the back door to the café. He grasped the knob and turned, inch by slow inch.

Something brushed against his legs, and he froze. The movement continued. Brush, brush, brush. One leg, then the other. He looked down to see Oreo twining about his ankles, looking up at him with wide eyes.

Greg let out a breath. He reached down and moved the animal aside. "Later, kitty. Just stay out of the way."

Slowly he turned the doorknob. Slowly he pushed open the door.

He hadn't taken a step inside before Oreo shot past him into the café.

Greg grabbed for her, but the cat was a black meteor streaking through the dim café, lit only by the emergency lights.

So much for the element of surprise.

Lindsay and Andi and I huddled together in the gap between the register counter and the pink lunch counter. Ahead of us was the door to the kitchen, behind us the café itself. I cradled my wrist in my good hand, cupping it through my fleece jacket. I tried to look weak and frail, a challenge since I'd spent my whole life trying to prove I was strong. The throbbing pain in my wrist made the mummery easier than it might have been.

Harl grabbed Andi, and she bleated in terror as he rested his hand on her shoulder and his gun against her throat. For whatever reason, the very nonchalance of the action more than all that had come before made me realize that we might not survive the night. Michael and Harl were men with everything to lose if we three lived.

I thought of Greg and what might have been and the injustice of his losing someone else he loved. *It's just not fair, Lord. It's just not fair.*

I thought of my mother and felt an unexpected ache. Was I going to die without resolving my feelings toward her, without forgiving? What was I going to say when I met God? *Well, Lord, I just didn't feel like making things right?*

"Where's the DVD?" Harl demanded.

Andi hunched her shoulders and squeezed her eyes shut.

"You're not an ostrich," Harl sneered. "You can close your eyes all you want, but we aren't going anywhere until you give us what we want."

Andi opened her eyes and glared at him with what I thought looked like contempt, an amazing thing considering who he was, what he'd done, and where we were.

"I happen to be praying," she said with dignity. "I'm asking God Him-self—not a mere archangel—to save us."

Chaz gave a strangled laugh. "That's funny." When no one else laughed, he said defensively, "You know, funny strange. Like who talks to God?"

I fought the insane impulse to raise my hand.

Michael ignored Chaz and nodded to Harl. He appeared happy to let Harl deal with Andi while he stood and watched, his gun aimed at my heart. At the rate it was pounding, it would jump from my chest at any moment and yell, "Shoot me and get it over with!"

"So where is it?" Harl asked again.

"In there." Andi pointed her chin toward the kitchen.

As good a place as any. All kinds of nooks and crannies, drawers and shelves offered cover for something as small as a disc.

"Everyone, move," Michael ordered.

Andi started for the kitchen, Lindsay right behind her.

"Knives," Chaz shouted. "There's knives back there."

Well, yeah. It was a kitchen.

"You'll just have to keep her away from them, won't you?" Harl's voice dripped with disdain, which the ever-sharp Chaz missed.

Twitching like a junkie in need of a fix—which was exactly what he was—Chaz charged into the kitchen. "There they are!" He threw his body between the big knives, slotted in front of a scrubbed cutting block, and little Andi as if he were a Marine ready to stand off a company of terrorists.

I thought of all the years I'd spent with a knife under my pillow, having to use it only once. How ironic that when I needed one again, Chaz—Chaz!—prevented me from getting to it.

But I had a better plan.

"Move it." Michael shoved at me again, and I staggered.

"My wrist!" I yelled it in spite of the fact that he hadn't touched me anywhere near my right arm. I fell back onto the stool behind the register. "Don't hurt me again!"

Michael, disgusted with my whining, ignored me as I started to pull myself upright. I put out my good hand to steady myself, dropped it below the counter, and grabbed for my weapon of choice: a canister of pepper spray I kept in case I ever wanted to fend off a burglar. Or a phony archangel. As I stood, I slid the spray into the side pocket in my jeans. I made my way out from behind the counter, moving toward the kitchen as requested.

"Where?" Harl demanded.

Andi looked at me, terror written all over her face.

I actually felt my stomach drop as I realized the DVD wasn't here in the kitchen.

Harl realized it too.

"Why you little—" He grabbed her by the hair and raised a fist to strike her.

At that wonderfully appropriate moment a black cat raced through the kitchen door, held open by Michael, bounded onto the cutting board, and leapfrogged onto Chaz, who screamed like a terrified little girl when Oreo landed on his shoulder. Oreo screeched too, dug in her back claws, and jumped down by way of the stove and scurried beneath Lindsay's pastry table.

There was a moment of absolute silence from everyone but Chaz who blubbered and brushed at his shoulder as if Oreo was still there.

Harl turned his gun on Oreo, visible only as a pair of unwinking eyes and a white bib.

"No!" Lindsay and I both yelled, racing to stand in front of our cat.

"No, Harl." Michael's voice was a whip. "No shooting here. Too much noise."

I watched Harl, fascinated as he struggled to obey Michael. There was a lot of resentment and anger there. Even if they got away tonight, someday it was all going to blow, and only one of those men would be left standing. My money was on Michael, though Harl would fight hard and dirty.

"How did that cat get in here?" Michael demanded, his eyes darting about the kitchen and into the café.

I shook my head. "I don't know how he got in. You saw him come downstairs with Lindsay, but he ran away."

"The back door must not have closed behind us, and she pushed her way in," Lindsay said. "She's a big, strong animal."

Michael turned to Chaz, now shaking doubly hard and muttering about demon cats and werewolves. "Go check that back door. Make sure it's closed and locked."

50

W hen Oreo went blasting past him, Greg knew he had just a few seconds to get deep into the shadows and assess the situation. Someone would be back to check the door to see how the cat had gotten in. He left the door open a few inches as if Oreo had pushed it, then stepped into the storage closet.

He heard Chaz's less-than-manly reaction to Oreo, not that Greg had room to criticize. He'd had his own "less than" performance just a couple of nights ago. Tonight would not be a repeat even if it literally killed him.

He heard Carrie and Lindsay explain Oreo's presence and defend the cat's honor with their lives.

Carrie, it's a cat! I can live without it but not without you.

When Michael ordered Fred—how had Fred gotten involved in this?—to stand down, Greg let out the breath he'd been holding.

"Go check that back door. Make sure it's closed and locked."

Who was Michael sending? Chaz? Fred? One of the girls?

He slid deeper into the closet and waited. Through the crack of the partially opened door he watched Chaz come, twitching and muttering to himself.

"I shoulda just left town." He ran a hand through his stringy hair. "I shoulda said, 'Pay me and I'll *tell* you where she is,' not 'I'll *show* you.' Demon cat. I shoulda just left town."

Chaz passed the storage closet, then reached for the back door. Quickly, silently, Greg moved behind him and pulled the Taser's trigger. Chaz gave an inarticulate gasp and went limp. Greg pulled him into the storage closet, laid him on the floor, and put him in the plastic restraints, hands behind his back, one foot attached to the leg of a large storage rack full of dishes and paper products. The last thing he wanted was a groggy Chaz stumbling out at the wrong moment.

Moving with stealth, Greg slid along the café's inside wall until he came to the counter. He dropped to a crouch and moved past the stools to the break between the pink counter and the register counter. He stuck his head forward for a quick glimpse to gauge what was happening in the kitchen.

And it was bad.

51

Relief coursed through me when I realized Oreo wasn't about to be shot. Of course Lindsay, Andi, and I were still likely to face that fate, but somehow knowing the cat was safe was satisfying.

But before I died, I could at least do half of something right. I turned to my sister who leaned against her pastry table beside me.

"Mom's here," I blurted.

"Shut up," Harl ordered.

"Mom? Here where?" Lindsay looked confused.

"In Seaside."

"Yo!" Harl yelled.

I hurried on before I lost my nerve. "And she came into the café."

"What? When?"

"I said shut up!" Harl let go of Andi and grabbed for me. I dodged. "Wednesday and today."

Lindsay blinked. "And you didn't tell me?" She looked from Harl to Michael, then back at me. I knew she was thinking that there was a very good chance she'd never see Mom now.

"She looks good, Linds. And she's got this handsome, nice husband. At least he seems nice."

"Mom's married." She said it with wonder. Given our experience with her, sticking with one man didn't seem something she'd be capable of.

"I'm sorry you didn't get to meet her."

"Yeah, me too."

"She wants to meet you. Her husband said."

"Are you deaf or something?" Harl snarled. "Shut up."

"Let them alone." Michael indicated Andi. "She's who's important. Get what we need from her and fast."

"It was my bitterness." I held out my hand palm up because I was without excuse. "I made your decision for you. I'm sorry. Can you forgive me?"

Lindsay got a dreamy expression in her eyes. "You know, I've wanted to see her for years. Just see her."

I shriveled a bit inside as I realized what my pettiness had cost my sister. "You can see her. It's okay with me. Get to know her. Love her." But as I looked at the guns focused on Linds and me, the chances seemed terrifyingly small.

Andi cried out in pain as Harl grabbed her again by the hair, and I temporarily forgot Mom.

"Leave her alone!" I cried.

"Don't hurt her," Lindsay cried. "She's a kid!"

We might as well not have spoken.

"No more lying, or I'll hurt you bad," Michael told her, a desperation I hadn't heard before creeping into his voice. "Maybe a bullet in some vulnerable spot or maybe I'll use one of those knives over there."

Andi started to cry.

I looked at the knives, blades sharp as Ricky could make them, and shuddered.

"Or maybe I'll hurt her." Michael grabbed me, his arm wrapping around my neck. I'd been so transfixed by the knives I hadn't seen him coming. He stroked the barrel of his gun down my cheek. "It'd be a shame if one of those knives damaged this lovely face."

"She doesn't know anything!" Andi cried.

"Get me that DVD."

"It's in the café."

"We're in the café."

"I mean in the dining area."

Harl put his face mere inches from hers. "You'd better be telling the truth this time."

"I am. I swear. It's under the pink counter."

The defeated way in which she spoke told me she was telling the truth. Lindsay opened her arms, and Andi ran to her, holding tight as her tears wet Linds's shoulder.

Harl almost danced out of the kitchen.

"Go." Michael pointed to the dining area, and Andi and Lindsay went. He pushed me ahead of him, walking in time with my steps as he kept the pressure about my neck steady. I tried to pull away, and he tightened his grip. Immediately I had difficulty breathing. I stopped fighting him.

Not now, girl. Relax. Wait.

Harl gave a happy cry. "Got it!" He held a jewel case high overhead.

And the world exploded.

52

Everything happened at once, or so it seemed to me.

The back door flew open, and Clooney came rushing in, armed to the teeth, Rambo in the flesh. I had no idea what the various guns dangling from his body were called, but they were big and ugly.

"Andi!" he screamed.

"Clooney!" She was looking at her greatest fear come true. "Run!"

Michael brought his gun up even as he kept his choke hold on me.

Clooney tripped over something and fell flat on his face.

Michael's bullet smacked into the back wall. The noise was deafening in the enclosed space.

I gave a brief thought to Chaz, who was supposed to have locked the back door. Had he been smart enough to run instead? He'd certainly been smart enough to stay out of Clooney's way.

"Get up!" Michael waved his gun in Clooney's direction, then at Andi. "Or I shoot her. I don't need her anymore."

"We don't need any of them anymore." Harl wiped nervous sweat off his top lip. He was as twitchy as Chaz, not with withdrawal but with the need to kill. And he'd just gotten another hostage.

"Patience, Harl," Michael said. "In time. I make those decisions. I am, after all, God's archangel."

The look of disbelief on Harl's face would have been funny in other situations. "Get a grip, Mike."

A loud voice amplified by a bullhorn called from outside, "Hello, the café. This is the police."

As relief surged through me, Michael whirled to face the window, moving so fast my feet left the ground as he spun me with him. I made a gagging sound as I struggled to gain my footing and relieve the pressure on my throat.

Harl snarled and swore. "Where did they come from?"

No one answered, but I knew. The coded message on the alarm system had worked. We would be saved!

Harl grabbed Andi and pulled her in front of him.

"Let go of me!" she screamed as she beat at his hands.

Clooney made an inarticulate growl as he struggled to his feet, his weaponry clinking and clanging.

Bright light poured into the café from outside, blinding all of us after so long in the dim illumination of the emergency lights. I squinted and could make out people and cars in the street. Or rather their silhouettes.

"This is Chief Gordon of the Seaside Police Department. Release your hostages and surrender."

"Never!" Michael yelled.

I could feel him trembling. What I didn't know was whether he was quivering with fear or fury. I suspected fury. Harl, on the other hand, stank with fear as he cowered behind Andi, quite a trick given her diminutive size.

Michael raised his gun to my temple, and I quickly rethought the I'm-saved concept.

I was afraid to move. My pepper spray was inches away, but Michael was on the edge. Even reaching for it might cause his finger to tighten on the trigger.

As I prayed feverishly, Lindsay raised her arm and brought it down with a rebel yell that would have made the Confederacy proud. It turned my blood to ice.

Harl screamed and let go of Andi, who fell to her knees. He grabbed his bicep where a paring knife was buried to the hilt. He turned green when he saw it. A single drop of blood slid down his arm. He raised disbelieving eyes to Lindsay, who was pressed back against her pastry table. The little knife she used to trim piecrusts was missing from its slot at the rear of the table.

Harl whimpered and his gun tumbled to the floor. "Mike?"

Andi grabbed the weapon and threw it beneath the stove.

Michael's gun lowered as he too stared at the knife. The choke hold eased.

My turn. I pulled my tear gas canister from my waistband and aimed it over my shoulder. I squeezed, praying I had the nozzle aimed where I wanted it. At the same moment Greg materialized out of the dimness and shot Michael with a Taser.

Michael let out a roar and collapsed. I stumbled toward Greg, who wrapped me in his arms, a spent Taser in one hand, a gun in the other, my own superhero. Clooney stood behind him, finally untangled from his personal armory.

And just like that, it was over.

53

The EMTs took Michael to the ambulance, his eyes red and watery, his muscles twitchy. As the effects of the Taser began to wear off, his arrogance slowly returned. He remained haughty even when Maureen Trevelyan started reciting, "You have the right to remain silent…"

He lay strapped to a gurney, staring over her head, as if she were beneath his notice, until she finished.

"Do you understand?" she asked.

"Do you understand?" he shot back, finally deigning to look at her. "I am Michael, God's archangel."

"Uh-huh. And I'm Maureen, Seaside's cop. I need to know if you understand what I just said."

"Of course I understand. I am Michael, Go—"

"Good," she interrupted. "Just what I needed to hear."

He looked at the ambulance, at the straps holding him down, and at Maureen who smiled at him without humor. Reality made a brief appearance. He looked around with panic in his eyes, his fingers splayed wide. Then Maureen nodded, the EMTs loaded him into the ambulance, and the door slammed shut, the first of many doors that would crash closed and lock behind him in the coming years.

Mac88 recorded the exchange between Michael and Maureen on his cell. As Maureen climbed into the passenger seat of the ambulance, he sent the Miranda episode around the world. This appearance by Michael on YouTube would be dramatically different from his previous ones.

As I looked at the chaotic scene, I thought the one thing missing was the television cameras.

And there came a van with the big ABC logo and an eager reporter who jumped out, a camera tech right behind him. Great. We'd not only be tweeted and YouTubed, we'd be on the eleven o'clock news.

The camera recorded Harl, police guard and EMT at his side, as he was brought outside, knife still protruding from his arm. He was whimpering like a baby. In the confusion and crowd, someone jostled him. He shrieked and doubled over. I knew it had to hurt, but did he have to vomit right outside my café?

"Arrest her! She stabbed me," he kept babbling. Everyone ignored him. He too was read his Miranda rights, then hustled into a second ambulance. They drove him away, a police car following.

Greg collected Chaz from the storeroom and walked him outside. It was all Chaz could do to stay on his feet. An EMT took one look and diagnosed his problem, not that it was hard. His nose was running, his eyes were watering, and he was twitchier than ever. His skin under the harsh lights was a blotchy gray.

An officer I didn't know walked over to Greg. "I'm to escort him to the hospital."

Greg held up a finger. "One minute. Chaz, can you hear me?"

Chaz sniffed and looked at him with glazed eyes. "S'all your fault. If you hadn't kicked me out—"

"You can hear me." Greg nodded and began reciting, "You have the right—"

"You're not allowed to say that!" Chaz pointed a shaking finger at Greg. "You aren't a cop. Only a cop can."

Greg blinked and stepped back. He looked around. Everywhere there were cops, flashing lights, and static. Emergency vehicles clogged the street, sirens sounding as men and women from nearby communities arrived to assist. It was everything he feared, everything that set memories screaming in 3-D Technicolor and high-def.

He stood without moving for a few moments. A look of wonder spread over his face. No dazed look. No withdrawal. Wonder.

He spotted me standing with Lindsay and Andi, waiting our turn to tell Chief Gordon our stories. His smile was a glorious thing to behold. I smiled back, and we met halfway.

"I did it," he said, his voice exultant. "I did what needed to be done."

I wrapped my good arm around his waist. "Yes, you did. That's because you're a cop." I kissed his cheek.

"I am," he said. "I'm a cop."

"Carrie! Lindsay!"

I dropped my head onto Greg's shoulder as I heard my mother's frantic voice. Joyous exultation to angry resentment at the sound of two words. I didn't want to deal with her. Not here, not now.

"In his own way, Michael was easier," I said.

"Understandable. No history. Just straight-out dislike." Greg kissed my temple. "You've done the hard things before. You can do this one now."

I made a sound of stubborn disagreement.

His hand settled on the nape of my neck, comforting, kind. "She needs you, Carrie—and you need her, whether you like it or not."

I couldn't decide which part of his statement I disagreed with more.

"Mom!" Lindsay rushed to Mom with open arms. My heart ached as I watched them embrace. The depth of their emotion scared me on several levels.

Would Linds come to resent me for all the years I'd kept them apart, though in my defense I hadn't done it maliciously? I'd pictured Mom never changing, and not contacting her had seemed wise. But I'd been protecting an adult who needed to be free to call her own shots, make her own decisions.

But what if she wanted to move to Atlanta to be close to Mom and Luke? That thought was a weight pressing so hard against my chest it was difficult to breathe. What would I do without my sister in my everyday life?

I looked at my mother and saw an emotional IED capable of blowing my life to smithereens.

Mary P joined the cozy circle of Mom, Lindsay, and Luke, everyone smiling and hugging. I felt abandoned all over again, which was ridiculous. All I had to do was walk to them, and I'd be welcomed.

My feet were stuck to the street where I stood.

"I've finally got a father," I mumbled, staring at Luke. "At my age. How strange is that?"

"He looks like a nice guy," Greg said. "Maybe he and my dad can become golfing or fishing buddies."

"Right. They can meet halfway in North Carolina."

Mom and Luke had both spotted me and were doubtless very aware of me not approaching.

"I'm scared," I whispered.

"Of course you are."

I clutched Greg. "Why can't I be more like Linds? Why can't I just run to Mom and love her? That's what I should do, right?"

"You're allowed to approach slowly and with caution if that's the way you need to do it, Carrie. No one expects years of pain to disappear in a moment."

"They did with Lindsay."

"She's not you. You bore all the fear and heartache, protecting her. I think what God is asking of you right now is that you're willing to take first steps. He's not asking you to respond like Lindsay. He's asking that you try as you."

If all I had to do was try... I felt I could breathe again.

"But—" He ran a knuckle down my cheek.

I nodded. "But I do have to try." I straightened my shoulders and turned toward my mother.

She and Lindsay stood with arms around each other's waists, and both of them were crying. Luke watched them with a slight smile. Then his eyes slid to me, and his eyebrow cocked in challenge. I gave him a grim little smile.

I grabbed Greg's hand. "Come with me."

"Of course."

Mom looked up and saw me approaching.

God, help me!

Six Months Later

Good morning, officer. May I get you some coffee?" I asked.

The cop nodded. "And one of my sister-in-law's grilled sticky buns, please."

"Coming right up."

I placed the order and got the coffee. When I set the cup down, Greg grabbed my hand.

"How's your morning been, Mrs. Barnes?"

I rested my arms on the counter and grinned at him. "Fine, Officer Barnes. How about yours?"

"Oh, for Pete's sake, stop mooning over each other." Mr. Perkins gave a little shudder as he sat on his usual perch. He'd had a bout of pneumonia over the winter that had concerned all of us, but he seemed back in form now that spring was here. Once a week he brought Cilla to the café for lunch.

"Once a week?" I'd teased him when the pattern became obvious back about the end of November. "You're not getting any younger, you know."

"It may be once a week here, but—" And he winked.

His smug expression made me laugh. "Mr. Perkins, you rogue."

"You know it," he'd said, bony chest swelling with pride.

Now I looked at him. "I can't smile at my customers?"

He gave a strangled laugh. "You've been out of town for a couple of weeks on your honeymoon. Didn't you smile enough then?"

"You can never smile enough." I leaned over the counter and kissed my cop.

Our wedding had been an interesting lesson in the expansive power of love. There was Mary P, in all practical ways my mother; my actual mother, who I was learning to like much to my surprise; and my stepfather, who walked me down the aisle. Lindsay, of course, was my maid of honor, and Jem stood as Greg's best man so he wouldn't have to choose among his brothers.

Mary P had once again been a great help to me when I was trying to figure out how Mom and Luke were supposed to fit into my life.

"But you're my mom," I had told her a short time after Michael's arrest. Mom and Luke were supposed to leave for Atlanta the next day, and I wasn't certain about visiting them at Thanksgiving as they wanted. "You were there when I needed you, and I love you."

She took my hands in hers and looked me in the eye. "Carrie, my dear girl, you know you and Lindsay are more precious to me than I can ever express. If I thought Sue showing up and wanting back in your life would take you away from me, I'd be terribly upset. I'd fight for you. But loving one person doesn't have to mean not loving another or loving another less."

"It feels that way," I said, torn inside.

Mary P shook her head. "Don't make it so hard, so black and white. It's not like we're given a limited quantity of love and we have to spread it out over those in our lives. Love will expand to include any and all you want to include in its circle. You can love your mother and me both."

The knot inside started to unravel.

"Think of it this way," Mary P said. "God's love expands to include all mankind in a general sense and His children in a specific sense. Does He ever say, 'Oops, I've reached my quota of love today. You can't become My child'? Of course not. And as His love expands to meet the demand, so does ours—if we let it."

Over the intervening months I'd found that loving many was easier than I'd imagined. And my true love had found his way too.

It had been a matter of days after his attempt to read Chaz his Miranda rights that Greg approached Chief Gordon about coming back on the force. After several talks with him and the other officers on the small force as well as a thorough psychological evaluation, Greg was reinstated. He did not miss property management one bit.

"Uh-oh," Mr. Perkins said. "Here he comes."

There was no need to ask who *he* was. If Mr. Perkins's tone of voice and Clooney's sudden scowl didn't give it away, Andi's little purr of pleasure as she walked past on her way to serve a table breakfast would have.

Bill swaggered in, unaware that Greg and I had been convinced he was a murderer at one point. He put a ten and a five on the counter. "Three eggs over easy, bacon well done, and a double order of wheat toast with lots of butter. Keep the change."

These days Bill was flush. He was working twenty-five hours a week at the GameStop in the mall on the mainland. He planned to go back to college in the fall, though I would believe it when I saw it. Bill was more a man of grand schemes than practical action.

"Oh, and a glass of OJ and a cup of coffee. I'll be back there waiting for Andi." He pointed to the back booth.

"And I'll be here waiting for my ulcer to enlarge," Clooney muttered. He pointed at me. "If nothing else, he's going to make me as religious as you are. I've never prayed so hard about anything in my life."

"Praying that he go away, no doubt," Greg said. "Disappear into the ether."

"If you're so worried, you should come to church with Andi." I grinned. "Bill came with her last Sunday."

Clooney made a disgusted noise. "Church. Who'd have ever thought?"

Whether he meant Bill or himself, I wasn't sure.

"Say, did you see that piece on Michael and Fred or whatever his name is?" Mr. Perkins asked. "It was on one of those TV news magazines last evening."

I nodded. "We watched it. Duplicitous thieves."

"Fred—"

"His real name is Harl Evans." Andi blew at her bangs in frustration. "I've been trying to contact my sister now that he's in jail to see what she's going to do—I mean, The Pathway is no more and I'm not sure about her marriage—but she won't respond." Her eyes filled with tears. "I worry about her."

Clooney slid an arm around her slim shoulders. "But you've got me, kiddo."

"Thank God." She gave him a hug and kissed his cheek.

"The thing on TV said your father was going to jail." Mr. Perkins was tactful as ever.

Andi made a face. "Can you believe it? My father!" She looked back toward Bill, who was studying the ceiling with amazing absorption as he waited for Andi and his food. "At least Bill doesn't mind dating a con's daughter."

"Hey!" Clooney turned her to face him, a big hand on each shoulder. "Any guy in the world would be lucky to have you like him, and don't you forget it. I don't want you ever thinking you have to settle. Why, you're a heroine, helping the police so much with your DVD and your testimony."

"You were great, Andi," Greg said. "I was proud of you."

"We all were." But I ached for her. I couldn't imagine how alone she often felt. Even in my darkest days I always had Lindsay.

She flushed under the praise. "All I did was tell them that Fred Durning wasn't Harl's name and that the real Fred Durning is one of the men belonging to The Pathway."

"They had a nifty little scam built around identity theft," Greg confirmed. "Join The Pathway, turn over everything to Michael, including credit cards and social security numbers, and he uses all your personal information to buy property for himself under a bogus company developed for him by Jase who, it turns out, was a computer genius."

"He'd probably still be happily scamming if it hadn't been for Jennie," Andi said. "With my father helping him."

"So would they all." Clooney held out his cup for a refill.

"Poor Jennie," Andi said. "I still miss her."

I gave Andi's shoulders a quick squeeze, and she gave me a wan smile.

"In a weird way I feel sorry for the real Fred and the others," I said. "They went to the compound with such high hopes."

Mr. Perkins snorted.

"They did," Andi said. "I know because of my family. For most of them their worst sin was being gullible. All they got for giving their trust was their name abused and their credit wrecked."

"Why resort properties on the East Coast?" Lindsay leaned on the pass-through. "I never understood the reason for that."

"No reason that we've been able to find out," Greg said. "Maybe it's just far from Arizona."

"And Michael liked to fish." Clooney reminded us.

"Greg's and Bill's orders are up, Andi, Carrie," Ricky called. "It's never as good as when I plate it."

I put the sticky bun down in front of Greg and dug in from my side of the counter. I savored my first bite, all sweet and spicy. As I cut another piece, I grinned at my husband.

He took my right hand in his, absently running his thumb up and down the scar left from my surgery. "Want to go fishing after I'm off duty?"

"If you promise to clean my fish."

"You know that's against the rules."

"I think we have to establish our own house rules, and I think they might be different from your parents'."

He assumed an expression of mock distress. "I think I feel a discussion coming on."

"Well, I could just throw back anything I catch whether it's legal or not."

"You drive a hard bargain."

"You'd better believe it, mister."

"Look, everybody." It was Mr. Perkins. "They're smiling again."

Greg swallowed his last bite and rose from his stool. He leaned over the counter and gave me a quick kiss. I watched him leave, wrapped in the rosy glow of love given and received.

As I collected our dirty dishes, my wristwatch clanked against the pink marble. I glanced at it and thought of the watch Clooney had given me the day I broke my wrist.

I smiled. Oh, yes. There was a time to every purpose under heaven.

Letter to Readers

The last year has seen me facing a new life, one that I didn't seek but which the Lord has allowed. I have become a widow.

How I wish it hadn't happened. If the Lord had asked me to write this part of my life, my scenario wouldn't be the one I'm living. Chuck would still be alive, healthy, whole. He was a wonderful guy, and I miss him and his love every day. It's very strange indeed that he's gone and life goes on both for me and around me.

It's interesting that the one line that irritates me most is the one people offer me as comfort. "Isn't it wonderful that Chuck's with the Lord!" they say.

Well, of course it is, especially when you think of the alternative. However my internal response is, *No, it's not! I want him here.*

Grieving is so individual.

When my friend Janny's mother died, her neighbor came over as soon as she heard and stayed, not wanting to leave Janny alone in her sorrow. When the neighbor's mother died, she hadn't wanted to be alone, and she transferred her feelings onto Janny. All Janny, an introvert, wanted was for her neighbor to go home and leave her alone to process her emotions.

Relationships are tricky enough when everything is fine. Just ask Carrie and Greg. When loss is involved, they are trickier still. I've been fortunate enough to have family and friends gather around and encourage me. They let me talk and grieve in my way and on my schedule. What a gift!

Gayle Roper

Acknowledgments

Thanks to the many whose expertise and imagination made *Shadows on the Sand* so much stronger than I could have alone:

Lucinda Barnett, who gave me my villain's name.

Katie Fleetwood, whose imagination gave me Carrie's Café.

Mike, chef and owner of Country Gardens Restaurant, who gave me some of his valuable time and wisdom, and makes the best crab cakes going!

Fay, Jodie, Pat, Denise, and Deb—Country Gardens ladies who not only feed me frequently but talked to me for the book.

Julee Schwarzburg, editor extraordinaire, who makes me so much better than I am.

To my dinner group friends—Bebe, Lois, Vicki, Barbara, and Linda—who have helped make the past months bearable. You women are fantastic, and I'll vacation with you all any day!

To my writers group—Georgia, Pat, Deb, and Nancy—thanks for being there for me!

And to my family—Chip and Audrey and their girls, Bri, Abbie, and Devan, and Jeff and Cindy and their two, Ashley and PJ—you've held me close and held me up. I love you.

Readers Guide

1. Carrie loves her café. Greg dislikes property management. What about your job? Why do you feel the way you do about it? Does God promise us jobs we love? Read Ecclesiastes 2:17; 9:10; and Colossians 3:23–24. What are your thoughts?

2. The watch Clooney gives Carrie is a symbol of what? Read Ecclesiastes 3:1, 4. Have you had experience with this principle?

3. What do you do when it doesn't appear to be God's timing for your heart's desire? Read Psalms 27:14 and 37:4. What do you think of these seemingly opposite truths?

4. Carrie says that distance helps her forgive her mother. What do you think of this idea?

5. In chapter 32, Carrie talks about the essence of genuine faith. Do you agree with her assessment? Read Hebrews 11:1.

6. In chapter 34, Carrie and Greg talk about what often draws men and women to cults that are outside the norm of American life and certainly outside orthodox Christianity. What are the main elements Greg says attract many? What is often the downfall of a cult?

7. When Carrie's mother arrives in Seaside, what is Carrie's reaction? What do you think your reaction would be if you had a similar history? Why is Lindsay's reaction so different?

8. Why are Carrie's mother and stepfather a sign of hope? Read 2 Corinthians 5:17 and Ephesians 2:1–5.

9. Mary Prudence is Carrie's "God-mother," a gift from the Lord. Does a mentor have to be this obvious? Have there been people in your life

who have been there at crucial moments with a word or a helping hand? Share your stories with others in the discussion group.

10. Greg concludes that he can never be all that Carrie needs any more than he was all that Ginny needed. Discuss this critical realization in light of romance novels.

OTHER NOVELS BY GAYLE ROPER

Fatal Deduction
Allah's Fire with Chuck Holton

SEASIDE SEASONS SERIES
Spring Rain
Summer Shadows
Autumn Dreams
Winter Winds